Adventure Bible

Daily Devotional for Kids

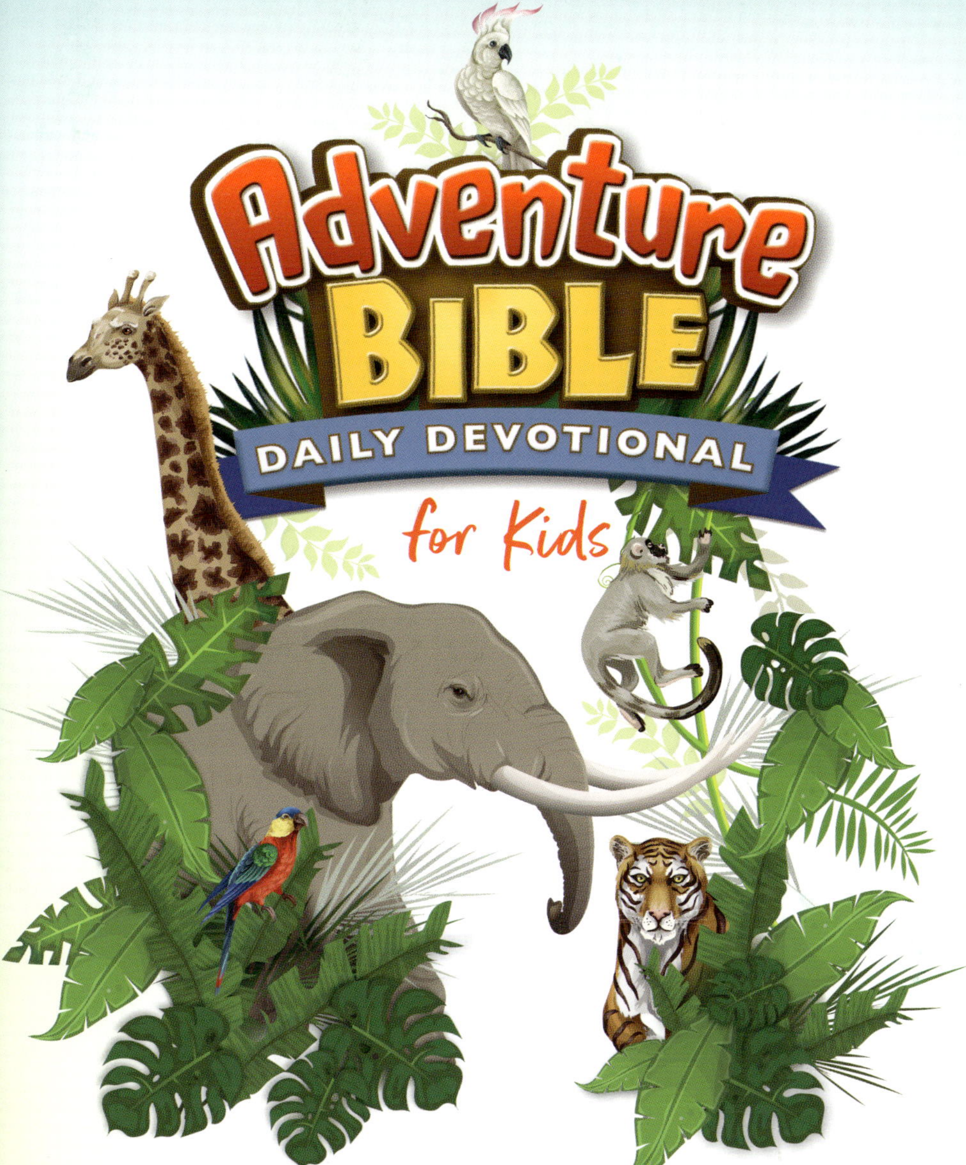

A 365-DAY GUIDE

TO UNDERSTANDING THE BIBLE

ZONDERkidz

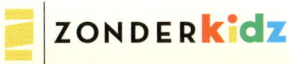

ZONDERKIDZ

Adventure Bible Daily Devotional for Kids
Copyright © 2025 by Zonderkidz

Material taken from the *NIrV Adventure Bible Book of Devotions for Early Readers: Polar Exploration Edition*, copyright © 2019 by Zonderkidz.

Published by Zonderkidz, 3950 Sparks Drive SE, Suite 101, Grand Rapids, Michigan 49546, USA. Zonderkidz is a registered trademark of The Zondervan Corporation, L.L.C., a wholly owned subsidiary of HarperCollins Christian Publishing, Inc.

Requests for information should be addressed to customercare@harpercollins.com.

ISBN 978-0-310-18125-5 (hardcover)
ISBN 978-0-310-18109-5 (audio)
ISBN 978-0-310-18126-2 (ebook)

Scripture quotations are taken from the Holy Bible, New International Reader's Version®, NIrV®. Copyright © 1995, 1996, 1998, 2014 by Biblica, Inc.® Used by permission of Zondervan. All rights reserved worldwide. www.Zondervan.com. The "NIrV" and "New International Reader's Version" are trademarks registered in the United States Patent and Trademark Office by Biblica, Inc.®

Any internet addresses (websites, blogs, etc.) and telephone numbers in this book are offered as a resource. They are not intended in any way to be or imply an endorsement by Zondervan, nor does Zondervan vouch for the content of these sites and numbers for the life of this book.

No part of this publication may be reproduced, stored in a retrieval system, or transmitted in any form or by any means—electronic, mechanical, photocopy, recording, or any other—except for brief quotations in printed reviews, without the prior permission of the publisher.

Published in association with Books & Such Literary Management, 52 Mission Circle, Suite 122, PMB 170, Santa Rosa, California 95409–5370, www.booksandsuch.com.

Zondervan titles may be purchased in bulk for educational, business, fundraising, or sales promotional use. For information, please email SpecialMarkets@Zondervan.com.

Without limiting the exclusive rights of any author, contributor, or the publisher of this publication, any unauthorized use of this publication to train generative artificial intelligence (AI) technologies is expressly prohibited. HarperCollins also exercise their rights under Article 4(3) of the Digital Single Market Directive 2019/790 and expressly reserve this publication from the text and data mining exception.

HarperCollins Publishers, Macken House,
39/40 Mayor Street Upper, Dublin 1, D01 C9W8,
Ireland (https://www.harpercollins.com)

Editor: Katherine Easter
Written by: Sherry Kyle
Cover Design: Sabryna Lugge
Interior Design: Denise Froehlich

Printed in Faridabad, India

25 26 27 28 29 30 31 / NT / 10 9 8 7 6 5 4 3 2 1

Introduction

Get ready for a 365-day adventure through God's Word with the *Adventure Bible Daily Devotional for Kids*.

This special devotional will help you grow closer to God, and you are sure to learn more about yourself and the world around you too! Each devotion has a Bible verse for you to think about, a topic that relates to your life, and a prayer or fun do-it-yourself activity.

You will learn all kinds of new things and interesting facts about the Bible, God, and his wonderful creation. From the artwork, biblical truths, and hands-on activities, you will have an adventure like no other. And if you happen to skip a day, don't worry! You can read the devotions any day of the year.

But there's more . . .

From the *Adventure Bible Daily Devotional for Kids*, you can also:

- Look up each day's verse in your Bible to read more
- Talk to your parents about the topics and interesting facts
- Do the action-packed activities with a friend

After all, why keep the adventure to yourself? So strap on your hiking boots and start the *Adventure Bible Daily Devotional for Kids* today!

DAY 1
Let the Adventure Begin!

See what amazing love the Father has given us! Because of it, we are called children of God. And that's what we really are!

—1 John 3:1

Ready for the best adventure of your life? Is it a boat ride on the ocean? A train ride through the mountains? A camping trip next to a stream? A hike through the jungle? Any of those places would be a blast, but this type of adventure is better than that!

The God of the universe wants a relationship with you. Yes, it's true! He created you, loves you, and calls you his child. Amazing, huh? And guess what? You can choose to love God back. How? By making him the center of your life. If you do that, you will be able to stand strong against any challenge that comes your way. Ready to start an adventure with the God who loves you? Awesome!

Grab a pen and a piece of paper and write a letter to God. Tell him everything you want him to know about you.

DAY 2
Special Gifts

God's gifts of grace come in many forms. Each of you has received a gift in order to serve others. You should use it faithfully.

—1 Peter 4:10

What do you love to do? Shoot hoops? Draw? Play an instrument? Most of the time we do what we enjoy because God has given us a special gift. But here's the thing: You're not supposed to keep that gift only for yourself. Sure, you can play basketball in your front yard. Or draw a pretty picture and hang it on your wall. Or sit inside your house and practice the piano. There's nothing wrong with that! However, God gave you your special gift to serve others.

When you share your gift with others, you are also serving God. Why not join a basketball team? Paint a picture for a friend? Or play the piano for the elderly people in a nursing home? You have the chance to inspire others and make people happy by using your gift. So be a faithful friend and glorify God with your gift!

Get out a piece of paper and draw a straight line down the center. On the left side list all the things you love to do. On the right side write down how you can use your gifts to serve others. Then take a leap of faith and do it!

DAY 3
Faith Not Fear!

Be strong and brave. Don't be afraid of them. Don't be terrified because of them. The Lord your God will go with you. He will never leave you. He'll never desert you.

—Deuteronomy 31:6

Do you ever get afraid when your teacher calls on you in class? Maybe you're scared to take a spelling test or a math quiz. Or maybe you're afraid of the dark and going to bed sends chills down your spine. Should you hide behind the person in front of you so that your teacher doesn't see you? Pretend to be sick so that you don't have to take a test? Sleep with your light on?

God will be with you when you are afraid. He will never leave you or desert you. It doesn't mean those jittery feelings will automatically go away. In fact, you may always get a bit nervous when speaking in front of the class, taking a test, or turning out the lights when it's time for bed. The difference is that you can be courageous because God is right there beside you.

Dear God, thank you for never leaving me alone. Help me to be strong and brave when I am afraid. Amen.

DAY 4
Friend Sharpener

As iron sharpens iron, so one person sharpens another.

—Proverbs 27:17

What type of pencil would you rather use: a sharp one or an unsharpened one? A sharp one, of course! That's because a sharp tip helps you write and draw better.

Do you have friends who help you be the best you can be? You know—the type of people who encourage you to be more kind, loving, and truthful? A kind person helps you be kinder. A loving person shows you how to be more loving. And a truthful person teaches you how to tell the truth. The Bible verse above talks about this very thing! Not only does iron sharpen iron, but good friends also sharpen each other to be better. Just as a pencil needs a good sharpener, you need good friends who sharpen you to be the best you can be.

Think of your best friends. What words would you use to describe them? Caring? Generous? Honest? If all you can come up with are negative words, like angry, mean, and unkind, then it's time to choose different friends.

DAY 5
Everyone Is Different

Christ has accepted you. So accept one another in order to bring praise to God.

—Romans 15:7

Have you ever noticed that everyone has their own likes and dislikes? Your sister may not love playing soccer like you, but she's a great singer. Your friend cheers for your least favorite sports team, but when you hang out, he always makes you laugh. Sometimes it's hard to accept and love people when they are different than you. You might be tempted to get frustrated with them, but doing that only makes the situation worse.

A better choice is to accept your siblings and friends for who God made them to be. Let's be honest—the world would be boring if everyone was alike! By accepting others, you stop expecting them to be just like you. We can be grateful and celebrate that God made everyone one of a kind. It makes the world a much more interesting place!

Dear God, thank you for accepting me for who I am, and for making everyone different. Help me to accept others. Amen.

DAY 6
Lions and Tigers and Bears!

Then God said, "Let us make human beings so that they are like us. Let them rule over the fish in the seas and the birds in the sky. Let them rule over the livestock and all the wild animals."

—Genesis 1:26

Many workers care for animals at the zoo. They feed the animals, help them get enough exercise, and make sure their cages are clean. What is your favorite animal? A giraffe? Dolphin? Maybe you love to walk through the aviary and see all the birds with their colorful feathers, or perhaps you enjoy the polar bears and penguins.

Did you know God wants you to care for animals too? Whether or not you have a pet at home, you can care for animals by taking care of the earth around you. Animals need a healthy place to live, and it is our responsibility to help them. By recycling plastic bottles, picking up trash, and walking or riding your bike instead of riding in the car, you are keeping God's earth clean and protecting his creations.

Talk with your parents about ways your family can care for animals and the earth. Visit an animal shelter or make a bird feeder for your yard. Small changes make a big impact!

DAY 7
Green Thumb

The word of God is alive and active. It is sharper than any sword that has two edges. It cuts deep enough to separate soul from spirit. It can separate bones from joints. It judges the thoughts and purposes of the heart.

—Hebrews 4:12

Do you have a green thumb? That means you have a special skill for growing plants and keeping them alive and healthy. How do you know if something is alive? Are your toys alive? Rocks? Water? No, those things are *nonliving* things. People, animals, and plants are examples of *living* things because they can grow, move, breathe, and do a bunch of other cool things.

The Bible says the Word of God is alive. When you read and listen to what the Bible says, God does something amazing to your heart and mind. He helps you grow, just like someone with a green thumb who keeps things alive. God's Word can change you from the inside out. Wow! Now that's powerful.

Try to keep a plant alive for a couple of weeks by watering it and making sure it gets the right amount of sun. Keep your heart and mind alive by reading the Bible every day too.

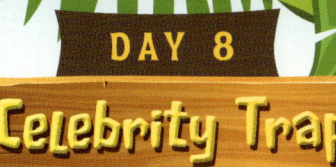

DAY 8
Celebrity Trap

Praise the Lord for the glory that belongs to him. Worship the Lord because of his beauty and holiness.

—Psalm 29:2

Do you watch television? Movies? Have a favorite band or singer? Sometimes we admire celebrities so much we want to be just like them—wear the same type of clothes, get the same haircuts, and talk and act like them too. But when you worship celebrities, you make them far more important than they are and compare their lives with yours. The truth is, celebrities are regular people who eat, sleep, and go about their day just like you. Lots of them are nice people, but their fame doesn't mean they're worth more in God's eyes.

But there is someone who is worthy of your worship. JESUS! He not only died for your sins, but he also made you (and the rest of the world), loves you, and has big plans for your life. Show God how much you love him today!

You can worship God in many ways, such as singing, praying, reading the Bible, and helping others.

DAY 9
Audience of One

Am I now trying to get people to think well of me? Or do I want God to think well of me? Am I trying to please people? If I were, I would not be serving Christ.

—Galatians 1:10

Who is the first person you talk to when something good happens in your life? Your friends? Parents? Siblings? What about when you get an A on a test? Or score a goal in soccer? It feels good when people clap for you and give you a high five. But sometimes, we worry too much about other people's opinions. Sometimes, all we care about are those cheers and high fives.

When you only want to please others, it means that what other people think matters more to you than what God thinks. The only audience you need to please is God! Make him number one in your life, because God's love and what he thinks about you is most important.

Dear God, thank you for loving me most. Help me to seek your opinion instead of the opinions of others. Amen.

DAY 10
Share God's Love

Dear friends, let us love one another, because love comes from God. Everyone who loves has become a child of God and knows God. Anyone who does not love does not know God, because God is love.

—1 John 4:7–8

When was the last time you told your parents you love them? Last month? Last week? Last night before bed? When was the last time you *showed* your parents you love them? You can show them by doing things like feeding the dog, taking out the trash, or cleaning your room without being asked. But your love for others doesn't have to stop there. You can write a letter to a friend, bring your teacher a thank-you gift, or bake cookies for your neighbor.

God created you and loved you first—that's why you and I get to show love to other people. It makes God so happy when we spread love to our friends, family, and communities! He always wants you to find ways to be loving and kind to the people around you.

Make a list of simple ways you can show God's love to others. Do one every day for a week. Sharing God's love with others will help you understand God's love for you.

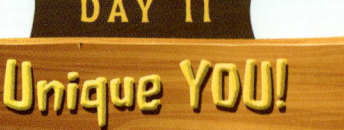

DAY 11
Unique YOU!

How you made me is amazing and wonderful. I praise you for that. What you have done is wonderful. I know that very well.

—Psalm 139:14

What do you look like? Do you have red hair, black hair, or are you blonde? Do you wear braces? Glasses? Do you have freckles? Are you tall, short, or in between? How would your friends describe you? Funny? Serious? Calm? Gentle? Quiet? Loud?

God made you special. There is no one else like you in the entire world. No one looks exactly like you (unless you have an identical twin, but even then there are differences!). No one has your personality, and no one thinks the way you do. You are special, and God designed you for a purpose!

Draw and color a picture of yourself. Write "God Made Me Unique" on the top and hang it on your wall.

DAY 12
Respecting God and Others

The Lord takes delight in those who have respect for him. They put their hope in his faithful love.

—Psalm 147:11

Have you ever wanted to laugh when someone falls down? Have you ever judged someone because they look different than you? Have you ever wanted to say a bad word to fit in or get attention? Respect is a big word and important to understand. Respect means you care about other people's feelings. Respect means you think good things about a person no matter how they look. Respect means you care about yourself too.

Did you know you can also show God respect? Yes, you can! You can talk to God and thank him for everything he's given you. You can listen to your parents without grumbling or complaining. And you can read your Bible and tell others about it. All these things show respect for God!

Dear God, thank you for your love. Help me show respect—to you and others. Amen.

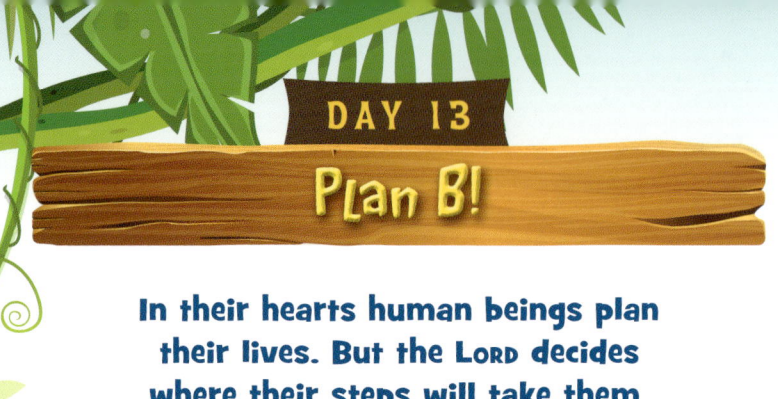

DAY 13
Plan B!

In their hearts human beings plan their lives. But the Lord decides where their steps will take them.

—Proverbs 16:9

Each day is a new adventure. Maybe today is an extra-special day, one that you have been planning for weeks or months. Maybe you are having your best friend over to your house for a sleepover. Maybe you are getting a new puppy. Or maybe you have your suitcase packed and are going on vacation!

It's good to make plans, but sometimes your day doesn't go as planned. Sometimes friends get sick and can't come over. Sometimes puppies need another week to grow before you can take them home. Sometimes you have to wait in the airport a long time before your plane leaves. No matter what, remember God is in control. He decides what is best and always has a better plan. The best part is that you can trust him to guide your steps each day!

Dear God, thank you for each new day. Help me to trust in you. Guide my steps today. Amen.

DAY 14
Praise God!

> **So the people said, "Lord, may your glorious name be praised. May it be lifted high above every other name that is blessed and praised."**
>
> **—Nehemiah 9:5**

Do you have a good singing voice? Maybe you've been singing for as long as you can remember, or maybe you don't remember the last time you hummed a tune. Maybe the only time you sing is in the shower or in front of your bedroom mirror. Many people are shy when it comes to singing in a large group of people, and others sing really loud.

Did you know God doesn't care if you sing like a professional or sound like a croaking frog? No matter what, it makes God happy when you sing and worship him. And guess what? It will make your heart happy too. By singing praise songs to God, you show him that you are thankful for all he has given you. So turn on the radio to a good Christian station and sing along!

The next time you hear your favorite Christian song or sing hymns at church, praise God with your voice!

DAY 15
What-If Game

Turn your worries over to the Lord. He will keep you going. He will never let godly people be shaken.

—Psalm 55:22

Do you play the what-if game? You know, when you ask . . .

What if the neighbor's dog bites me?
What if the dentist finds a cavity?
What if a spider crawls on my pillow at night while I sleep? Eeek!

It's easy to worry about situations like these, but there's a reason the Bible tells you to pray and give your worries to God. He cares about every what-if question you have. When you pray, God calms you and gives you peace when you are tempted to worry. He also watches over you and gently reminds you that he's in control. Truth is, most of the things you worry about will never happen, but it's good to know God cares and will listen.

Dear God, thank you for being in control of my life. Help me to trust you instead of playing the what-if game. Amen.

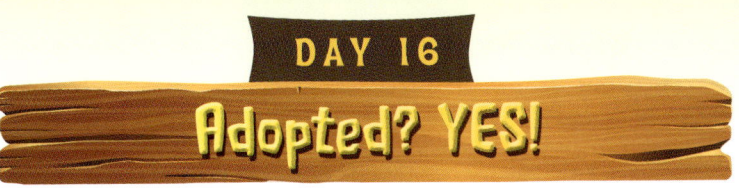

DAY 16
Adopted? YES!

So he decided long ago to adopt us. He adopted us as his children with all the rights children have. He did it because of what Jesus Christ has done. It pleased God to do it.

—Ephesians 1:5

Are you adopted? How awesome that someone chose you to be their very own! If you're not adopted, do you know someone who is? Most likely you do. Maybe you don't really know what adoption means and it sounds unfamiliar to you. You don't need to be scared to talk about it. Adoption is a wonderful process where parents raise children as part of their families, even if they aren't related by blood.

Did you know God adopted you into his family? If you believe in Jesus and what he did on the cross, you are a child in God's family. God loves you so much, and he always will!

Unscramble the letters: He DPEAOTD us! Hint: It pleased God to do it!

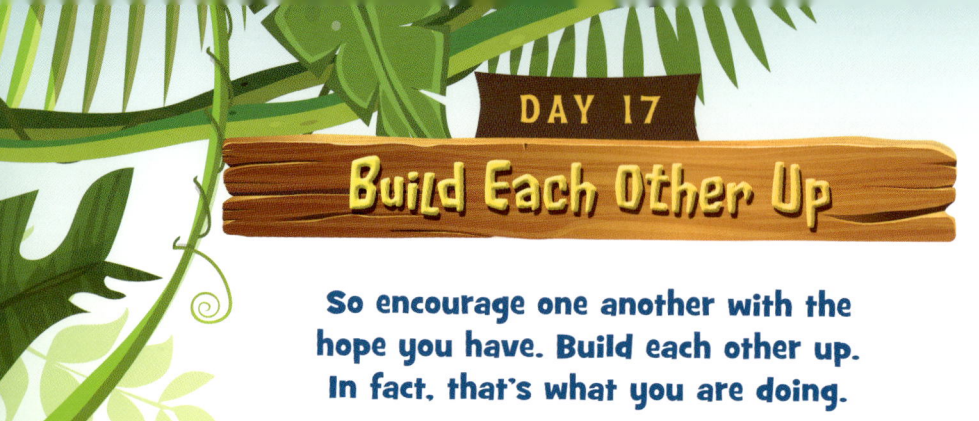

DAY 17
Build Each Other Up

So encourage one another with the hope you have. Build each other up. In fact, that's what you are doing.

—1 Thessalonians 5:11

Do you have a friend who is going through a hard time? Maybe your friend got a bad grade on a test. Maybe their parents are fighting. Or maybe they didn't make the team. Life can be difficult sometimes. When tough stuff happens in your friend's life, what do you do? Hope it blows over soon and ignore them until it does? Or do you listen and offer encouragement? Building up your friends, especially during difficult times, will give them the confidence they need to get through it. And when it's your turn to have a bad day, because everyone does, your friend will hopefully be there for you too.

Jesus encouraged people, and he tells us to build up others as well. You demonstrate God's love when you speak kind words. And guess what? When you encourage others, you build up yourself too.

Spend some time with your friend or even bring them a small gift, like cookies or some other treat. It shows them how much you care.

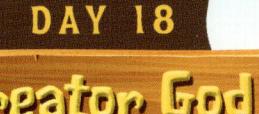

Creator God

In the beginning, God created the heavens and the earth.

—Genesis 1:1

Have you ever made something you were proud of? Your creation might not be perfect, but it doesn't matter—nothing ever is. You can be very proud of your work when you do your best. It could be a painting, a birdhouse, or a knitted scarf. Did you hang that painting on your wall? Place the birdhouse in the tree? Wear the scarf to school on a chilly day? The fact that you made it with your two hands should bring a smile to your face.

Did you know God is the Creator with a capital C? God created the heavens and the earth and everything in it. Have you ever seen an orange and pink sky at sunset, or a field of purple flowers, or a white snowcapped mountain? God made them all! And when God created the heavens and the earth, he said what he had made was very good.

Go outside and look up at the sky. Do you see clouds? A clear sky? The moon and stars? Remember, God made them all!

Those Bullies

Don't answer a foolish person in keeping with their foolish acts. If you do, you yourself will be just like them.

—Proverbs 26:4

Have you ever been bullied or treated in an unkind way? In life, there are people who say and do mean things. What do you do? Do you respond back with mean words, or do you show them God's love? Loving those who are mean can be hard, but the Bible says if you answer a bully in the same way he has treated you, then you will be just like him. Yikes! You don't want to be foolish, right?

Then how can you show respect to those who hurt you? First, walk away if you think the bully is trying to pick a fight. Next, tell an adult about it. An adult can help a bully understand his hurtful behavior. It takes a lot of courage to stand up to bullies, but with God's help you can do it!

Dear God, thank you for showing me how to love others. Help me to have courage to stand up to those who try to hurt me. Amen.

DAY 20
Going Fishing!

"Come and follow me," Jesus said. "I will send you out to fish for people." At once they left their nets and followed him.

—Matthew 4:19–20

Have you ever gone fishing? Before you go, you need to pack a fishing rod and reel, bait, along with water, snacks, sunscreen, bug repellant, and a first aid kit. You'll also want to make sure you find a good fishing spot. And for safety, have an adult bait your hook and teach you the best way to cast and grip your rod. Remember to have a lot of patience and always have fun!

Did you know Jesus wants you to fish for people too? That may sound strange, but fishing for people means telling others about Jesus. Like fishing for fish, you need the right equipment. By knowing what the Bible says, you can share it with others. You have to go to the right fishing spot, or where the people are. You also need a lot of patience. Not everyone you tell about Jesus is going to believe in him, but don't give up! Catching fish is exciting, but introducing someone to Jesus is out-of-this-world amazing!

Go fishing! Read your Bible every day and see what happens when you tell a new person about Jesus.

DAY 21
Give from Your Heart

Each of you should give what you have decided in your heart to give. You shouldn't give if you don't want to. You shouldn't give because you are forced to. God loves a cheerful giver.

—2 Corinthians 9:7

Are you a cheerful giver? What do you do when your friend is in need and you have twenty dollars in your piggy bank? What about when someone forgets to bring their lunch to school? Those are tough questions to think about. It's not easy being a cheerful giver when you've been doing a lot of chores to save up for something. It's not easy to share your lunch when your mom makes your favorite sandwich.

Do you have to be rich to give? Nope. The Bible says it doesn't matter how much money you have. But God does want your heart to be in the right place. What does that mean? God wants you to carefully think about giving before you do it. The important thing is to give because you want to. When you give cheerfully, your heart will be happy too.

Dear God, thank you for everything you've given me. Help me to give to others with a cheerful heart. Amen.

DAY 22
God Chooses YOU!

You are a holy nation. The Lord your God has set you apart for himself. He has chosen you to be his special treasure. He chose you out of all the nations on the face of the earth to be his people.

—**Deuteronomy 7:6**

Have you ever been the last one picked for something? Has a teacher ever ignored your raised hand? Or maybe you wanted the lead role in the school play and instead got put in the chorus? Does it feel as though other kids are always the ones chosen over you? It hurts when you're the last one standing and never picked. You may wonder if something is wrong with you. You may feel discouraged.

Did you know God chose you before you were born? Yes, the God of the universe chose you to be a part of his family—not because you are good enough, smart enough, or talented enough, but because he loves you. You didn't do anything to deserve it or earn it. God chose you because of his love and grace. You are God's special treasure!

Write a letter to God and tell him about a time you weren't chosen for something. Thank him for choosing you to be his special treasure.

DAY 23
Ouch, That Hurts!

"Forgive other people when they sin against you. If you do, your Father who is in heaven will also forgive you. But if you do not forgive the sins of other people, your Father will not forgive your sins."

—Matthew 6:14-15

Has anyone ever done something to make you mad? Maybe your brother grabbed the controller when it was your turn to play video games. Maybe your sister took the last slice of pepperoni pizza even though your mom said you could eat it. Maybe a friend shared your secret even though they promised they wouldn't tell a soul. Ouch, that hurts! Truth is, humans make mistakes and sometimes hurt each other. But what should you do about it? Let it roll off your back? Hold a grudge?

In Matthew 6:14–15, the Bible says forgiveness works two ways. If you can't forgive others, then you can't expect others to forgive you. Wow! Time to rethink that grudge, huh? Remember, there will come a time when you hurt someone and need forgiveness. Forgiveness doesn't mean the wrong that was done doesn't hurt, or you need to instantly trust that person again. Forgiveness means that you show grace to your sibling or friend and let go of the issue.

Write a story about something that made you mad and why it was unfair. Read it several times aloud, then throw it away. Time to forgive and move on!

DAY 24
New Every Morning

The LORD loves us very much. So we haven't been completely destroyed. His loving concern never fails.

—Lamentations 3:22

Have you ever hidden under a blanket during a thunderstorm? Or gone down to the basement during a tornado? Or crawled under the kitchen table during an earthquake? Natural disasters can be scary, but the more you know about them, the better prepared you will be. The best thing to do is have a family meeting to discuss where you will go and what you will do. But what if you're still frightened?

God can bring you comfort during a storm. His love never changes and never runs out. In fact, he always loves you—today, tomorrow, and forever! The Bible says his love is new every morning, like the sun rising with each new day! During a natural disaster, ask God to change your fear with faith. He is faithful and will make it happen.

Dear God, thank you for loving me each day. Help me to have faith instead of fear. Amen.

DAY 25
What Did You Say?

"Whoever has ears should listen."
—Matthew 11:15

Have you ever wondered how your ears hear your friend's laughter? Your favorite song on the radio? A whisper? Here's how it works: Ears are made up of three parts—the outer ear, or the part that collects sound; the middle ear, which turns the sound into vibrations; and the inner ear, which turns the vibrations into nerve signals for your brain. Pretty cool, huh?

Since God gave you such amazing ears, it's important to use them in the right way. How well do you listen to your parents when they ask you to do something? Do you listen to your teacher's instructions, or do you zone out in class? What about when your friend is trying to tell you something important? One of the best ways to show that you truly care about someone is to listen to them. God listens to you. Take time to listen to others.

Think about all the people you listen to each day. How can you show them you care by listening better? Remember to thank God for being a faithful listener.

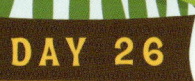

DAY 26
The Devil Made Me Do It

You are tempted in the same way all other human beings are. God is faithful. He will not let you be tempted any more than you can take. But when you are tempted, God will give you a way out. Then you will be able to deal with it.

—1 Corinthians 10:13

Have you ever eaten too much candy? Taken something from your sibling's closet that wasn't yours? You might say, "I couldn't help myself. Something inside me made me do it!" The devil is the one who puts those thoughts in your mind. Satan tempts you to do the things that go against what the Bible says is true, but he can't *make* you do anything. The choice is up to you. So when you are tempted, what should you do?

Talk to God! God's Word says he will not let you be tempted any more than you can take. And when that time comes, he will provide a way out! The best thing to do is memorize this Bible verse so you can swap temptation with God's truth!

Dear God, thank you for providing a way out when I'm tempted. Help me memorize Scripture so I can resist the devil. Amen.

DAY 27
Being Kind Is a Choice

The LORD is holy and kind. Our God is full of tender love.

—Psalm 116:5

Do you like to go first while playing a game? Be the first person in line? Always get your way when hanging out with friends? When you have a "me first" attitude, there is no room to be considerate of others.

Being kind is a choice. You can choose to let someone else go first. You can choose to let a friend pick the movie you're going to watch. These simple acts show kindness to the people around you.

God shows you kindness by caring for your needs. He loves you, watches over you, and provides for you. He also sent his Son, Jesus, to die on the cross to take the punishment for your sins. When you are kind to others, you are putting others first and sharing God's tender love with them.

Write down twenty ways you can be kind to others. Then start doing them! Sharing God's love feels great!

DAY 28
Giving Thanks

Always give thanks to God the Father for everything. Give thanks to him in the name of our Lord Jesus Christ.

—Ephesians 5:20

Do you tend to grumble and complain? Maybe you have to stay home and you'd rather hang out with friends. Maybe it's a rainy day and you'd rather play outside. Or maybe it's time to go to bed and you'd rather stay up late. It's easy to be thankful when you're having fun, doing well in school, and everything is going your way. But it's a lot harder to be grateful when you break your favorite toy, fall down and skin your knee, or a parent is making you eat something you don't like.

How do you thank God the Father for everything all the time? It's easy! You can have a grateful heart because no matter what happens, God loves you! He can show you how to be thankful even when life stinks. There are many things to be thankful for every day. Look around you. You can probably find a hundred things to be thankful for right now!

Make a "Give Thanks" banner to hang in your room. Cut out ten triangle shapes from construction paper and write G-I-V-E-T-H-A-N-K-S, one letter per triangle. Attach to a long piece of string or yarn with tape and hang in your room so that you can remember to be thankful every day.

DAY 29
Be Joyful Today

The LORD has done it on this day. Let us be joyful today and be glad.

—Psalm 118:24

What is your favorite day of the year? Christmas? Your birthday? Last day of school? It's fun to count down on a calendar and look forward to those special days. What about today? What if nothing special is happening? What if today is the worst day ever? Can you still be joyful? Can you choose joy no matter what type of day God gives you?

Each day is a gift and created by God. The fact that you are alive and breathing makes today a good day. To have another day with friends and family makes today a good day. When you wake up each morning, you have a choice of how you will greet your day. Will you be joyful for the day God made no matter what?

Do you have a calendar on your bedroom wall? If not, you can make one! Grab paper and a marker and make five rows of seven days. Write Sunday through Saturday on the top, then ask a parent for help to fill in the numbers. Remember to be joyful each day!

DAY 30
Sit By Me!

My brothers and sisters, you are believers in our glorious Lord Jesus Christ. So treat everyone the same.

—James 2:1

Does it matter to you whether someone is rich or poor? What if a new student walked into your classroom wearing the expensive shoes you've been dreaming about for months? What if someone walked in wearing dirty clothes and smelling like they hadn't had a bath in weeks? Who would you eat lunch with? Would you invite the rich kid to sit by you and tell the dirty one to take a hike?

If you're tempted to treat some people better than others, you're not alone, but God says that's a sin. He wants you to treat everyone the same. It doesn't matter to God if someone is rich or poor, clean or dirty. What matters most to God is showing love to all people. Besides, when you judge people by how they look, you are only trying to make yourself look better. And that's not cool. So love everyone like Jesus does!

Dear God, thank you for the people in my life. Help me to treat everyone the same. Amen.

DAY 31
Are You Laughing Yet?

He will fill your mouth with laughter. Shouts of joy will come from your lips.
—Job 8:21

How would you describe your laugh? Do you giggle? Snicker? Howl? Shriek? Roar? Snort? A good joke can make you smile and sometimes you might giggle because you're nervous, but most of the time you laugh because someone else is laughing. Have you ever laughed so hard you had to clutch your stomach and gasp for air? Laughter is good for you and one of the easiest ways to change a bad mood. Besides, life is full of funny situations.

Did you know laughter is mentioned in the Bible at least forty-two times? The Bible says God laughs too. Psalm 2:4 says, "The God who sits on his throne in heaven laughs." He has a great sense of humor. After all, God is the one who created all the funny things in this world! Truth is, if you want to be more like God, laugh!

Tell a joke to a friend. Laugh for no reason. Thank God for giving you a sense of humor!

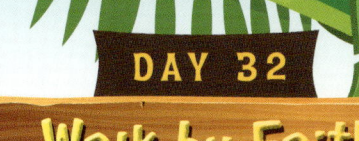

DAY 32
Walk by Faith

We live by believing, not by seeing.
—2 Corinthians 5:7

Your eyes gather information about people, places, and objects all day long until you close them to go to sleep at night. That is a lot of information for your brain! Look around you. What do you see? The cookie jar? Your cozy bed? A large, hairy spider? Eek! Each one of these things makes you feel something different. Seeing the cookie jar might make your mouth water, glancing at your bed might make you feel sleepy, and a scary-looking spider may make you feel afraid. But you shouldn't let what you see and feel decide every move you make.

The Bible says you should live your life based on your faith in Jesus instead of on what you see going on around you. Walking by faith means you believe God has a good plan for your life whether or not things are going right. When you trust in God and pray for him to guide your life, you will experience peace. All you need is courage and a little bit of faith. Put your trust in God. He will guide you each step of the way.

Think about the things you see throughout your day and how they make you feel. Now think about Jesus and how much he loves you. Ah, peace!

DAY 33

Antarctica, Mount Everest, and Other Cool Stuff

He placed the earth on its foundations. It can never be moved.
—Psalm 104:5

Did you know Earth really isn't round? It is sphere-shaped, but it's flatter at the North and South Poles. Seventy percent of Earth is water, and ten percent of the Earth's surface is ice. Brr! Antarctica is the largest and coldest desert, and the highest mountain on the Earth's surface is Mount Everest of the Himalayas, with a height of 29,032 feet. Did you also know there are one hundred fifty million kilometers between the Earth and the sun?

There are many more interesting facts about Earth, but the most important one is that God created it. He made every hill and valley, desert and forest, river and ocean. He not only created Earth, but he placed it where he wanted it to be.

Next time you take a ride in the car, look closely at the landscape and praise God for making our planet!

DAY 34
God's Masterpiece

We are God's creation. He created us to belong to Christ Jesus. Now we can do good works. Long ago God prepared these works for us to do.

—Ephesians 2:10

What is one thing you really like about yourself? Is it your hair? Your personality? The way you help others? Is there one thing you would change if you could? Maybe you wish you were better in school, knew how to draw, or played sports. Do you think God made a mistake when he made you?

You are God's masterpiece, not just in how you look on the outside, but also how he made you on the inside with your personality and your likes and dislikes. God made you for a purpose. There is no one else like you! Your friends and family need you. Your school needs you. Your neighbors need you. If you were not needed, God would not have made you. You can be sure that God has a perfect plan for you—just as you are.

Dear God, thank you for making me for a purpose. Help me to love the person you made me to be.

DAY 35
Fantastic Feet

The Lord and King gives me strength. He makes my feet like the feet of a deer. He helps me walk on the highest places.
—Habakkuk 3:19

Take off your shoes and socks and wiggle your toes. The average foot has thirty-three joints, twenty-six bones, nineteen muscles, and one hundred seven ligaments. Do you have sweaty feet? Don't be surprised. You have 250,000 sweat glands in each foot! How much of your foot touches the floor when you stand? If everything touches, you have flat feet, otherwise you've developed arches. Did you know standing is more tiring than walking? Yep! When you walk, it boosts circulation and helps you burn calories.

After a long day, your feet may be too tired to stand or walk. Tough situations in life are like that too. They can get you down and make you tired. This verse talks about how God gives us strength during hard times. You can trust God to lift you up when you are down. When you depend on God for strength, he will make your steps stable and secure.

Take good care of the feet God gave you. Have a parent show you how to care for them properly so they work just right.

DAY 36
Green Stuff

"No one can serve two masters at the same time. You will hate one of them and love the other. Or you will be faithful to one and dislike the other. You can't serve God and money at the same time."
—Matthew 6:24

There is a difference between a need and a want. A *need* might be a new backpack for school or new clothes when yours are too small. A *want* may be the latest toy or gadget or popcorn and candy when you're at the movie theater. A need is something that is important to buy, while a want is a choice. Shopping is fun and buying something new feels good, but the feeling doesn't last long and the next thing you know, you want to buy something else. Pretty soon your closet is jam-packed, and your bookshelves are overflowing with stuff!

It's hard to keep our priorities straight when we live in a world that likes stuff. The Bible says it's impossible to love God and money at the same time. You have to choose what is more important. One way to remember that God is more important is to be generous. Every time you give, you are changing from the inside out and are becoming more like God.

Find a charity you can donate some of your old clothes or toys to. It feels good to give!

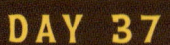

What's That Sweet Smell?

God considers us to be the pleasing smell that Christ is spreading.

—2 Corinthians 2:15

What is your favorite smell? Crayons? Bubble gum? Suntan lotion? Chocolate chip cookies baking in the oven? The "smell device" inside your nose is called the olfactory (ol·-fac·to·ry) epithelium (ep·i·the·li·um). You have more than ten million scent receptors, which can distinguish up to ten thousand different smells. When the tiny odor molecules pass through your nose, the receptors send messages to your brain, which tells you what you smell. That is how you know when your mom is wearing perfume or when your dad's cooking fish for dinner.

Have you taken a good whiff of yourself lately? No, not your stinky gym clothes or your favorite shampoo. When you show your love for God in your words and actions, you have the sweet fragrance of Christ. Take the sweet aroma of God everywhere you go!

Get permission to cut a flower from a yard and put it in a small vase with water. Put the flower where you will smell it often to remind yourself to be the aroma of Christ.

DAY 38
Model Airplanes and Spaceships

Ezra had committed himself to study and obey the Law of the Lord. He also wanted to teach the Lord's rules and laws in Israel.

—Ezra 7:10

Have you ever built something after reading an instruction manual? Maybe you tried to build a model airplane or spaceship. Or maybe you helped create a delicious meal by following directions in a cookbook. The cool thing is when you commit to study, learn, and practice how to do something, you'll be able to teach someone else how it's done.

That's exactly what it was like for Ezra. He was a high priest. He spent many hours, days, and years studying the Bible. Ezra set his heart on knowing God's Word so he could teach it to others.

What about you? Are you studying the Bible? Whether you go to church regularly or not, you can read your Bible and know what it says so you can share what you've learned with others. Jesus taught everywhere he went, and so can you!

Dear God, thank you for pastors and all their hard work. Help me to study the Bible so that I can share it with others too. Amen.

DAY 39
My Family

God gives lonely people a family.
—Psalm 68:6

How many people are in your family? Are you the oldest, middle, youngest, or are you an only child? Do you ever wish you had your friend's family or something different than what God gave you? It's easy to think your friends have a better life, but no family is perfect.

Some kids live in two homes because of divorce, splitting their time between their parents. Other kids live with a single parent, grandparents, or aunts and uncles. And some kids live with foster parents because their birth parents are unable to care for them. Your family might look different than your friend's family, but God has a plan and it is perfectly okay. Remember, no matter what type of family you have, God loves you and wants you to do your best in the family he gave you.

Draw and color a picture of your family. Hang it on your wall and thank God for the family he gave you.

DAY 40
God's Gifts

But the Israelites replied to the Lord, "We have sinned. Do to us what you think is best. But please save us now."
—Judges 10:15

The God of the universe loves you and wants a relationship with you. Yes, it's true! But there's one thing that's stopping you on this adventure—sin. Sin keeps you from having a relationship with him. What exactly is sin? Is it only big things, like lying, cheating, stealing, or hurting someone? No! Disobeying your parents or being mean to your sibling is a sin too.

Did you know the Bible says everyone sins? But don't worry, God thought of everything! He sent Jesus to earth to die on the cross for your sins. Amazing, huh? Salvation from sin and eternal life in heaven are God's gifts to you when you believe and ask forgiveness for your sins. Are you ready to admit your sins, believe Jesus died on the cross, and commit to spending time with him? Awesome!

If you are ready, say this prayer: Dear God, please forgive me of my sins. I believe in Jesus and that you sent him to earth to die on the cross for my sins. I want to live my life for you. Amen.

DAY 41
Get Moving!

Don't you know that your bodies are temples of the Holy Spirit? The Spirit is in you, and you have received the Spirit from God. You do not belong to yourselves. Christ has paid the price for you. So use your bodies in a way that honors God.
—1 Corinthians 6:19-20

Do you like to play sports? Maybe you are on a soccer team or enjoy gymnastics. Or maybe baseball or football is more your thing. But what if you'd rather play video games, read a book, draw, or do your homework than exercise? Is moving your body that important? The answer is yes! Your heart is a muscle, and it works hard at pumping blood throughout your body. By regularly doing aerobic activity, your body will be in great shape and you'll give your heart a workout.

Does God really care if people exercise? Yes, he does! He made your body and wants you to take care of it. When you exercise, it shows God you are grateful for the body he's given you.

Get your body moving sixty minutes every day! Ride your bike around the neighborhood, take a long walk, or play a game of tag. Ask your parents to join you. They need exercise too.

DAY 42
Your Temple

Don't you know that you yourselves are God's temple? Don't you know that God's Spirit lives among you?

—I Corinthians 3:16

When was the last time you ate cookies, a doughnut, or a slice of pie? What about chips? Special treats are fun to eat every once in a while, but they have a lot of fat and sugar, which isn't the best thing for your body. Eating fruits and vegetables, as well as dairy products, like cheese, milk, and yogurt, and the protein found in beans, eggs, meat, and nuts is important to staying healthy.

The Bible says that your body is God's temple. Part of taking care of your temple is eating healthy. That doesn't mean you can never eat french fries or another slice of pizza. God is more concerned about your heart. Yes, God wants you to eat healthy, but he cares more about your relationship with him.

Spread some peanut butter on apple slices or celery sticks or make a smoothie with a cup of milk, ice, and fresh fruit. Enjoy!

DAY 43
Love Like Jesus

"I give you a new command. Love one another. You must love one another, just as I have loved you. If you love one another, everyone will know you are my disciples."

—John 13:34–35

Has your mom or dad ever asked you to be kind to your sibling? You might have thought, *It's not fair! How can I be nice when he's not being nice to me?* When those around you are mean, it's natural to want to treat them the same way, but God asks you to love them and show that you love Jesus.

Did you know God's love was the same during Bible times as it is today? Because he loves you, he wants you to love others. Sometimes loving other people is difficult, especially if they are different than you or push you away. Remember, God loves everyone. He loves your parents, siblings, and your friends. He also loves bullies, grouchy neighbors, and those in prison. God wants you to love others too. Just as you can recognize a police officer, firefighter, or a nurse by their uniform, the best way for people to see that you are a Christian is by your love for others.

Draw a picture of a big heart. In the center write the words "Love Like Jesus." Whenever you're having a difficult time loving someone, write their name inside the heart to remind yourself to love them like Jesus does.

DAY 44
Sweet Dreams

**In peace I will lie down and sleep.
Lord, you alone keep me safe.**
—Psalm 4:8

Do you like to go to bed or would you rather stay up late? How many hours of sleep do you get at night? Your brain needs sleep so that you can stay awake at school and remember what you learn. When you get enough sleep, you are able to concentrate, solve problems, and think of new ideas. Your muscles, bones, and skin grow and fix injuries while you sleep. Sleep is also important to keep your body healthy and fight illness.

It's hard to go to sleep if you're worried about a big test, or if you feel your parents treated you unfairly. But you can lie down and have peace if you trust God to take care of you. He will help you do your best at school, and help you honor your parents even when you disagree with them. When you put your trust in God, you can count on a good night's sleep!

Turn off the screens and establish a bedtime routine, such as brushing your teeth, putting on comfortable pajamas, and reading a book. After you turn out the light and get comfortable, close your eyes and ask God to give you peace.

DAY 45
Working for God

Work at everything you do with all your heart. Work as if you were working for the Lord, not for human masters.

—**Colossians 3:23**

What kind of chores do you do at home? Do you take out the trash? Help with the dishes? Clean your room? What type of attitude do you have when you do those chores? Do you have a cheerful attitude, or do you grumble and complain? Do you do the job as quickly as you can, or are you careful to do your best?

The Bible says you are to work at *everything* with your whole heart, which means no chore is too small when you are working for the Lord. So have a cheerful attitude and do your best when you take out the trash, wash the dishes, and clean your room. You know you are working for the Lord when you want to please God.

Dear God, thank you for seeing even the small things I do. Help me to do my best with a cheerful attitude. Amen.

DAY 46
The Small Voice

Peter replied, "All of you must turn away from your sins and be baptized in the name of Jesus Christ. Then your sins will be forgiven. You will receive the gift of the Holy Spirit."

—Acts 2:38

Have you ever received a gift on a day that wasn't Christmas, your birthday, or a special holiday? Maybe a parent bought you an ice cream cone on the way home from school. Maybe a friend loaned you their favorite book. Or a teacher brought in a yummy treat. How did you feel? Loved? Cared for? Special?

God gave you an amazing gift too! He gave you the gift of the Holy Spirit. The Holy Spirit lives inside you and helps you make good choices. He also comforts you and reminds you how much God loves you. Next time you get a surprise gift from someone, think about God's gift to you—his Holy Spirit.

Dear God, thank you for the gift of the Holy Spirit. Help me listen to the small voice inside me so I can make good choices. Amen.

DAY 47
Where's My Bible?

Some people worship the worthless statues of their gods. They turn away from God's love for them.
—Jonah 2:8

It's fun to play video games, collect toys, and have special treasures. God has given you everything you have, and it's okay to enjoy them. But if you can't stop thinking about your video game or toy during breakfast, when you're at school, and when it's time to go to bed, then it's possible you've made that item into an idol.

An idol is something that has taken God's place in your heart. Does your Bible have a thick layer of dust on it? Is it hiding under your bed? If the answer is yes, then you know you need to spend time with God. Read your Bible and pray. Ask God to help you put him first. Go outside and look around at the flowers and trees and all that God has made. Remember that nothing is more important than spending time with him.

Tell a parent if you are making something into an idol. Ask them to help you put it away for a while so you can put God first.

DAY 48
Learning the Important Stuff

"Sell what you own. Give to those who are poor. Provide purses for yourselves that will not wear out. Store up riches in heaven that will never be used up. There, no thief can come near it. There, no moth can destroy it."

—Luke 12:33

Have you ever had a garage sale? Was it easy or hard for you to sell your stuff? Sometimes it's hard to let go of things because of the fun memories. Besides that, there's a possibility you might need it someday or maybe the person who buys it won't take care of it the way you do. Don't let your fears stop you from making someone happy!

Truth is, Jesus doesn't want you to worry about stuff. He wants you to build your treasure in heaven, not on earth. Building treasure in heaven means you do things to help others, like giving your stuff to the poor, helping someone in need, or being a friend to someone who is lonely. When you show love to others, you are storing up riches in heaven.

Go through your closet or toy chest and find some toys you don't play with anymore. Ask a parent to help you find a local charity so that you can donate your stuff to someone in need.

DAY 49
Stick It Out

But Ruth replied, "Don't try to make me leave you and go back. Where you go I'll go. Where you stay I'll stay. Your people will be my people. Your God will be my God."

—Ruth 1:16

Have you ever wanted to quit something when it seemed difficult? Maybe you're on a soccer team and find yourself on the bench more than out on the field. Maybe piano lessons are a lot harder than you thought they would be. Maybe you're having a tough time reading or doing your math homework.

Ruth from the Bible was in a difficult situation too. Her husband died and her mother-in-law, Naomi, asked Ruth to leave her. But Ruth wasn't going to leave Naomi, even though Ruth had the possibility of starting a new life with a new husband near her family. Talk about commitment! Do you have the kind of faithfulness that will stick it out when things get tough? Are you all in?

Stick it out! Kick the ball around, practice the piano, study a bit longer, or do what it takes to commit to whatever is difficult right now. If Ruth can do it, so can you!

DAY 50
Obey Your Parents

Honor your father and mother. Then you will live a long time in the land the Lord your God is giving you.

—Exodus 20:12

When was the last time you kept watching television or playing a game when the adult in the house asked you to help with a chore? When was the last time you stayed up late when your parents told you to go to bed? When was the last time you rolled your eyes at your mom or dad when they asked you to do something you didn't want to do?

Your parents aren't purposely being mean or trying to ruin your fun when they ask you to do something. Instead, they are helping you discover how to take care of yourself, learn right from wrong, and make wise choices. No, grown-ups aren't perfect, but God put adults in charge, and he wants you to obey them. It isn't always easy to obey when you don't agree with your parents or like their rules, but when you obey the adults in your life, you are learning how to honor God.

Draw a picture of your family. Put a circle around the adults in charge. When you obey them, you honor God!

DAY 51
Say "YES" to God

"It's possible that you became queen for a time just like this."

—Esther 4:14

Have you ever helped a younger sibling with their homework? Have you ever played a board game or read a book with an older person in a nursing home? Have you ever given money from your piggy bank to help your church or school? Have you ever told an adult when you've seen someone getting picked on? God calls everyone, including you, to help when needed.

In the Bible, there was a young queen named Esther who was called by God to do something brave. She was asked to help save God's people from Haman, an evil man who had a wicked plan to kill all the Jewish people in the kingdom. First, Esther prayed, then she went to the king for help to stop Haman's plan. This was very courageous because Esther could have been killed for going right to the king without asking him first. Because Esther listened to God, she saved an entire nation! God has a special purpose for you too. Will you listen to him today?

What is something God is calling you to do? Help a sibling? Visit someone who is lonely? Help with a fundraiser? Stop a bully? Be brave like Esther!

DAY 52
Hair, Hair, Everywhere!

"In fact, he even counts every hair on your head! So don't be afraid. You are worth more than many sparrows."

—Luke 12:7

What color hair do you have? Brown? Black? Red? Blond? Is your hair curly, wavy, or straight? Short, long, or somewhere in between? Did you know hair above the skin is considered dead? That's the reason it doesn't hurt when you get a haircut! On average, you lose 50–100 strands of hair every day—just look at your hairbrush! It is important to take care of your hair because it protects your head from the sun, as well as keeps your head warm on cool days and cool on warm days.

Did you know God counts every hair on your head? Yes, he does! God not only knows the number of hairs on your head, but he is watching over you every minute of the day. He cares about the biggest and the smallest details of your life. If you ever feel afraid, remember this verse. Because you are important in God's eyes!

Next time you shampoo your hair, remember you are so important to God that he counts every hair on your head.

DAY 53
The Mighty Ocean

But Lord, you are more powerful than the roar of the ocean. You are stronger than the waves of the sea. Lord, you are powerful in heaven.

—Psalm 93:4

Do you live by the ocean? Maybe you've taken a vacation along the coast or have seen the ocean on television shows or movies. If you've never heard the roar of the ocean, ask an adult to help you search the internet to hear what it sounds like. You'll be blown away by how powerful it is!

The Bible says that God is more powerful than the roar of the ocean and stronger than the waves of the sea. Wow! Did you picture God to be so big? Because God is so mighty, he is bigger than the waves in your life and stronger than any storm that comes your way. So when you feel anxious or overwhelmed, remember you have a big God who will help you weather the rough seas.

Dear God, thank you for being so powerful and mighty! Help me go to you during the difficult times or storms of life. Amen.

DAY 54
God Formed YOU!

"Before I formed you in your mother's body I chose you. Before you were born I set you apart to serve me. I appointed you to be a prophet to the nations."

—Jeremiah 1:5

Incubation is the process of keeping fertile eggs warm. Did you know chicken eggs incubate for twenty-one days? Much like babies, eggs don't all hatch on their exact due date. Some hatch as early as day nineteen and others wait until day twenty-three. But they never take God by surprise!

Just like God forms chickens inside of eggs, he formed you inside your mother's body. Yes, God knows you and calls you by name. In the Bible, God called a man named Jeremiah, someone he picked as a prophet to tell others about him. Before you were born, God chose you to do important things for him too. And like Jeremiah, you are never too young to make a big impact!

Look through photos of when you were young. What are some things you can do now that you couldn't then? Remember, before you were born, God set you apart to serve him!

DAY 55
Let the Tears Flow

"Blessed are those who are sad. They will be comforted."

—Matthew 5:4

Has something big and terrible ever happened to you? Has one of your grandparents died? Or a pet? Maybe your parents are divorced or your best friend moved away. Or maybe you know someone who is very sick. Maybe the sick person is you! You may feel afraid, angry, or worried. The sad events in your life will bring out strong emotions, and you may be surprised by everything you are feeling.

The best thing to do is to let all those feelings out. Don't stuff them inside or pretend nothing is wrong. Instead, tell God how sad you are. Cry to him. Let him know you are hurt and having a tough time. When you release your grief to God, he will comfort you and heal your broken heart. But what if you don't feel better? Talk to an adult. He or she can get you the help you need.

Go to a quiet place and pray. Tell God what is making you sad. Let your feelings out. Remember, it's okay to cry.

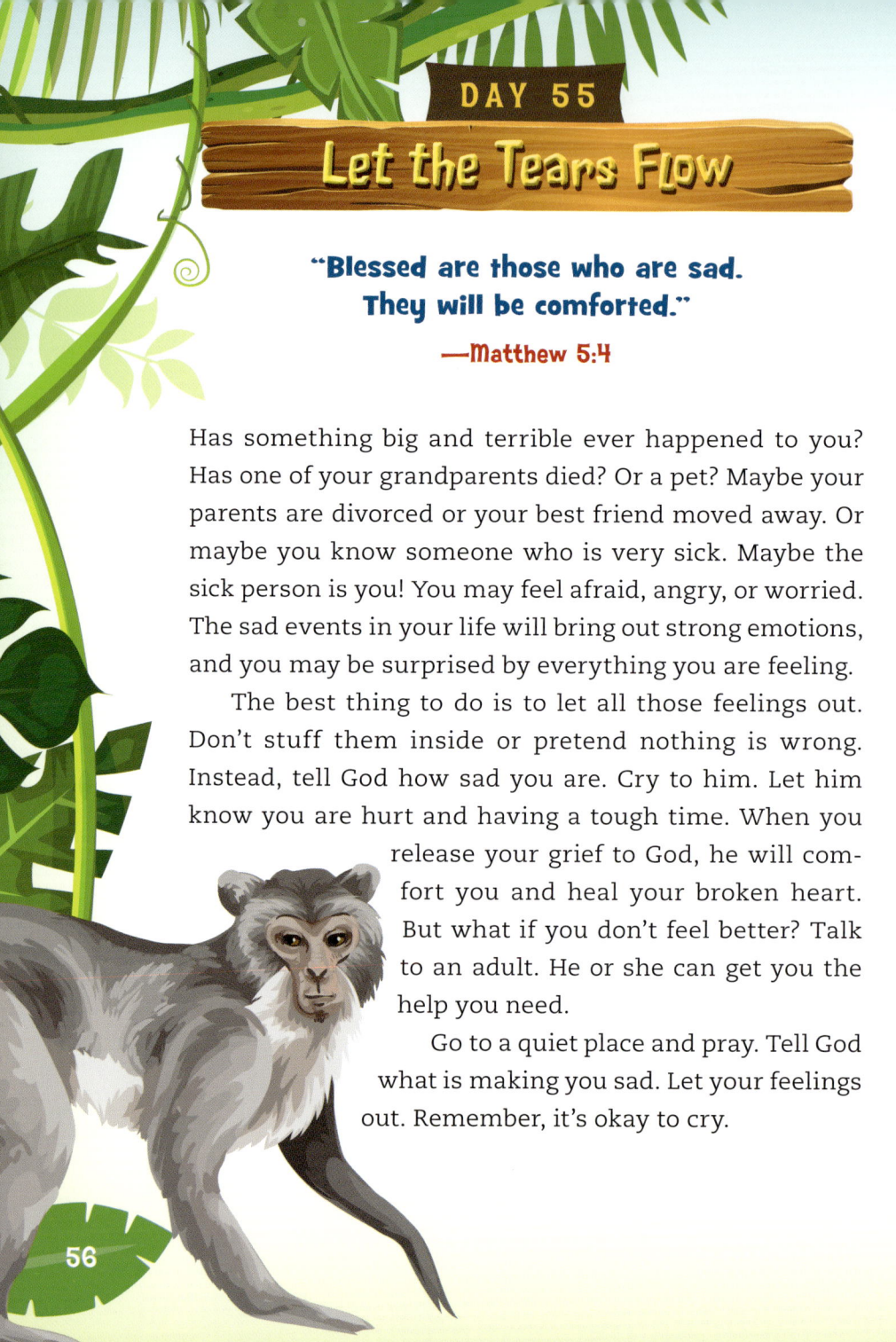

DAY 56
Knock, Knock. Who's There?

Here I am! I stand at the door and knock. If anyone hears my voice and opens the door, I will come in. I will eat with that person, and they will eat with me.

—**Revelation 3:20**

Knock, knock.
Who's there?
Harry.
Harry who?
Harry up and answer the door!

As funny as that joke is (or isn't), the truth is no one likes to wait for someone to answer the door. Do you have a "no closed doors" policy at your house, or do your parents let you hang out in your room with the door shut?

Jesus is knocking at the door of your heart. It is up to you whether you open it and invite him into your life. When you pray and accept Jesus into your heart and believe in him, you are answering the door and opening up to the better life he has for you. Jesus is knocking at your door. Have you let him in?

Create a door hanger. Write "Jesus is Knocking" on it to remind yourself to invite him into your heart.

Jealous No More

Are you jealous? Are you concerned only about getting ahead? Then your life will be a mess. You will be doing all kinds of evil things.

—James 3:16

Are you jealous of anyone? Maybe someone in your class got a better grade than you on a test. Maybe your teammate scored a goal, and you didn't. Maybe your friend has her own room, and you have to share. In situations like these, it's easy to want what someone else has. But being envious of other people prevents you from being grateful for the person God created you to be.

Yes, God made you to be unique! It is difficult to do what God wants you to do when you are focused on other people. Spelling might be hard for you, but you might be good at math. You might not be the star player on the team, but you encourage everyone to do their best. Maybe you don't have your own room, but you know how to share. You have your own gifts and talents. So instead of being jealous of others, thank God for making you to be *you*.

Dear God, thank you for the gifts and talents you've given me. Help me not to be jealous of others. Amen.

DAY 58
Small Fibs and Big Lies

Don't lie to one another. You have gotten rid of your old way of life and its habits. You have started living a new life. Your knowledge of how that life should have the Creator's likeness is being made new.

—Colossians 3:9-10

Have you ever told a white lie? You know, the kind of lie that feels as if it's no big deal, like the time you said, "I'm fine," when you were really having a bad day. Or when your friend asked if you liked his haircut and you said, "Yes," even though it looked like it was cut by a lawnmower! Sometimes people tell lies so that they don't hurt people's feelings. Sometimes people tell lies to get out of trouble, or to avoid getting into trouble.

Did you know God sees all lies the same? The Bible says telling lies is a sin. You might think small fibs don't hurt anyone, but even those lies make God sad. And if you're able to tell white lies, you might be tempted to tell big ones too. The good news is that God will forgive your sins when you ask! Telling the truth takes a lot of courage, but you can be honest with God and others in a loving and respectful way.

Who was the last person you told a lie to? Tell God about it, then go to that person and be honest with them in a loving and respectful way.

DAY 59
Promise Keeper

God isn't a mere human. He can't lie. He isn't a human being. He doesn't change his mind. He speaks, and then he acts. He makes a promise, and then he keeps it.

—Numbers 23:19

Name all your friends. Who is your best friend? What do you like to do together? A faithful friend is there for you during happy times and sad times. A faithful friend doesn't make a promise and then change his mind. A faithful friend keeps his promises.

God is a faithful friend. Because God isn't human, he doesn't change his mind or tell lies to get out of sticky situations. In fact, God always means what he says. He knows everything, and he keeps his promises. You can be confident God will never change, and you can trust that he will always be by your side!

When was the last time you changed your mind or broke a promise to someone? Praise God that he means what he says and keeps his promises.

DAY 60
Two-Stepping with Jesus

Let them praise his name with dancing. Let them make music to him with harps and tambourines.

—Psalm 149:3

Do you like to dance? Maybe you've taken ballet lessons or tap. Maybe you've square danced during PE at school. Maybe you've never had training and just like to move to the beat. Or maybe you'd rather eat a plate full of peas than be caught dancing! There are many different styles of dance, from ballroom and hip-hop to line dancing and ballet. Did you know people have always danced? Several thousand years ago, people put pictures on pottery and stone to describe their dances.

When you're a Christian, Jesus is your dance partner in life. Your relationship with him is like a dance. The more you get to know him by praying and reading your Bible, the more in step you will be. Show him how much you love him today by two-stepping with Jesus!

Turn on some worship songs and praise God with dancing!

DAY 61
Pass the Fruit

But the fruit the Holy Spirit produces is love, joy and peace. It is being patient, kind and good. It is being faithful and gentle and having control of oneself. There is no law against things of that kind.

—Galatians 5:22–23

What is your favorite fruit? Is it apples, bananas, or pears? Maybe it's blueberries, raspberries, or strawberries. Or perhaps you like grapes or peaches. Fruit is good for you because it has vitamins and minerals that help you stay healthy and energized. Did you know that cucumbers, peppers, and tomatoes are considered fruit because they have seeds? How many pieces of fruit do you eat in a day?

The Holy Spirit produces a different type of fruit in your life when you follow Jesus. As you spend time with God, you will have more love, joy, peace, patience, kindness, goodness, faithfulness, gentleness, and self-control. You can't have any of those fruits by yourself. The only way you can produce the fruit of the Spirit is by trusting God with your whole heart.

Add fruit to your dessert. Cut up or slice fresh fruit and put it on top of frozen yogurt and think about how you can show others God's love through the fruit of the Spirit.

DAY 62
By Your Side

"Joshua, no one will be able to oppose you as long as you live. I will be with you, just as I was with Moses. I will never leave you. I will never desert you."

—Joshua 1:5

Have you ever felt all alone? Maybe you're an only child and wish you had a sibling to play with. Maybe your best friend has moved away. Or maybe your parents accidentally forgot to pick you up after school. When you feel invisible, you may feel sorry for yourself and wonder if anyone cares. At times like these, it's important to talk with a trusted adult about how you are feeling.

Just as God was with Joshua and Moses, God is always with you. He loves you and watches over you every minute of every day. He promises never to leave you or abandon you. And guess what? You will do great things with God by your side. You will learn how to find things to do when you are by yourself. You will find close friends when others move away. And you will forgive your parents when they make mistakes. With God by your side, you are never alone.

Dear God, thank you for always being by my side. Help me to talk to you when I feel alone. Amen.

DAY 63
Terrified!

They all saw him and were terrified. Right away Jesus said to them, "Be brave! It is I. Don't be afraid."

—Mark 6:50

Has someone ever come up from behind and scared you? Your heart probably felt as if it was going to beat right out of your chest. Have you ever needed to go to the hospital for stitches? Perhaps you fell off your bike or out of a tree. That out-of-control feeling and knowing you are going to hurt yourself is scary! Have you ever been in a car during a rainstorm? The pounding sound on the roof of the car might have made you feel helpless and unsafe.

The same thing happened to the disciples in the Bible. They were in a boat in the middle of the Sea of Galilee when the wind whipped up. As they pulled hard on the oars, they saw something coming toward them and thought it was a ghost! Yikes! Talk about a scary situation. But it wasn't a ghost. It was Jesus! He told them to be brave and not to be afraid. After that, the wind died down, and they were completely amazed. What scary situation has frightened you lately? Jesus wants you to know that he is there for you too.

Can you be brave today?

Draw a picture of a boat on a piece of paper or create the shape of a boat with wooden craft sticks. Remind yourself of what Jesus said to the disciples by saying it aloud: "Be brave! It is I. Don't be afraid."

DAY 64
One Big Family

So also we are many persons. But in Christ we are one body. And each part of the body belongs to all the other parts.

—Romans 12:5

How many people are in your family? Do you belong to a team or club? You might be on a sports team or part of a youth organization in your church or community. It's nice to be a member of something because it makes you feel loved and accepted. And in a family, club, or team, each member is important. Can you imagine a baseball team without a pitcher or a Girl Scout troop without a leader? Of course not!

When you believe in God, you belong in God's family. As his child, you also belong to his church. Did you know the people in your church are called the body of Christ? Just like your ears, eyes, hands, and other parts of your body belong and work together, every person in your church is needed and belongs too. When you are part of God's family, you not only belong to him: everyone in the church is your brother and sister in Christ.

Gather a few friends and form a club. Decide on how you will help people in your church or community. Remember, you are a part of God's family!

DAY 65
Choose JOY!

Finally, my brothers and sisters, always think about what is true. Think about what is noble, right and pure. Think about what is lovely and worthy of respect. If anything is excellent or worthy of praise, think about those kinds of things.

—Philippians 4:8

Are you having a good day or a bad day? Maybe everything is going great! You enjoy school and your friends, and you're getting along with your siblings. But maybe your day (or week or month) isn't going the way you planned. Your grades stink, your friends are being mean, and your siblings ignore you or want to pick a fight.

Did you know you can be joyful no matter what your day is like by changing the way you think? You can choose to focus on what is true, right, excellent, and worthy of praise—like God's creation and how much he loves you—or you can think about all the bad stuff that happens, including what you hear on the news and on television. The more you read the Bible and spend time with God, the more positive and joyful you will be. But if you are still having trouble thinking about the good, talk to an adult to help you find good things in each day.

Choose joy by writing down all the good things that happened today, then thank God for each one.

DAY 66
Big Trouble

He said, "When I was in trouble, I called out to the Lord. And he answered me. When I was deep in the place of the dead, I called out for help. And you listened to my cry."

—Jonah 2:2

When was the last time you got into big trouble? You might have disobeyed your parents, made a bad choice at school, or said or done something you knew you shouldn't. Maybe you get into trouble a lot. You may have a lot going on at home and the only way you know how to handle it is by acting out. By now you've probably figured out that you get a lot of attention for that kind of behavior, but this isn't the kind of attention you want.

Jonah got into big trouble when he didn't listen to God. When he disobeyed God, he ended up in the belly of a very big fish for three days. Talk about a fishy situation! But Jonah realized his gigantic mistake and called out to God for help. God not only was paying attention and listening to Jonah, but he also answered his cry and commanded the fish to spit Jonah out on dry land. Ah, freedom! When you are in trouble, call out to God. He will listen and answer you too!

Dear God, thank you for listening to me and answering my prayer. Help me to stay out of trouble and obey you. Amen.

DAY 67
Magnetic Power

God's power has given us everything we need to lead a godly life. All of this has come to us because we know the God who chose us. He chose us because of his own glory and goodness.

—2 Peter 1:3

Have you ever played with a magnet? It's amazing how powerful a magnet can be when it's near a metal object. You can attract metal objects or push them away, depending on which side you use.

God sees *everything* and hears *everything*. God is all-powerful. That means he is in control of everything and can do anything! He is stronger than the heaviest mountain on earth and more powerful than the fiercest storm in the sky. This big, all-powerful God chose *you*! He not only chose you, but he also gave you everything you need to follow him. Like the magnet, you have to stay close to God to have his power work in your life. Read your Bible, pray, and tell him that you want to put him first before anything else. Thank God today for the gift of his power.

Grab a magnet and a small metal object and discover the magnet's power. Consider God's power in your life and remember he chose YOU!

DAY 68
Going to Battle

Put on all of God's armor. Then you can remain strong against the devil's evil plans.

—Ephesians 6:11

Temptations are everywhere. Ads pop up constantly on television and online for the latest movie, junk food, or video game. The desire to have all those things can push you to make poor choices. And when you fixate on the things that are tempting you, you become focused on yourself instead of helping other people. Every day you make decisions about what you say, what you do, and how you act, and the devil would like nothing better than for you to fall into his trap. So what do you do?

In order to stand strong when the devil tempts you, put on the armor of God. What is that, you ask? As a Christian, you've been given the Holy Spirit to give you power, as well as spiritual weapons, such as the Bible and God's promises, to fight off the evil forces of this world. By putting on the armor of God, you can fight off the devil's schemes.

Dress for battle every day by asking God to help you fight off the devil's schemes. To find out more about God's armor, read Ephesians 6:10–18.

DAY 69
Keeping the Peace

> "City of Zion, be full of joy! People of Jerusalem, shout! See, your king comes to you. He always does what is right. He has won the victory. He is humble and riding on a donkey. He is sitting on a donkey's colt."
>
> —Zechariah 9:9

Are you a peacemaker, or do you like to pick a fight? Sometimes it's hard to be a peacemaker and do what is right when your sibling teases you or your friend always seems to get their way. You need God's help and a big dose of humility to keep the peace. Did you know kings in the Bible chose peace over fighting too?

The king mentioned in Zechariah 9:9 rode a donkey into Jerusalem instead of a warhorse. During this ancient time, leaders rode horses to war and donkeys if they came in peace. Did you know Jesus also rode a donkey into Jerusalem? Yes, this verse is a prophecy of Jesus's entry into the city on the first Palm Sunday. Like a peaceful king of long ago, Jesus also is humble and righteous and comes in peace. Will you choose peace too?

Draw a picture of a king riding a donkey and consider how you can be a peacemaker the next time you have to make a choice between fighting and peacemaking.

DAY 70
It's All Good

We know that in all things God works for the good of those who love him. He appointed them to be saved in keeping with his purpose.

—Romans 8:28

Do you know someone going through a difficult situation right now? Truth is, bad stuff happens—to you and those around you. But the Bible says that everything works together for good for those who love God. How, you ask?

When you love and rely on God to carry you through the tough stuff, he gives you peace. And guess what? God cares about the tough stuff as well as the smaller things too, like whether or not you made the team, got a good grade on your test, or had a fight with your friend. We don't know God's plan, but he sees the whole picture. Whatever you are going through, remember God's promise to work everything out for good.

Dear God, thank you for seeing the whole picture. Help me to remember that even when the bad stuff happens, you will work everything out for the good. Amen.

DAY 71
Strong as a Tree

"But I will bless anyone who trusts in me. I will do good things for the person who depends on me. They will be like a tree planted near water. It sends out its roots beside a stream. It is not afraid when heat comes. Its leaves are always green. It does not worry when there is no rain. It always bears fruit."

—Jeremiah 17:7-8

Whom do you trust? Your parents? Your teacher? Your best friend? It's good to trust the important people in your life, as long as you remember that they are human and sometimes make mistakes. What about celebrities or influencers you see on television or online? Can you trust them? Truth is, you're probably only seeing what they want you to see, rather than the full picture.

Is there someone you can trust? Yes—God! He's the one who always tells you the truth. If you put your trust in God and depend on him, he will make you strong and do good things in your life. He will bless you when you stay connected to him. You can trust in God. He knows everything and wants the best for you at all times.

Connect with God by going outside and sitting under a tree. Thank God for being trustworthy today!

DAY 72
Got Milk?

Like newborn babies, you should long for the pure milk of God's word. It will help you grow up as believers.
—1 Peter 2:2

What do you crave? Chocolate chip cookies? The latest toy or video game? Someone to notice you or your achievements? The dictionary defines a craving as something you want, long for, and greatly desire. Satan wants you to crave food, material things, and recognition, but these things won't help you grow. God knows what you really need—his Word, the Bible! Did you know that it's okay to crave? God made you that way. Most of all, he wants you to crave him.

A newborn baby needs to eat every couple of hours—that's eight to twelve times per day! Just like a newborn baby craves milk, when you are hungry for God and his Word, you will want to read the Bible and learn more about him. Every time you crave something, remember all you need is God's Word. You will grow up into a strong believer when you spend time with him.

Pour yourself a glass of milk and enjoy. Now read your Bible for the best milk of all!

DAY 73
Only a Prayer Away

When you hope, be joyful. When you suffer, be patient. When you pray, be faithful.

—Romans 12:12

Every family goes through difficult times. A new job, a move, money issues, and relationship problems are some of the things that can put stress on a family. What about you? Is your family going through a tough time right now? It's hard to put on a brave face or go to school and see your friends when things are not happy at home. And sometimes it's hard to concentrate or do your homework. Are you the type of person who keeps everything inside, or have you told someone about it?

It's best to talk with your parents, a teacher, a counselor, or pastor about how you feel. It's their job to guide and help you through the tough times. But don't forget to pray too. God knows what your family is going through! He is faithful and will give you joy in the middle of your pain, and the patience to go through it. You can be strong during tough times because God has a plan. You can trust him.

Ask your parents to tell you about a time God brought them through a difficult situation.

DAY 74
Learn to Be Wise

It is much better to get wisdom than gold. It is much better to choose understanding than silver.

—Proverbs 16:16

Do you like school? What is your favorite subject? Is schoolwork hard for you or is it easy? Having a good education is important. The more you learn, the better job you'll have in the future. But being smart and having a lot of knowledge is different than having wisdom. How? Knowledge is having a lot of information in your head, like knowing the capital of Alaska (Juneau) or how many bones are in the human body (206), but wisdom is being able to make good choices.

Do you think it is better to have a lot of money or to have wisdom? The Bible says it is better to get wisdom and understanding than to have gold and silver. Really? Why? When you search the Bible for godly wisdom, you will understand what is valuable, true, and what is worth far more than riches. And if you need to make a decision and you don't know what to do, ask God for wisdom. That's how you learn to be wise!

Dear God, thank you for helping me learn. Help me to be wise and choose understanding so that I can make good choices. Amen.

DAY 75
Secret Treasure

But Mary kept all these things like a secret treasure in her heart. She thought about them over and over.
—Luke 2:19

What is a special memory you treasure? A birthday? Riding your first bike? An outing with your dad or mom? A slumber party with a friend? Laughing with a sibling? It's fun to remember special times.

Mary, Jesus's mother, had a special memory too. After Jesus was born, shepherds from the field came to worship him. They told Mary and Joseph that an angel of the Lord had appeared to them and said that a Savior had been born. After they found Mary and Joseph, and the baby Jesus lying in a manger, they told everyone what they had seen and heard. The people were amazed! Everything that Mary knew about her precious baby boy was true! He was Christ the Lord!

You won't ever experience what Mary and Joseph did, but that doesn't mean you shouldn't treasure your special memories. God wants you to think about the blessings in your life. After all, he gave them to you! What secret treasure is in your heart?

Create a secret treasure chest from an old shoebox and store souvenirs inside, such as photos, movie ticket stubs, or any small object that reminds you of special times with family and friends.

DAY 76
Great Delight

The Lord your God is with you. He is the Mighty Warrior who saves. He will take great delight in you. In his love he will no longer punish you. Instead, he will sing for joy because of you.

—Zephaniah 3:17

Whom do you love? No, not the mushy kind of love, but the I-can't-imagine-my-life-without-you type. Maybe it's a grandparent or your mom and dad. Maybe it's a sibling or a friend. When you love someone, you smile when you think about them and you look forward to the next time you see them.

God thinks about YOU that way too! He not only loves you, but he takes great delight in you. The Bible says he sings for joy because of you. God loves you no matter what! That means he loves you whether you are having a good day or a bad one. God, the Mighty Warrior, is with you and rejoices over you because you are his child! How cool is that?

Write a simple love song for God and think about how he delights in you and sings for joy because of YOU.

DAY 77
Please Come In!

Welcome others into your homes without complaining.
—1 Peter 4:9

When was the last time you invited someone over to play? Was it a week ago? Last month? Last year? Do you like it when friends come over to your house, or do you have a difficult time sharing your toys? What if they want to play a board game or kick a soccer ball in the backyard and you don't? What do you do then? Do you go along with it, or do you grumble and complain?

There is a fancy word for welcoming people into your home—it's called hospitality. When you show hospitality, it means you are friendly, warm, and generous. You give friends the food in your refrigerator, let them play with your toys, and allow them to choose which parent-approved movie to watch. It's not always easy to let others play with your stuff and decide what to do, but God welcomes you into his family and he wants you to welcome others.

Invite a friend over to your house to play. Remember to show hospitality.

DAY 78
Lost and Found

Jesus answered, "I am the way and the truth and the life. No one comes to the Father except through me."

—John 14:6

Have you ever been lost? At first you might not have known you were lost until you looked around and noticed you were by yourself. Suddenly your stomach probably felt sick and your hands might have started to sweat! It's a scary feeling when you don't know where your parents are.

Truth is, you can't be found on your own. You need someone to help you, like your parents, the police, or a store clerk. (Phew! What a relief.) The same thing happens before you know Jesus. When you are lost in your sin, you can try to make good decisions on your own, but every path leads you down the same dark road. Jesus can help you find your way! He is the only way to God, the Father. He is truth. He is life. And you are found when you put your trust in him.

Dear God, I feel lost inside, but I want to be found. Help me put my trust in you because you are the way, the truth, and the life. Amen.

DAY 79
True Confidence

The Lord will be at your side. He will keep your feet from being caught in a trap.
—Proverbs 3:26

Have you ever tripped over your own feet? It's easy to do when you are growing. What about tripping over a step, the curb, or the edge of a rug? When you are by yourself, maybe you can laugh it off and move on, but what happens when someone sees it happen? Does your face turn red from embarrassment? Do you get mad at the person (or yourself)? Or do you have confidence to shrug it off and keep going?

You can have confidence that God will always be by your side. He loves you on the days you trip up and make a mistake, and he loves you even if you don't love him back. The good news is when you give God your heart and follow him, he will keep your feet from being tangled up and help you make good decisions.

Go outside and hop on one foot and then the other. Now jump rope. Think about how God keeps your feet from being caught when you follow him.

DAY 80
Sweet as Honey

Your words are very sweet to my taste! They are sweeter than honey to me.

—Psalm 119:103

What kind of food do you like to eat? Sweet? Sour? Salty? Bitter? Do you know your tongue has ten thousand taste buds? Check out your tongue in the mirror! See all those bumps? Those are your taste buds. Each taste bud has tiny, sensitive hairs that send messages to the brain to tell you how something tastes. But don't give your tongue all the credit. The uppermost part of your nose has special cells that help you smell the food when you chew. Between your taste buds and your nose, your brain discovers the sweet taste of honey or the sour taste of a Granny Smith apple.

Did you know your words can also have a sweet taste? When you encourage someone who's having a bad day, say something kind to a friend, or respond in a positive way to your parent or siblings, your words will have a sweet taste to those who listen. The Bible, or God's Word, is also sweeter than honey because when you read it you grow closer to him.

Do a "taste test" with a sibling or friend. Take turns blindfolding each other and try samples of food (peanut butter, maple syrup, yogurt, etc.) to see if you can guess what it is. As you do this, think about saying sweet words to others.

DAY 81
Nothing Better

A person can't do anything better than eat, drink and be satisfied with their work. I'm finally seeing that those things also come from the hand of God.

—Ecclesiastes 2:24

What is your favorite day of the week? Monday? Friday? Maybe you look forward to the weekend when you can sleep late and don't have school. Or perhaps you like relaxing Sunday afternoons after you've gone to church. Or maybe you like any day of the week as long as you are having fun!

God wants you to enjoy each day. Yes, it's a blast to go to fun places like restaurants, the movies, or the zoo, but you can be content on regular days too when you eat your meals at home and work hard during school. Some days you might get bored with peanut butter and jelly sandwiches or wish you could play instead of doing your math homework. But when your belly is full and you have finished your work, you are satisfied. And that is good!

Enjoy each bite at your next meal, and smile when you do your schoolwork! God gave you food to eat and work to do. Thank him today!

DAY 82
Be Happy

You gain a lot when you live a godly life. But you must be happy with what you have.

—I Timothy 6:6

Does your best friend have more toys than you? Live in a bigger house? Get better grades in school? Sometimes it's difficult to be happy with your new video game when your friend has had it for months. Sometimes it's hard to share a room with a sibling when your friend tells you how great it is to have her own space. And sometimes it's tough to enjoy playing board games when your friend wins all the time. How can you be happy with what you have when your friend has more than you?

It may not seem fair, but God knows best. He wants you to be happy with what he has given you instead of comparing your life with others' lives. Do you have a bed to sleep in? Food in your belly? Clothes to wear? Toys to play with? If you answered "yes," then be happy with what you have. They are gifts from God!

Dear God, thank you for giving me everything I have. Help me to not compare myself with others. Amen.

DAY 83
God's Beautiful Nature

He owns the deepest parts of the earth. The mountain peaks belong to him. The ocean is his, because he made it. He formed the dry land with his hands.

—Psalm 95:4–5

Do you like to go outside? Nature not only gives us water to drink and air to breathe but also food to eat and land to live on. Did you know you can use all five senses when you are outside? You can *see* the big mountains. You can *hear* the wind rustling the leaves on the trees. You can *smell* the beautiful flowers. You can *taste* an apple from an apple tree and *touch* the cool ocean water or grass beneath your bare feet.

God made nature, and everything belongs to him. You can help God take care of the earth. By helping God care for the earth, you show respect and appreciation for the beautiful planet God created.

Discover the age of a tall tree by having a parent or friend help you wrap a measuring tape around the widest part of the trunk. The number of inches is close to the age of the tree in years. Cool, huh?

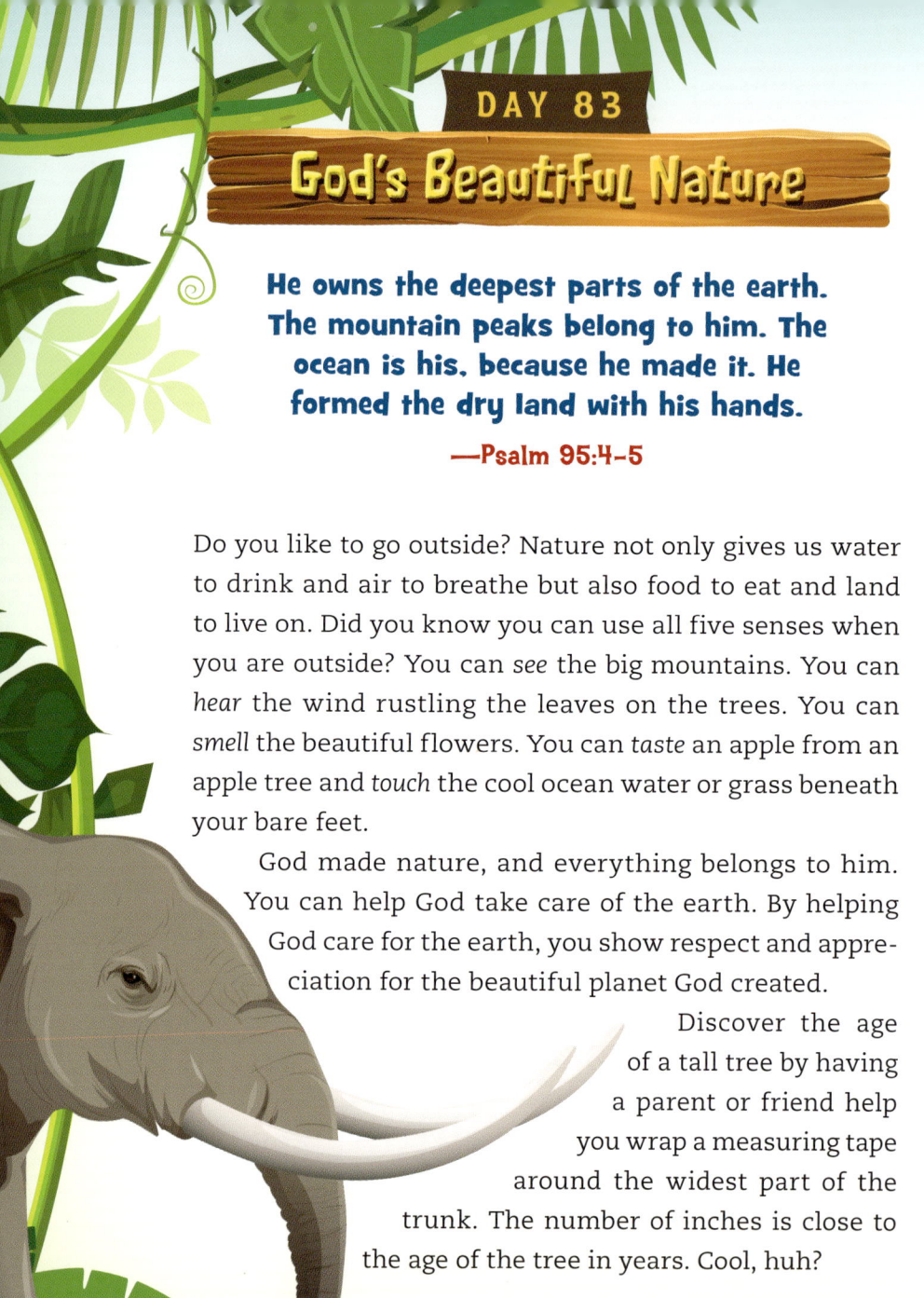

DAY 84
How's Your Heart?

They can't understand the truth. They are separated from the life of God. That's because they don't know him. And they don't know him because their hearts are stubborn.

—Ephesians 4:18

Have you ever felt your heart beating hard in your chest after you've ridden your bike or taken a run? Did you know the average heart beats 80 times per minute and 4,800 times per hour? That's about 115,000 times per day. Wow! And when you exercise, your heart beats faster and harder. That's because your heart is a muscle that pumps blood throughout your body.

The Bible talks about the heart in a different way. Sometimes our hearts can be hard or stubborn when we want our own way instead of following God. You know, like the time your parents told you to eat your vegetables and you didn't, or when they asked you to go to bed and you played a video game in your room. When your heart is stubborn, you are separated from God. So be a kid after God's heart and follow him.

Dear God, thank you for my heart. Help me to follow you and not be stubborn. Amen.

DAY 85
Birds of a Feather

"So don't be afraid. You are worth more than many sparrows."

—Matthew 10:31

Have you ever seen a sparrow? Sparrows are small brown and gray birds that love to eat seeds, insects, and berries. They are social birds that live in flocks and have a life span of four to five years. They build nests in bushes and trees and sometimes under house eaves. You may spot a sparrow near a bird feeder, in a tree, or flying around in your garden.

God loves sparrows. He feeds them and cares for them. But do you know whom God loves more than sparrows? YOU! He not only feeds you and cares for you, but he watches over you. He sees when you wake up and when you go to sleep. He sees when you play and when you do your chores. He sees when you are happy and when you are sad. God not only sees you, he loves and cares for you too. So when you're afraid, remember that you are worth more than many sparrows!

Grab a pinecone from the park or your yard and spread peanut butter and honey all over it. Roll it in birdseed on a plate, then hang it on a tree branch with yarn. Wait for the birds to come, and remember how much God loves you.

DAY 86
Handy Hands

May the Lord our God always be pleased with us. Lord, make what we do succeed. Please make what we do succeed.

—Psalm 90:17

Look at your hands and wiggle your fingers. Human hands are different than the paws of most animals because humans have opposable thumbs. That means your thumbs and fingers work together so that you can pick things up and do things like hold a pencil, type on a computer, play video games, and carry things. Did you know no human being has the same fingerprints as you? That's right—the only person to have your fingerprints is you!

Just as you have unique fingerprints, God made you to do unique things. You may use your hands to take care of someone, pet an animal, play an instrument, paint, or write a story. Some people use their hands to talk through sign language. When you honor God with your hands, he will help you succeed.

Before you eat, wash your hands so that you don't pass germs to your mouth. Make sure you use soap and scrub both sides of your hands, in between your fingers, and under your nails. Don't forget your wrists too! After you rinse your hands with water, dry them off on a clean towel.

DAY 87
T for Trouble

The Lord is good. When people are in trouble, they can go to him for safety. He takes good care of those who trust in him.

—Nahum 1:7

Have you ever climbed a rock wall? Here's how it works: first, you get strapped into a harness that is attached to a long rope. The rope is hooked to a pulley at the top and then clipped to an adult's harness or to the rock wall at the bottom. Some days you might be able to climb all the way to the top with no problem. Other days you might get scared and feel as if you can't climb anymore. In fact, your hands may start to sweat. You may even feel like you're about to fall.

Life can be like that too. You're having a good day, then suddenly you accidentally hit a ball through someone's window, spill something all over the floor (again!), or leave a wad of gum in your pocket and ruin a load of laundry. Talk about *trouble*! What do you do? You can go to God and put your trust in him. He will help you apologize and make things right. Just like the harness and rope keep you from falling when you climb a rock wall, God is your safety.

Find a friend and climb a rock wall. As you climb higher, remember you can trust in God. He is your safety in times of trouble.

DAY 88

Truly Sorry?

But Zacchaeus stood up. He said, "Look, Lord! Here and now I give half of what I own to those who are poor. And if I have cheated anybody out of anything, I will pay it back. I will pay back four times the amount I took."

—Luke 19:8

Have you ever said sorry to someone, but you didn't mean it? Maybe you were a tiny bit sorry, but not *totally* sorry. Everyone feels that way sometimes, but that doesn't make it okay.

Zacchaeus was a rich tax collector. He wanted to see Jesus, so he climbed up in a tree because he was too short to see. When Jesus passed, he stopped and said, "Zacchaeus, come down at once. I must stay at your house today." The people were surprised Jesus would stay at the house of a thief. Zacchaeus was so touched by Jesus's words his heart changed. He gave back the money he took from people.

When you are truly sorry and ask God to forgive your sins, your heart will be changed and you'll want to do something about it.

Create a tree snack by using pretzels for the trunk and branches and grapes for the leaves. Think about how you can have a change of heart when you are truly sorry for your sins.

DAY 89
Do the Right Thing

The Lord has shown you what is good. He has told you what he requires of you. You must act with justice. You must love to show mercy. And you must be humble as you live in the sight of your God.

—Micah 6:8

What would you do if you saw someone sitting alone at recess? Would you look away and pretend you didn't see them, or would you ask them to play? What if you saw someone crying or in need of food? Would you ignore them, or sit by them and listen? Would you eat your entire lunch, or offer to share?

Have you ever wondered what God wants you to do? He wants you to act justly—to do the right thing. But what does that mean? Acting justly is taking action when God asks you to do something. He is the only one who can truly make things right, but God created you to participate in his plan. The Bible is full of examples of how God used unlikely people to bring about justice, and he can use you too! When you help the lonely, bullied, and hungry, you are sharing God's love and justice with the world.

Gather some clothes and toys you've outgrown or don't need, and give them to someone in need. Now that's doing the right thing!

DAY 90
Gentle Words

Tell them not to speak evil things against anyone. Remind them to live in peace. They must consider the needs of others. They must always be gentle toward everyone.

—Titus 3:2

Has someone ever said something mean about you? Did your feelings get hurt? Were you mad? Did you say something mean back? Or were you the one who said something mean first? Maybe you're not getting along with your siblings. Maybe you had a fight with a classmate or a friend. What should you do?

When you love Jesus, you shouldn't speak evil of anyone, and you shouldn't quarrel or pick a fight. Instead, you should be gentle and considerate of others, even toward people who aren't nice to you. So if someone makes fun of you, don't say mean words back. If you want to explode, take a deep breath. Showing God's love to your siblings, classmates, and friends means you should speak with kind words and treat them with respect.

Practice being gentle by saying kind words to someone right now. When you are considerate of others, you will live in peace.

DAY 91
Jesus Is My Friend

"I have called you friends. I have told you everything I learned from my Father."

—John 15:15

Do you have a best friend? A best friend is someone who loves you just the way you are and helps you be the best you can be. A best friend is there when you need him. A best friend listens and builds you up. A best friend sticks up for you. Do you have a friend like that? Friends on earth grow and change, and sometimes they disappoint you or move away. But there is one friend who will never do that!

Did you know Jesus is your best friend? No one loves you like Jesus, and no one knows you better than he does. You can talk to him anytime. You can talk to him anywhere. He not only wants what is best for you, he gave his life for you by dying on the cross for your sins. You are important to Jesus, and he will guide you when you put your trust in him. Jesus is not only your best friend, but he is Christ the Lord.

Dear God, thank you for being my best friend! Help me to put my trust in you. Amen.

DAY 92
Mold Me

"Lord, you are our Father. We are the clay. You are the potter. Your hands made all of us."

—Isaiah 64:8

When was the last time you played with modeling clay? It's fun to mold objects with clay, like an animal or car! The fun part is reshaping it into something else. But don't leave it out for too long or else the clay gets hard, and you won't be able to mold it anymore.

A potter is someone who makes bowls, plates, and pots with clay. In the Bible it says God is a potter and people are like clay. There was a prophet named Isaiah who wanted God to change the hearts of the people. Their hearts had become hard like clay. Isaiah knew God could soften their hearts and mold them into the kind of people he wanted them to be. When you stray away from God, ask him to soften your heart and mold you. God is the best potter of all!

Make homemade modeling clay by mixing together 1 cup of flour and 1/4 cup of salt. Next, mix 1/2 cup of warm water with a few drops of food coloring. Slowly pour the water and food coloring mixture into the flour and salt. Stir until combined and then knead with your hands. If the dough is sticky, add more flour. Have fun!

DAY 93
Let Your Light Shine

Let us consider how we can stir up one another to love. Let us help one another to do good works.

—Hebrews 10:24

Have you ever gone camping with your family? It's fun to set up a tent, sit around a campfire, and roast marshmallows. You can also make s'mores and tell stories under the stars. When you go camping, your family learns to love and work together.

Did you know being part of a church family is like that too? When you are part of a church, you learn to love others and work together. You need a church family to grow your faith like a campfire needs many logs to burn brighter and longer. When you don't go to church, your light will only burn for a short time. But with your church family by your side, your faith will stay strong and your flame will keep burning.

Make a fort inside your house using furniture and blankets. Invite your family for an indoor camping trip. Take turns sharing what your church family means to you.

God's Steadfast Love

His great love is new every morning. Lord, how faithful you are! I say to myself, "The Lord is everything I will ever need. So I will put my hope in him."

—Lamentations 3:23–24

Do you feel like you've blown it? Maybe you yelled at your mom or dad. Maybe you had some bad thoughts. Or maybe you did something that you know was a sin. Do you wonder how God can still love you? That kind of thinking is a lie from Satan and will only make you feel worse.

The truth is, God's steadfast love for you never changes. That's right—God's love never ends! So when you yell, have a bad thought, or do something wrong, God still loves you because his love is unconditional. It's never too late to make things right with God because he never gives up on you! As you get out of bed, remember today is a new day and God's faithfulness is new every morning.

Go outside and let the sun shine on your face. Now close your eyes. God's love and faithfulness are like the warmth of the sun, which is new every day.

DAY 95
Thirsty?

"But anyone who drinks the water I give them will never be thirsty. In fact, the water I give them will become a spring of water in them. It will flow up into eternal life."

—John 4:14

Do you like to drink water? Your body needs a drink every few hours, even more if you live where it's hot. In fact, water is more important for your body than food, because more than half of your body weight is made up of water. Most of your blood is made up of water, and water is in your lymph system, which helps fight infection. Did you know water is inside your cells and bones too? You need water to keep your body healthy and strong.

Have you ever tried eating something salty without drinking water? Just like your body craves water after eating a bag of chips or salty popcorn, your soul craves something too—Jesus! Your soul is the invisible part of you that thinks, feels, makes choices, and basically makes you YOU! The only thing that can satisfy your soul is a relationship with God. When you follow Jesus, your soul will never be thirsty again.

Drink a big glass of water and thank God for the gift of Jesus, the only one who satisfies your soul.

DAY 96
Mouth Guard

LORD, guard my mouth. Keep watch over the door of my lips.

—Psalm 141:3

Have you ever said something you didn't mean? Maybe you were sad. Maybe you were mad. Or maybe you were hungry or tired. Perhaps you were joking around and someone's feelings got hurt. Or maybe you lied to get out of a sticky situation.

There are many verses in the Bible that talk about being careful about what you say. Words have power, and they can either build someone up or tear someone down. Once you say something, you can't take it back. It's like trying to stuff toothpaste back into the tube after you've squeezed it out. Impossible! But God can help guard your mouth from saying words that are hurtful. When you pray, ask him to keep watch over your lips. He can help you use your words in a positive way.

When you brush your teeth today, think about saying words that build people up instead of tearing them down.

DAY 97
Are You Beautiful?

But the Lord said to Samuel, "Do not consider how handsome or tall he is. I have not chosen him. The Lord does not look at the things people look at. People look at the outside of a person. But the Lord looks at what is in the heart."

—1 Samuel 16:7

Do you know someone who is handsome or pretty? You might think of a celebrity or someone on the cover of a magazine. Or maybe a friend or somebody else you know comes to mind. What makes them nice to look at? Pretty hair? Great smile? Fancy clothes? Just because someone is beautiful on the outside doesn't mean they are beautiful on the inside.

Did you know God doesn't care about outward appearance? Yes, he wants you to take care of yourself by taking baths, brushing your hair and teeth, and wearing clean clothes. But that is not what makes you beautiful. What matters most is having a kind and caring heart toward others. This type of beauty is what God wants for you. How can you be beautiful? Listen to a friend, take care of a pet, or help your parents with chores. No matter what you look like on the outside, inner beauty is what lasts.

Take a bath or shower and think of ways you can be kind and caring toward others.

Golden Rule

"In everything, do to others what you would want them to do to you. This is what is written in the Law and in the Prophets."

—Matthew 7:12

Have you heard of the Golden Rule? It's what Jesus said in this verse about treating others the way you want to be treated. How do you do that? God wants you to love others the way he loves you. Here are some ideas:

- Accept people for who they are, even when they are different than you.
- Give a compliment or encourage a friend.
- Say "please" and "thank you."
- Listen to and respect others.
- Talk to others with a kind and gentle voice.
- Forgive.
- Love those who are hard to love.

It takes a lot of courage to follow the Golden Rule. And it's not always easy. But when you treat others the way you'd like to be treated, you are putting God's love in action.

Draw a picture showing someone acting out the Golden Rule from the list above.

DAY 99
Sneaky Snake

The serpent was more clever than any of the wild animals the L<small>ORD</small> God had made. The serpent said to the woman, "Did God really say, 'You must not eat fruit from any tree in the garden'?"

—Genesis 3:1

Serpent is another word for snake. Did you know there are 2,500 species of snakes? Here are some other snake facts: Snakes are long, flexible reptiles. They are meat eaters and have flexible jaws, which allow snakes to eat prey bigger than their heads! Snakes shed their outer skin every few months. Some snakes are poisonous and some use camouflage to hide in their surroundings.

In the beginning, Adam and Eve lived in the garden of Eden. God told them that they could eat from any tree in the garden, except from the tree of the knowledge of good and evil. But the serpent tried to get the woman to eat that fruit anyway. Just as the serpent tempted the woman to eat the fruit, Satan tempts you today. But instead of listening to Satan's lies, believe the truth of the Bible and be ready to do what it says. God will help you withstand temptation when you rely on him.

Dear God, thank you for the Bible and for always telling me the truth. Help me listen to you instead of Satan's lies. Amen.

Time to Eat!

Then Jesus said, "I am the bread of life. Whoever comes to me will never go hungry. And whoever believes in me will never be thirsty."

—John 6:35

Have you ever wondered why your stomach makes funny noises when you're hungry? Actually, your stomach and small intestines make noises all the time, but the noises aren't as loud when you have food in your stomach. A couple hours after you eat, your stomach sends signals to your brain to get the stomach muscles moving again. Growl. Time to eat!

Many times throughout the Bible, Jesus shares a meal with people because he knows how important food is to live. In this verse, however, Jesus isn't talking about the garlic bread you ate with your spaghetti last night. Jesus is saying he is the bread. When you have a friendship with Jesus, you will never be hungry or thirsty for anything else again.

Eat a slice of bread and think about how Jesus is the bread of life.

DAY 101
Let's Go Fly a Kite

The disciples were amazed. They asked, "What kind of man is this? Even the winds and the waves obey him!"
—Matthew 8:27

Have you ever flown a kite? You need the right flying conditions, including the right amount of wind. When the wind is between 5–25 mph, your kite is able to dance across the sky when you pull in and let out the line. The best place to fly a kite is a clear, open area away from roads and power lines, such as on the beach or in an open field. Of course, never fly a kite in stormy weather and stay away from trees!

Did you know God controls the wind? In this verse, the disciples were amazed when Jesus calmed the wind and waves. They realized there was no need to worry because God is in control. Just like you don't control the wind when you fly a kite, you don't control circumstances that happen in life. So be like the disciples and put your trust in God. He is the only one in control.

Fly a kite and give your worries to God. Remember that he is in control.

DAY 102
Planting Seeds

The soil makes the young plant come up. A garden causes seeds to grow. In the same way, the Lord and King will make godliness grow. And all the nations will praise him.

—Isaiah 61:11

Have you ever planted flower seeds in soil and had them grow into plants? You need to water the soil and make sure it gets the right amount of sunlight. You also need patience because plants don't appear overnight. One day the seeds will sprout, and the plants will come up out of the soil. Over the next few weeks, you'll notice how the plant changes and grows. Soon you will see beautiful flowers.

Your relationship with God is like a seed planted in soil. In order to grow, you need to spend time with God by reading your Bible and praying. Soon you'll sprout up and others will see the change in you. You will continue to grow and spread God's love to others. By sharing your faith, you may encourage someone else to plant a seed for God. Who knows? You might plant a whole garden!

Ask a parent to help you plant a few seeds in a cup. Follow the directions on the seed packet and watch them grow into plants. Don't forget to tend to your relationship with God too!

DAY 103
The Rock!

"So then, everyone who hears my words and puts them into practice is like a wise man. He builds his house on the rock. The rain comes down. The water rises. The winds blow and beat against that house. But it does not fall. It is built on the rock."

—Matthew 7:24–25

Rocks are fun to collect when you're outside exploring. You can skip rocks across a lake or pond, or play games with rocks, such as hopscotch or tic-tac-toe. Rocks are also used for building houses. In fact, the most important part of a house is the base, or foundation. When houses were first built, stones were used to create a thick foundation so the houses wouldn't sink. When a house has a firm foundation, it will stand for a very long time.

To be wise, Jesus says you need to build your house upon a rock. Wind and rain may beat against the house, but it stays strong. By reading your Bible and doing what it says, you are building your life on the solid rock of Jesus. Put his words into practice so that when the hard times come, your foundation will be firm.

Find a rock in your yard that fits inside the palm of your hand and write "Jesus" on it with a permanent marker. This will remind you to rely on him.

DAY 104

Sand

> "But everyone who hears my words and does not put them into practice is like a foolish man. He builds his house on sand."
>
> —Matthew 7:26

Have you ever built a sandcastle? Maybe you live by the beach or near a park with a sandbox. Either way, you can build an awesome sandcastle with a plastic shovel and a couple of buckets. You've probably discovered the key to a great sandcastle is to use a little water. By mixing sand and water, and patting it down, you'll be able to form towers. But if you use too much water, your sandcastle will fall down.

As cool as sandcastles are, they don't last. One big wave or stormy day and they fall apart. What about the hard days or storms in your life? Do you stay strong, or do you crumble like a house built with sand? Building your life on what others say instead of the truth of the Bible would be as foolish as building a house on sand. Instead, trust Jesus and do what he says. If you do, you will be wise.

Build a sandcastle and remember to put God's Word into practice so that you won't crumble like a house built with sand.

Guard Your Heart

Above everything else, guard your heart. Everything you do comes from it.
—Proverbs 4:23

When you play football, you wear a helmet, a mouth guard, shoulder pads, and body padding. When you play soccer, you wear shin guards. And when you play baseball, you wear a mitt. When you play sports, your body needs to be protected. If you don't protect your body, you might end up with bruises, broken bones, or missing teeth!

Did you know the Bible says your heart needs protection too? But how do you guard something that is on the inside? You can protect your heart by being careful about what you see and hear, and what you think about. By watching good shows, reading good books, and listening to uplifting music, you will fill your heart and mind with good things. Just like your body needs to be guarded when you play sports, your heart needs to be guarded from the bad things in the world around you.

Put on a helmet and ride your bike around the neighborhood. Think of ways you can guard your heart so that whatever you do and say will be pleasing to God.

DAY 106
Thank You Very Much

Lord, I will give thanks to you with all my heart. I will tell about all the wonderful things you have done.

—Psalm 9:1

When was the last time you said thank you? When someone passed food around the table? Opened the door for you? Gave you a gift? It's important to be polite and show good manners. So when your mom or dad washes your clothes, makes you dinner, or drives you to school, remember to say thank you. When your grandma knits you a sweater or plays a board game with you, remember to say thank you. When your friend stands up for you, remember to say thank you.

God also wants you to thank him for all he has given you. Tell him how grateful you are for your home, your toys, and your family. God cares for you and wants to hear what is on your heart. And it makes him happy when you thank him for all the wonderful things he has done.

Dear God, thank you for everything you have given me. Help me remember to say thank you to others. Amen.

DAY 107
Give a Shout

Then I heard the noise of a huge crowd. It sounded like the roar of rushing waters and like loud thunder. The people were shouting, "Hallelujah! Our Lord God is the King who rules over all."

—Revelation 19:6

Have you ever heard the sound of a big crowd? The mighty ocean waves? Or the loud crash of thunder? Maybe you went to a baseball game and cheered with the crowd. Maybe you took a vacation to the beach and listened to the roar of the ocean waves hitting the shore. Or maybe you ran for cover during a rumbling thunderstorm.

The Bible says people will shout their praises to God in heaven with a loud, "Hallelujah!" The word "hallelujah" means "God be praised." When was the last time you gave a loud shout of praise to God? You don't have to wait until you get to heaven to worship God. Go ahead and try it! And the next time you hear a loud crowd, the roar of ocean waves, or the rumbling of thunder, let it remind you that God is your king who rules over all.

Go outside and shout praises to God, saying, "Hallelujah! God is King and rules over all!"

Faith in Action

I pray that what we share by believing will help you understand even more. Then you will completely understand every good thing we share by believing in Christ.

—Philemon v. 6

Do you have a friend you can tell all your secrets to? Someone you can listen to and encourage? Someone who also shares your faith? Maybe this special person is a friend from church or school. Maybe they're on your soccer team or from your neighborhood. Maybe this person is your sibling. The important part about having a Christian friend is that you can encourage each other to make good choices because you both believe in Jesus.

In this book of the Bible, Paul asks Philemon to put his faith in action by forgiving somebody for doing something wrong. By encouraging Philemon to forgive, Paul was being a good Christian friend by helping him make a good choice. Sharing your faith with a Christian friend means you build each other up and put your words into action because of what Jesus did for you on the cross.

Do you or a Christian friend need to forgive someone? Put your faith in action and do it today.

DAY 109
Hannah's Prayer

So after some time, Hannah became pregnant. She had a baby boy. She said, "I asked the Lord for him." So she named him Samuel.

—1 Samuel 1:20

During Bible times, when a woman had a baby it was viewed as a gift from God. If a woman didn't have a child, people thought she must have done something wrong. Hannah was sad because she didn't have a baby, so she prayed about it. She prayed with her whole heart. She promised that if she had a son, she would give him back to God to serve him. God answered her prayer and gave her a son. And Hannah kept her promise and dedicated Samuel to the Lord.

Have you ever wanted something so badly that you prayed to God for it with your whole heart? Maybe you wanted a new baby brother or sister. Maybe you wanted a horse or a dog. Maybe you made a promise like Hannah. It's up to God whether he answers your prayer with a yes or a no. Many times, he wants you to wait. But if he answers your prayer and gives you what you asked for, it's up to you to follow through and do what you've promised.

Don't give up praying for what you want. God hears your prayers. Trust that he knows what is best.

DAY 110

Power Inside You

God gave us his Spirit. And the Spirit doesn't make us weak and fearful. Instead, the Spirit gives us power and love. He helps us control ourselves.

—2 Timothy 1:7

Has the power ever gone out in your neighborhood? One minute the electricity works, then *poof!* It's out. Suddenly, you can't watch television, play your favorite video game, or read with the light on. How does it make you feel to be without power? Frustrated? Scared? Out of control?

Did you know God gave you power through the Holy Spirit? When you accepted Jesus as Lord, the Holy Spirit came inside you and helps you achieve things you wouldn't be able to do on your own. The Holy Spirit helps you be brave when you are afraid, helps you love when you are upset, and gives you self-control when you are tempted. Ask the Holy Spirit to fill you up with his power each day so that you will know what he wants you to do. God gave you the Holy Spirit to be your special helper. Listen to what he is saying to you today.

Turn your bedroom light on, read a good book, and thank God for giving you the gift of the Holy Spirit. Remember to rely on his power.

DAY III
Hidden Treasure

Call out for the ability to be wise. Cry out for understanding. Look for it as you would look for silver. Search for it as you would search for hidden treasure.

—Proverbs 2:3-4

When was the last time you went on a treasure hunt? Maybe you went geocaching with a parent. Maybe you hunted for shells or sand dollars on the beach. Or maybe you searched for objects hidden in a book. Whatever you are looking for, it's fun to locate treasure!

God wants you to search for wisdom and understanding as if you were looking for hidden treasure. You don't become wise by listening *only* to your feelings. You may feel like eating a whole bag of candy, but that doesn't make it a wise choice. You may feel like staying up all night to watch television or play video games, but that isn't wise and will make you feel exhausted. You become wise and gain understanding by asking God. If you want to find God's hidden treasure, search for his wisdom in the Bible. Talk to God and listen to his words.

Go on a scavenger hunt and search for hidden treasure. Ask God for wisdom and understanding so that you will be more like him.

DAY 112
Ticktock

The Lord who rules over all says, "Think carefully about how you are living."
—Haggai 1:5

How do you spend your time? How many hours per day do you run, jump, move, or play? How long do you read? What about playing video games or watching television? How much time do you spend with your family and friends? What about going to school and doing homework? Of course, you also need to count how many hours you sleep and the time it takes to eat and get ready for bed. Are you surprised at how you spend your time?

God wants you to spend your day with him by your side. When you ask him to be with you throughout the day, your day will look a lot different. You'll notice when your mom needs help with chores or if she just needs a hug. You'll see when your sibling needs a shoulder to lean on. You'll stop to listen to a friend. You'll help a neighbor without being asked. And you'll adjust your attitude when things don't go your way. When you invite God to be by your side, you'll spend your time on what matters most to him.

Dear God, thank you for always being by my side. Help me spend my time wisely.

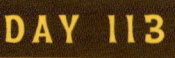

God Is Good

Look to what is good, not to what is evil. Then you will live. And the Lord God who rules over all will be with you, just as you say he is.

—Amos 5:14

Are you having a good day? Even if today is a bad day, you can find something that is good. Has someone done something nice for you? Have you done something good to brighten someone else's day? Even if your good deed went unnoticed, God sees you.

What about if someone is mean to you? Do you have to be good then? Doing a good deed or being kind to someone who is mean shows that person there is good in the world. And when you do good things, it points people to God.

You can find joy knowing that God is good even when you are not. When you don't understand what God is doing in your life, you can trust that he is good and that he cares for you.

Write "God is good!" on a piece of paper or index card. Tape it to your mirror to remind yourself that God is good all the time!

DAY 114
What Did You Say?

Let the words you speak always be full of grace. Learn how to make your words what people want to hear. Then you will know how to answer everyone.

—Colossians 4:6

Do you jump at the chance to correct your sibling or friend when they make a silly mistake, or do you give them grace? Do you complain when things don't go your way, or are you thankful for everything God has given you? Do you talk about others behind their backs, or do you speak words of kindness?

The way you talk reveals what is in your heart. If you say kind and good things, you have a heart full of grace. But if you constantly correct, grumble, and gossip, you're revealing a negative and bitter heart. In order to speak words that are full of grace and build others up, you need Jesus in your heart. The next time you talk with someone, speak words that show God's love.

Are you having a difficult time saying kind words? Before you go to bed tonight, ask God into your heart so that you can speak words that build others up.

DAY 115
"On Fire" for God

The Lord your God is like a fire that burns everything up. He wants you to worship only him.

—Deuteronomy 4:24

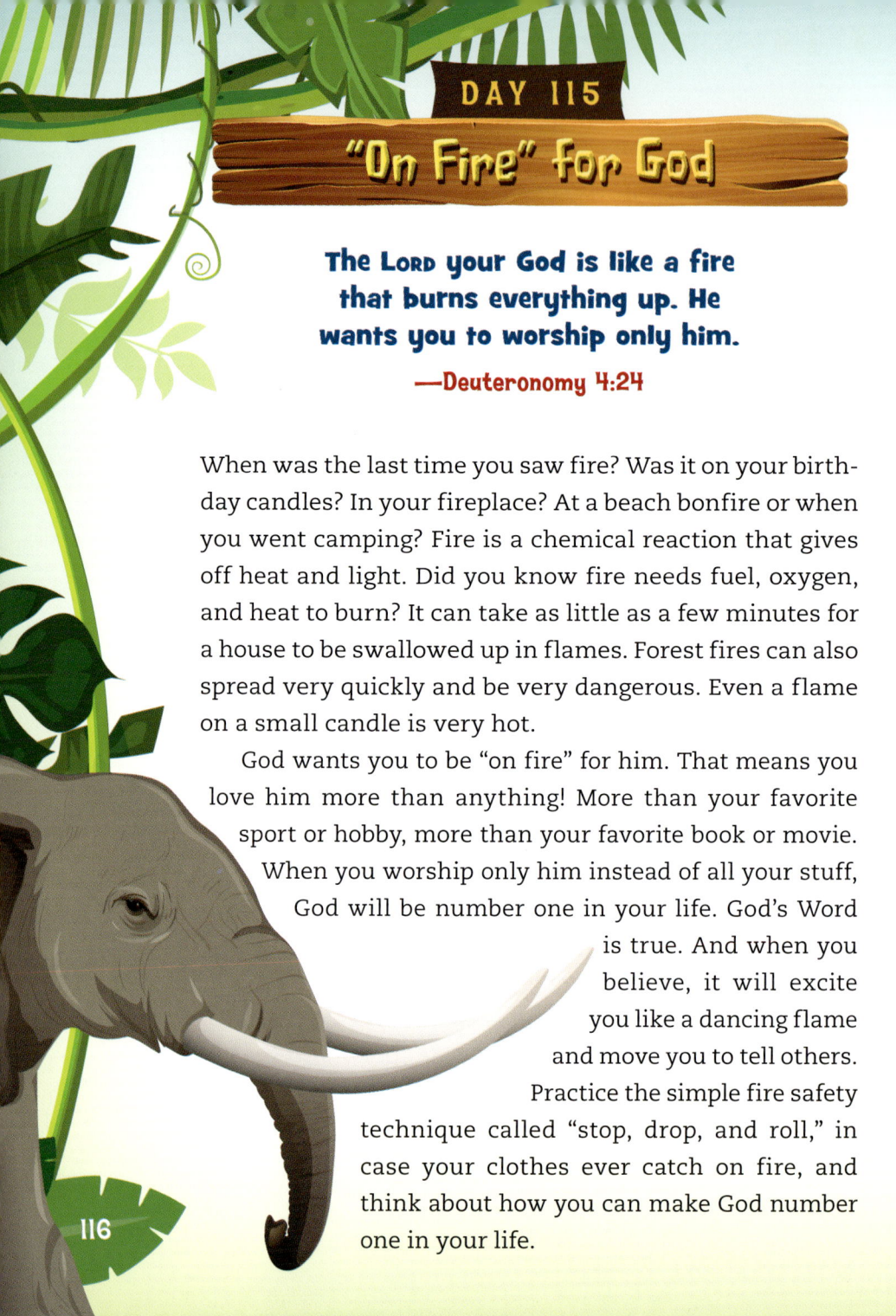

When was the last time you saw fire? Was it on your birthday candles? In your fireplace? At a beach bonfire or when you went camping? Fire is a chemical reaction that gives off heat and light. Did you know fire needs fuel, oxygen, and heat to burn? It can take as little as a few minutes for a house to be swallowed up in flames. Forest fires can also spread very quickly and be very dangerous. Even a flame on a small candle is very hot.

God wants you to be "on fire" for him. That means you love him more than anything! More than your favorite sport or hobby, more than your favorite book or movie. When you worship only him instead of all your stuff, God will be number one in your life. God's Word is true. And when you believe, it will excite you like a dancing flame and move you to tell others. Practice the simple fire safety technique called "stop, drop, and roll," in case your clothes ever catch on fire, and think about how you can make God number one in your life.

God Is Truth

I have no greater joy than to hear that my children are living by the truth.

—3 John v. 4

Have you ever been caught telling a lie? Maybe you saw something that could get someone else in trouble. What did you do? Telling the truth is always the right choice. Yes, you or your friend might be punished for lying, but the truth is more important than avoiding negative consequences.

Did you know Satan tells you lies too? Like when he says you're not good enough, cute enough, or smart enough. Those lies are far from the truth. What about what you hear on television and see online? Is that the truth? Not always.

The Bible teaches that Jesus is the truth and that he will always tell you the truth. God's Word, the Bible, is also the truth. When you spend time reading the Bible, you will discover how God wants you to live. What God tells you in the Bible is always the truth. If you want to know the best way to live, seek the truth. Seek God.

Dear God, thank you for always telling me the truth. Help me read the Bible so that I seek the truth. Amen.

DAY 117
A Heart Thing

With all my heart I want the temple of my God to be built. So I'm giving my personal treasures of gold and silver for it. I'm adding them to everything else I've provided for the holy temple.

—1 Chronicles 29:3

Did you know that God really owns all your stuff? Yes, he does. God is just letting you use it here on earth. Have you ever thought about giving your treasures to God? It doesn't mean you have to give away your favorite toy or all the money in your piggy bank, but it has to cost you something. What if you don't have much to give?

In Old Testament times, people gave a *tithe* of ten percent of their crops to the storehouse. Today, many people give ten percent of what they earn to the church. You should never give out of pressure, only if you want to. In fact, God doesn't make you give. He wants you to decide in your heart what you want to give. But when you put God first and trust him to take care of your needs, you will have a willing heart. And if you give, you will discover that God will bless you more than you can imagine.

Do you have books, clothing, or toys that you can give to someone in need? Give from the heart.

DAY 118
What Should I Pray?

But you, dear friends, build yourselves up in your most holy faith. Let the Holy Spirit guide and help you when you pray.

—Jude v. 20

Do you ever wonder what you should pray? Maybe you're going through a tough situation and you don't know what to do. Maybe you have a choice to make and you're afraid to make the wrong one. Or maybe everything is fine and you don't feel the need to pray.

The good thing is, when you give your heart to Jesus, the Holy Spirit guides and helps you when you pray. Even when you think you know what to pray, the Holy Spirit prays for you. So when you're going through a tough time, let the Holy Spirit guide you and help you when you pray. When you have a choice to make, let the Holy Spirit guide and help you when you pray. And when everything seems to be going fine, let the Holy Spirit guide and help you when you pray. Thanks to the help of the Holy Spirit and Jesus's sacrifice on the cross, you can go boldly to God in prayer.

Dear God, thank you for the gift of the Holy Spirit. Help me come to you in prayer. Amen.

DAY 119
Special Treasure

"The day is coming when I will judge," says the LORD who rules over all. "On that day they will be my special treasure."

—Malachi 3:17

Do you have a special treasure? Maybe it's a stuffed animal, a handmade blanket, or a new toy. Maybe your special treasure is a letter or a book, such as your Bible or diary. How do you feel when you hold that treasure in your hand? Does it make your heart happy and bring you comfort? Do you think of the person who gave it to you?

The Bible says that God calls you his special treasure. As his child, you make God happy! You are God's jewel, his treasured possession. He bought you with the highest price imaginable, the blood of Jesus, and you are beautiful in his eyes. It doesn't matter what others think of you. You can be joyful knowing God sees you as his precious treasure.

Give your special treasure a big hug and think about how you are God's jewel, his treasured possession.

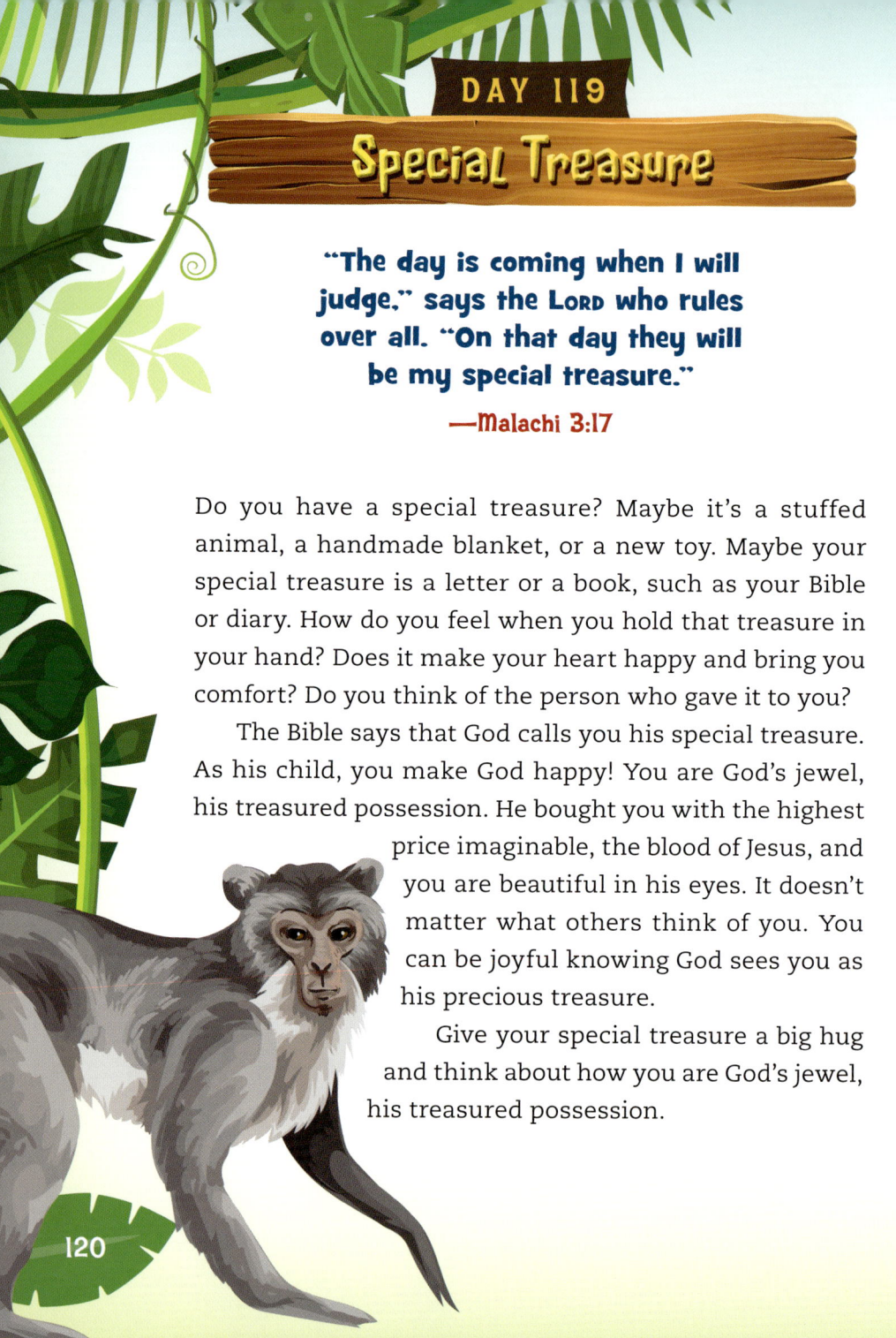

DAY 120
Jesus Is Calling YOU!

"My sheep listen to my voice. I know them, and they follow me. I give them eternal life, and they will never die. No one will steal them out of my hand."

—John 10:27-28

If you closed your eyes when someone in your family was speaking, would you know who it was? Of course you would, because you know them. You've heard them speak countless times and can recognize their voice. What about your teacher? Or your friends? Would you know their voices? What about someone you just met? The more you know someone, the easier it is to identify them by their voice.

The Bible calls Jesus the Good Shepherd and his children the sheep. The more you spend time with Jesus by reading your Bible and praying, the more you will be able to hear his voice speaking to you. Did you know Jesus knows you better than you know yourself? It's true. This verse also says when you follow Jesus, you will be safe in his hands and live forever with him. Do you hear Jesus calling you? Listen for his voice today.

Do you know when Jesus is speaking to you? If not, spend more time with him so you can recognize his voice.

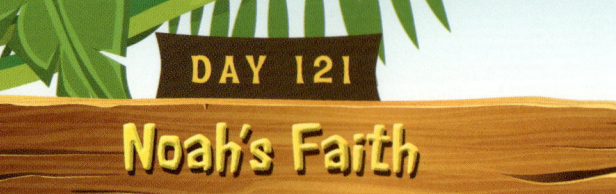

DAY 121
Noah's Faith

Noah had faith. So he built an ark to save his family. He built it because of his great respect for God.

—Hebrews 11:7

Has someone ever asked you to do something that seemed impossible? Maybe your team needed you to score the winning run when you hadn't hit the ball all season. Maybe your parents asked you to do better in school even though you were still having a hard time with math. What if God asked you to build a big boat to fit two of every animal because a huge flood was coming? Talk about a seemingly impossible situation!

That's exactly what God asked Noah to do. God told Noah to build the ark. Noah had a choice to make. Have faith and build the ark even though it seemed impossible or turn away and disobey God. Noah made the right choice by doing everything the Lord commanded him to do. What about you?

Play a memory game with a friend. The first person says, "Noah took a (name an animal) on the ark." The next person repeats what the first person says and adds an animal. Keep taking turns adding animals. Whoever remembers all the names of the animals wins.

DAY 122
When You Are Weak, He Is Strong

"My grace is all you need. My power is strongest when you are weak." So I am very happy to brag about how weak I am. Then Christ's power can rest on me.

—2 Corinthians 12:9

Are you strong? Maybe you help with chores like carrying the groceries or laundry. Maybe you are in gymnastics or football. You need a lot of strength for those things. Having a strong body is healthy, but sometimes you might feel weak. This kind of weakness has nothing to do with your muscles. You might get frustrated or scared when you feel you can't do something God calls you to do. Like when he asks you to invite a friend to church or speak to someone who needs encouragement.

Jesus teaches that you can become strong because of your weakness. You can become strong by leaning on God's strength to help you. After all, if you could do the things that frustrate or scare you without God, then you wouldn't rely on his power. God won't let your weakness stand in the way of what he wants you to do. God's strength is all you need.

Dear God, your grace is all I need. Help me to become strong even when I'm weak. Amen.

Father's House

> "There are many rooms in my Father's house. If this were not true, would I have told you that I am going there? Would I have told you that I would prepare a place for you there?"
>
> —John 14:2

How would you describe your home? Is it big or small? Do you have your own bedroom, or do you share with a sibling? Have you ever wondered what it's like to live in another town? What about another state or country? It's fun to sometimes think about what it might be like living somewhere far away.

The disciples wondered the same thing when Jesus talked about heaven. He said he was going back to heaven to prepare a place for them—and for you too! When the time is right, Jesus promises to return and take all those who believe in him to their heavenly home. There is room for everyone. Yes, someday you will live in the Father's house with Jesus! Isn't that exciting?

Draw a picture of what you think heaven looks like.

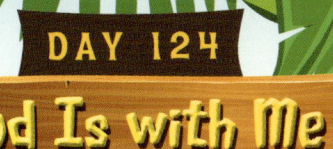

God Is with Me

Even though I walk through the darkest valley, I will not be afraid. You are with me. Your shepherd's rod and staff comfort me.

—Psalm 23:4

Are you sick? Maybe you have an illness that has lasted a long time. Maybe you know someone who is sick. Or maybe a close friend or relative has died and you feel sad. You might even feel afraid. Times like these can make you feel like you're walking through a dark valley.

A dark valley is a dangerous place for sheep because animals such as bears, cougars, coyotes, snakes, and wolves might be hiding behind rocks or in caves. But the sheep don't have to be afraid because the shepherd is there to rescue the sheep when they are in trouble. He'll use his rod to protect them from wild animals. And if a sheep gets caught in some briars or stuck up on a ledge, the shepherd will use his staff to pull them out of danger.

Like a good shepherd, God is watching over you and will protect and comfort you when you are afraid. He is always with you. You can put your trust in him.

Talk to God about your fears. Remember that he will protect and comfort you. He is always with you.

DAY 125
Light of the World

Jesus spoke to the people again. He said, "I am the light of the world. Anyone who follows me will never walk in darkness. They will have that light. They will have life."

—John 8:12

Do you have a night-light in your room? A night-light helps you find your way in the dark. You can put one in your bedroom, the hallway, or the bathroom. And if you wake up in the middle of the night and need a drink of water, you'll be grateful the night-light is on. Without light, you might stub your toe or bang into something. It's hard to walk around in the dark. It's much easier to navigate your way if you have light.

Just as a night-light shows you the way in the dark, Jesus is the Light of the World that shows us the way to God. Just as a night-light keeps you from stubbing your toe or banging into things, a relationship with Jesus keeps you from making bad choices. Jesus will light your way.

Before bed, plug in a night-light so that you can see your way if you wake up in the dark. Remember Jesus is the Light of the World and will show you which way to go.

DAY 126
Prince or Pauper

He doesn't favor princes. He treats rich people and poor people the same. His hands created all of them.

—Job 34:19

Does it ever feel like some kids have everything? A big house, a nice car, and expensive clothes. Why is it that some kids are rich while other kids are poor? You may wonder if it's fair. But no matter how much money you have, there is always someone with more. Does God love rich people more? Or does he love you more if you're poor?

The truth is, God loves all people the same. The amount of material possessions you have doesn't matter to God. What is important to him is your heart. Yes, food, clothing, and shelter are needed to live, but God wants you to focus on spiritual things that are eternal, like whether you have a relationship with him. Rich or poor, he created you. Everyone is equal in his eyes.

Dear God, thank you for creating me. Help me focus on spiritual things instead of material possessions. Amen.

DAY 127
Don't Give Up

May the Lord fill your hearts with God's love. May Christ give you the strength to go on.

—2 Thessalonians 3:5

Sometimes it's overwhelming to do the same thing every single day, especially if you don't like what you have to do. Schoolwork. Chores. Practice. Maybe you'd rather watch cartoons all day in your pajamas. Maybe you just want to sleep in a few more hours and stay home and play. Maybe you are overwhelmed because your family is going through some tough stuff, and you feel like giving up.

When you feel overwhelmed, remember Jesus is with you and will give you strength for each day. His love will carry you through. Instead of thinking about everything you have to do, think about how God is in control and how he will give you strength for each step. When you let God lead you, your heart will be filled with his love, and you'll stay strong.

Before you get out of bed in the morning, say this simple prayer: Dear God, thank you for filling me up with your love and strength today. Help me to take one step at a time. Amen.

Holy Toothbrush

"'You must be holy. You must be set apart to me. I am the Lord. I am holy. I have set you apart from the other nations to be my own people.'"

—Leviticus 20:26

Do you share your toothbrush? Do you use your toothbrush for something besides brushing your teeth, like cleaning the toilet? Of course not! That would be gross. Your toothbrush is set apart for one purpose, to clean your teeth.

Did you know that as a follower of Jesus, you are set apart for a special purpose? Instead of thinking and acting like the world, you are set apart to serve him and become more like Jesus. When you spend time with God, you will start to resemble him. Even though you still look like yourself when you look in the mirror, you will look like God in the way you think and live. When you want to be holy, you want to be set apart for God and to please him.

Brush your teeth and think about how you are set apart for God to be holy.

DAY 129
Grace, Mercy, and Peace

God the Father and Jesus Christ his Son will give you grace, mercy and peace. These blessings will be with us because we love the truth.

—2 John v. 3

How do you show God's love to others? Do you make a card for someone when they're sick? Give gifts to your teacher? Clean your sibling's room? All those actions are kind and thoughtful, but you can also demonstrate God's love by giving grace, mercy, and peace. How do you do that?

You can offer grace to others when you choose to respond with a kind word instead of saying something mean. You can show mercy by forgiving someone who has wronged you. And you can encourage peace by standing up for a friend who is being bullied or picked on and telling an adult who can help.

Because you love God and the truth, God the Father and Jesus Christ his Son will give you grace, mercy, and peace. That's a promise!

Think of ways you can show God's love to others. Remember to offer grace, show mercy, and encourage peace.

Winning the Prize

I push myself forward toward the goal to win the prize. God has appointed me to win it. The heavenly prize is Christ Jesus himself.

—Philippians 3:14

Have you ever won a prize? Maybe you won an art award. Maybe you won a ribbon for running a race, or your sports team won a trophy. Or maybe your teacher picked you as the star of the week. How did it make you feel? Happy? Excited? Proud? Maybe you've never won a prize, and the thought makes you sad. Maybe you have a hard time sticking with something and tend to quit before you get to the finish line.

Have you ever tried to win a race by running backward? Of course not! That would be silly. You might bump into people, fall down, or lose track of where you're going. Your relationship with God is like that. Instead of looking behind at past mistakes, you need to keep your eyes focused on Jesus. Read your Bible. Pray. When you look forward and press on toward the goal, you will win the prize—a better relationship with Jesus.

Run around the block and consider how you can push yourself forward toward winning the heavenly prize of Jesus!

DAY 131
Who Is Perfect?

"God's way is perfect. The Lord's word doesn't have any flaws. He protects like a shield all who go to him for safety."

—2 Samuel 22:31

Do you try to be perfect? Maybe you get angry or upset when you make a mistake. Maybe you refuse to try new things or are afraid of being humiliated or embarrassed. Truth is, no human is perfect. Nobody. All you can do is your best. God loves you unconditionally, flaws and all.

Did you know God is perfect? Yes, he is. God and his Word are flawless. You don't need to try to be perfect. Jesus's blood on the cross covers you. Depend on God to help you when you get frustrated, upset, or afraid. Do your best and remember God loves you just the way you are.

Try something new! Eat something you've never had before. Ride your bike on a new path. Or invite a new friend over to your house. Do your best and remember only God is perfect!

God Knows Your Name

"The gatekeeper opens the gate for him. The sheep listen to his voice. He calls his own sheep by name and leads them out."

—John 10:3

What is your name? How do you spell it? Do you have a middle name? What does your name mean? If you don't know, ask your parents or guardian. They might say they just liked the name, or they named you after a family member, or because they liked the meaning. Your name is important to who you are.

Even though there are billions of people in the world, God knows you by name. He knows your family and where you live. He knows what you like and what you don't like. He knows everything about you. He knows you better than you know yourself. God loves you like a shepherd loves his sheep. Listen to his voice. He's calling you by name.

Write your name in big bubble letters and color it in. You can draw designs inside each letter or fill them in with a solid color. Be creative. Remember, God knows your name.

DAY 133
Little Bird

Anyone who runs away from home is like a bird that flies away from its nest.

—Proverbs 27:8

Have you ever wanted to run away? Maybe you were mad at your parents because they wouldn't let you do something you wanted to do. Maybe you had an argument. Or maybe you did something that you felt ashamed of and didn't want to tell them. Did you pack a bag? Walk down the street? When it got dark, did you forget why you wanted to run away and return home?

The Bible says that anyone who runs away from home is like a bird that flies away from its nest. That bird is now on its own. You may think it would be great to not have any rules and to make your own decisions, but just like a little bird you will need to find food to eat and a safe place to sleep. The truth is, if you stray from home, you are more likely to find trouble. Instead of running away, learn how to calm yourself down. Read a book. Listen to music. Write in a journal. Talk to your parents or a trusted adult. Tell them how you are feeling. Running away is never the answer.

Dear God, thank you for always being there for me. Help me to share my feelings with someone I trust. Amen.

DAY 134
Whale of a Story

"Go to the great city of Nineveh. Preach against it. The sins of its people have come to my attention." But Jonah ran away from the Lord. He headed for Tarshish.

—Jonah 1:2-3

What would you do if your mom asked you to help the mean kid at school? Would you obey even though it would be hard?

In the Bible, God told Jonah to go to Nineveh to preach to the people there. But Jonah didn't want to be a missionary to his enemies at Nineveh. He didn't want God to show mercy to the people there. He wanted God to destroy them. So, he ran away to Tarshish. You might think that is the end of the story, but that was only the beginning for Jonah.

He discovered you can't run away from God. Because of his disobedience, he ended up in the belly of a big fish! But after three days and three nights, the big fish spat him out. Jonah learned his lesson and went to Nineveh. Just as God didn't let Jonah disobey, he won't let you either. He wants you to obey even when it's tough.

Go to the library and find a book about fish. As you learn some fun facts, think about how you can obey even when it's difficult!

DAY 135
Got Hope?

Let us hold firmly to the hope we claim to have. The God who promised is faithful.

—Hebrews 10:23

What is hope? Is hope wishing for a certain gift for your birthday or Christmas? Is hope wishing your team wins the game? Or that you don't make a mistake at your piano recital? Is hope faith?

Hope is expecting God to answer your prayers.
Hope is knowing God has a plan.
Hope is believing without seeing.
Hope is God's gift to you.
Hope is a person—Jesus Christ.

In the Bible, you will discover that God keeps his promises. You can be confident that God listens to your prayers, and you can expect him to give you an answer. The answer may not always be yes, but you can trust that he knows best. You can have hope because you have God in your heart.

What are you hoping for right now? Talk to God about it and believe he will answer your prayer in the best way for you.

DAY 136
God's BIG Plans

"I know the plans I have for you," announces the Lord. "I want you to enjoy success. I do not plan to harm you. I will give you hope for the years to come."

—Jeremiah 29:11

What do you want to be when you grow up? A teacher? A doctor? A firefighter? Where do you want to live? Out in the country? In a big city? Maybe you don't know what you want to be when you grow up or where you want to live. You don't know what tomorrow will bring. That's okay, because God does. He's had big plans for you ever since you were born.

Yes, God made you for a special purpose. He wants you to succeed, and his plan is to give you hope. Do you enjoy playing a musical instrument? Building with your hands? Taking care of others? When you discover God's plans for you, you will find joy in the person God made you to be.

Imagine yourself as a grown-up. Ask God to show you the plan he created just for you, and take small steps to make it happen.

DAY 137

Snowflakes

"Come. Let us settle this matter," says the Lord. "Even though your sins are bright red, they will be as white as snow."

—Isaiah 1:18

Freshly fallen snow is clean and beautiful. And so much fun! You can build a snowman, go sledding, and have a snowball fight. Did you know that snowflakes are made when ice crystals form on bits of dust? Each snowflake is made from two hundred crystals and looks white because of the reflection from the sun, even on a cloudy day.

Just like a snowflake forms on a bit of dirt, you have sin in your life that makes you dirty and separates you from God. But God loves you so much that he provided a way to make you clean again. When you admit your sin and ask for forgiveness, Jesus covers your sin with his blood and washes your sins clean. Then you are beautiful in his sight, like freshly fallen snow.

With a parent's permission, cut out a snowflake from a round coffee filter. Fold it in half three times until you have a pointed end and a rounded end. Make as many cuts as you like, then open it up and hang it on your window. Just like this snowflake, God will make you beautiful and clean when you confess your sins and seek forgiveness.

DAY 138
Tiny Bit of Faith

"If you have faith as small as a mustard seed, it is enough. You can say to this mountain, 'Move from here to there.' And it will move. Nothing will be impossible for you."

—Matthew 17:20-21

How big is your faith? Is it the size of your pinky finger? A tennis ball? Your dog or cat? Maybe your faith is as big as Montana or as small as a marble. Does it matter to God how much faith you have?

The Bible says if you have faith as small as a mustard seed, it is enough. A mustard seed is so small you can hardly see it. God just needs you to have a little bit of faith. After all, it's not about the size of your faith, it's about how big and powerful God is! That's why even a tiny bit of faith in God goes a long way. Did you know once a mustard seed is planted, it grows into a tree big enough for birds to live among the branches? It's true! And like the mustard seed, when you trust in God, your faith will grow a little more each day.

Create a bookmark with construction paper and write the above verse on it to remind you that it's not about the size of your faith, it's about how big and powerful God is!

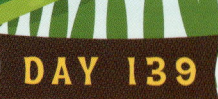

DAY 139
Wearing the Crown

King Solomon was richer than all the other kings on earth. He was also wiser than they were.

—2 Chronicles 9:22

If you were king or queen, what would be your first decree? To make the world a kinder place? To help the poor? To keep people safe? Would you clean up trash? Have more holidays? If you were king or queen, would you eat your vegetables? Go to school? There would be a lot to do if you wore the crown. Would you make wise decisions?

You don't need a lot of education or money to have the kind of wisdom God talks about in the Bible. God's wisdom is knowing him and what his Word says so that you can live a life that pleases him. King Solomon asked God for wisdom so that he could lead the people in a way that honored God. You can have the same wisdom God gave King Solomon. If you ask God for wisdom and search your Bible for guidance, you can make wise decisions and lead others to Jesus.

Take turns being king or queen with a sibling or friend. Make wise decisions by asking God for wisdom and searching your Bible for answers.

DAY 140
Kids Can Change the World

But Jesus asked the children to come to him. "Let the little children come to me," he said. "Don't keep them away. God's kingdom belongs to people like them."

—Luke 18:16

In the New Testament, the disciples tried to stop the parents from taking their children to Jesus, but Jesus said to let the children come to him. Jesus loves children. Jesus loves YOU! Many times, kids think they can't do big things for God until they are adults, but that is far from the truth. With faith in God, you can change the world! How, you ask?

You can tell others about Jesus. You can raise money for causes, such as cancer awareness or clean water. You can donate items to homeless shelters or visit the elderly in nursing homes. Even the smallest action can change someone's life. A smile. A note. A kind word. As God's child, you can be a bright, shining light for Jesus. Remember, Jesus said God's kingdom belongs to people like you!

Consider how you can change the world for Jesus. Walk dogs, have a lemonade stand, or sell crafts to raise money for a cause you believe in. You can do it!

DAY 141
The Waiting Game

Here is something I am still sure of. I will see the Lord's goodness while I'm still alive. Wait for the Lord. Be strong and don't lose hope. Wait for the Lord.
—Psalm 27:13-14

What are you waiting for? Christmas? Your birthday? Or maybe your very own phone? It's difficult to wait for something to happen. Even adults have a hard time waiting. But every day there are situations where you need to be patient. You wait in line. You wait for the bus. You wait for your friends to come over. Throughout your life, you are going to spend a lot of your time waiting.

Did you know God is never in a hurry? Sometimes he answers your prayers right away, and sometimes he makes you wait. Do you ever feel as though whatever you are waiting for isn't important to God? No matter how long it takes, God loves you and is busy working in your life. The important thing to remember is God's timing is best. And if you're able to trust God while you wait, you will be able to trust him every day.

Write down everything you are waiting for. Pray about each one. Sometimes the answer is yes, sometimes the answer is no, and sometimes the answer is wait. God always answers your prayers!

DAY 142
True Forgiveness

Be kind and tender to one another. Forgive one another, just as God forgave you because of what Christ has done.

—Ephesians 4:32

Have you ever been bullied at school? Does your sibling call you names? Do you have a mean neighbor? Did you know if you are kind to those who hurt you, you have a better chance of winning their heart? It's true. Kindness leads to forgiveness.

Forgiving others means you understand how much God has forgiven you. When you feel God's forgiveness, it will be easier for you to forgive others. You will know if you have truly forgiven someone when you don't think about the hurt anymore and can pray for them, even if it doesn't come easily. God will take care of your situation and make things right. Until then, be kind and keep forgiving.

Dear God, thank you for forgiving me of my sins. Please help me to forgive the people who have wronged me. Amen.

DAY 143
New Heart

I will give you new hearts. I will give you a new spirit that is faithful to me. I will remove your stubborn hearts from you. I will give you hearts that obey me.

—Ezekiel 36:26

Do you like to be in charge? Maybe you like to tell your siblings what to do. Maybe you like to be the boss of your friends. Maybe you argue with your parents. There is a word for this type of behavior. It's called stubbornness.

Stubborn people have a hard time admitting they are wrong. But if you ask Jesus into your heart, ask God to forgive you, and seek his help every day, he will change you on the inside. Then you will get along better with your siblings. You will listen to your friends. And you will obey your parents. When you focus on God, you will be faithful to him instead of insisting on having your own way. You will have a new heart. One that is obedient to God.

Cut a large heart out of construction paper. Write "New Heart" on it and hang it in your room to remind yourself to be obedient to God. When you are faithful to him, you won't always insist on having your own way.

DAY 144
Watchful and Ready

"So keep watch. You do not know on what day your Lord will come."
—Matthew 24:42

When was the last time you saw a fire truck with its lights flashing, speeding down the street? That means there is a fire somewhere or that someone needs medical help. Firefighters are trained to respond to an emergency at a moment's notice. They do not know when they will be called. They also make sure the fire truck is well-equipped with whatever supplies they might need. The firefighters are watchful and ready.

The Bible also tells you to keep watch because you do not know the day Jesus will return. Like a firefighter, you can be prepared by keeping your mind and body well-equipped. You can get your heart ready through prayer and reading your Bible. You can get your mind ready by making wise choices. You can get your body ready by going out and sharing the good news about Jesus with others. Honor God with your life, so that when he comes, you will be ready.

The next time you see a fire truck or ambulance with its lights flashing, pray for the person needing help and remember to prepare your heart for Jesus's return.

God's Family Tree

May the Lord our God be with us, just as he was with our people who lived long ago.

—1 Kings 8:57

A family tree shows the people you are related to, such as your parents, grandparents, and great-grandparents. Do you know who is in your family tree? You might be related to kings, queens, presidents, or other well-known people. Whether the members of your family are famous or not, God loves families and has been helping families for generations.

There are family trees listed in the Bible. One example is in Matthew 1:1–16 where it lists fathers, mothers, and sons from Abraham to baby Jesus. Did you know no more family trees were written down in the Bible after Jesus was born? That is because Jesus is our connection to God. Once you accept Jesus into your heart, you become part of God's family tree. You can't get more famous than that! Cool, huh?

Ask your parents to tell you about your family tree. Write down all the names of your family members as far back as they can remember. You are part of God's family tree when you accept Jesus into your heart.

DAY 146
Slow Down

Anyone who is patient has great understanding. But anyone who gets angry quickly shows how foolish they are.

—Proverbs 14:29

Do you get angry sometimes? Why do you get angry? Is it because a parent woke you up to get ready for school and you wanted to sleep? Did someone say something that frustrated you? Maybe you slammed your finger in the door or broke your favorite toy. Everyone gets angry sometimes, but it's how you handle your anger that counts.

The Bible talks about slowing down when you are angry or when your feelings are hurt. When you slow down, you will be more patient. How do you do that when you are about to lose your cool? Think! If you think when you start getting angry, you will take the time to consider your reaction. Are you going to scream or answer with kind words? Are you going to fight or keep your cool? Are you going to hurt others or settle the matter peacefully? By slowing down to think, you will know the right things to do and say.

The next time you feel angry, remember to take the time to think before you lose your cool. When you are patient, you will have great understanding.

DAY 147
Do You Care?

Don't do anything only to get ahead. Don't do it because you are proud. Instead, be humble. Value others more than yourselves.
—Philippians 2:3

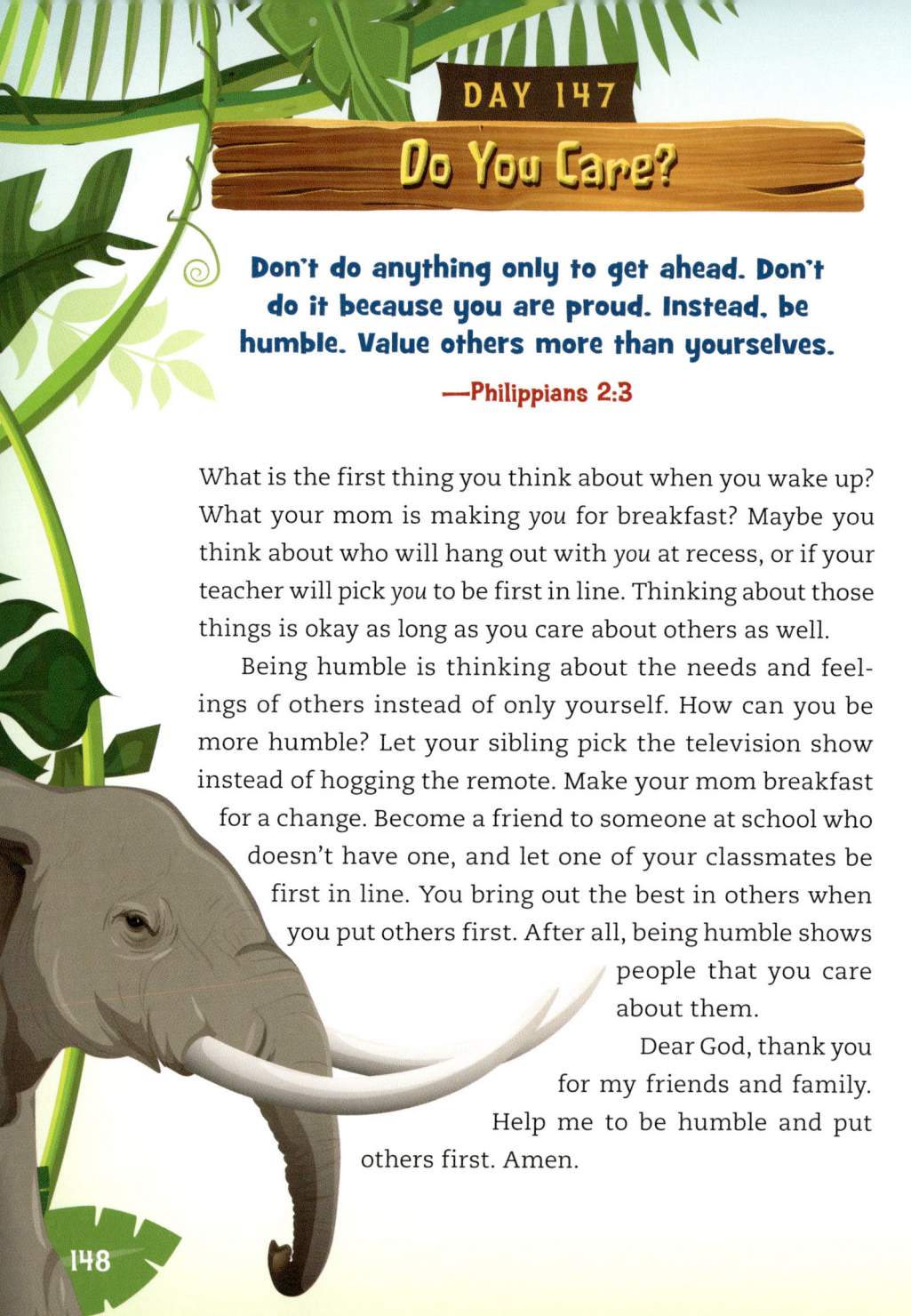

What is the first thing you think about when you wake up? What your mom is making *you* for breakfast? Maybe you think about who will hang out with *you* at recess, or if your teacher will pick *you* to be first in line. Thinking about those things is okay as long as you care about others as well.

Being humble is thinking about the needs and feelings of others instead of only yourself. How can you be more humble? Let your sibling pick the television show instead of hogging the remote. Make your mom breakfast for a change. Become a friend to someone at school who doesn't have one, and let one of your classmates be first in line. You bring out the best in others when you put others first. After all, being humble shows people that you care about them.

Dear God, thank you for my friends and family. Help me to be humble and put others first. Amen.

DAY 148

Footsteps

They kept walking along and talking together. Suddenly there appeared a chariot and horses made of fire. The chariot and horses came between the two men. Then Elijah went up to heaven in a strong wind.

—2 Kings 2:11

Have you ever had someone you love die? Maybe it was a grandparent, or your neighbor. When someone is no longer living on earth, you may wonder what life is going to be like without them. You can't talk with them, or sit next to them anymore. But if they loved Jesus, you can have peace knowing they are in heaven.

There were two men in the Bible named Elisha and Elijah. As they were walking along, a chariot made of fire came between them, and a strong wind carried Elijah up to heaven. What a surprise for Elisha! Elijah had been his mentor and friend—someone he looked up to. When Elijah was gone, Elisha followed his example by performing miracles like Elijah.

You too can keep your loved one alive in your heart by following in their footsteps. Were they kind? Joyful? You can be that type of person too. More importantly, you can follow Jesus's example. He is your friend, and you can be like him.

Place one foot on a piece of paper and draw around it. Color it in and write, "Follow Jesus" across the top.

DAY 149
Be Ready

But make sure that in your hearts you honor Christ as Lord. Always be ready to give an answer to anyone who asks you about the hope you have. Be ready to give the reason for it. But do it gently and with respect.

—1 Peter 3:15

Do you know what you believe? As a Christian boy or girl, it's good to talk with your parents, Sunday school teacher, or pastor so that you can be ready to talk about what you believe to anyone who asks. You don't need to argue with someone if they disagree with you. You only need to tell them with a kind and gentle voice about God's love and the hope you have in Jesus.

One of the best ways to share what you believe is to tell the story of how you became a Christian. Don't worry if you are asked tough questions. It's okay if you don't know all the answers. God doesn't expect you to know everything. He just wants you to share what you've seen him do in your life.

Create a prayer journal and write down your prayers. Then you'll have a lot of hope-filled stories to share.

DAY 150
Gracious God

Return to the L‍ord your God. He is gracious. He is tender and kind. He is slow to get angry. He is full of love.

—Joel 2:13

Do you picture God as tender and kind? What about slow to get angry and full of love? You might be thinking of a time you did or said something wrong. Was God tender and kind, slow to anger and full of love *then*? Even though God isn't happy when you sin, he wants you to seek forgiveness and follow him.

There was a time in the Old Testament when God sent his prophets to warn the people about their disobedience. God promised he wouldn't punish them if they would stop sinning and follow him. Why would God do that? God warned the people because he is tender and kind, slow to get angry and full of love. He warns you too. Listen to the Holy Spirit inside you. He will tell you when you are doing something you shouldn't. Ask God for forgiveness and follow him.

Dear God, thank you for being tender and kind, slow to get angry and full of love. Point out sin in my life and help me follow you. Amen.

DAY 151
Be Like Jesus

Dear friend, don't be like those who do evil. Be like those who do good. Anyone who does what is good belongs to God. Anyone who does what is evil hasn't really seen or known God.

—**3 John v. 11**

Have you ever noticed that little children often copy what you do and say? Maybe you have a little sister or brother who wants to dress like you or have the same haircut. Maybe he or she wants to play the same sports or hang out with you and your friends. Or maybe you are the one who is imitating someone else. Is it a friend? Family member? Someone on television? The most important person God wants you to imitate is Jesus. Did you know you were made in God's image? That means you were created to be like him.

When a friend makes fun of someone, do you do it too? When a sibling disobeys your parents, do you join in? When an actor uses bad language, do you repeat what they say? God wants you to be like those who do good, not evil. God wants you to be like Jesus.

Take a large piece of aluminum foil and press it against your face, creating an impression. It may look a bit like you, but it's not you. In the same way, you are created in the image of God, to be like him.

God's Name Is Holy

"Do not misuse the name of the L ORD your God. The L ORD will find guilty anyone who misuses his name."

—Exodus 20:7

If God's name is special, why do some people use it like a swear word? You have probably heard it used this way on television, in movies, at school, and in your neighborhood. Perhaps you, or someone you know, have misused God's name too.

When people misuse God's name, they are disrespecting God in the worst possible way. It makes him sad when he hears his name used that way. Would you feel hurt if people used your name as a swear word?

God's name is precious and holy. He wants people to praise his name, not use it as a bad word. Throughout the Bible, God says kind and loving words when he speaks about his children. Shouldn't people respect and honor him too? You can't control what others say, but you are in control of the words that come out of your mouth. Practice showing God respect today!

Dear God, thank you for being holy. Help me to show respect by praising your name. Amen.

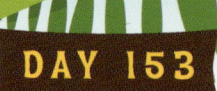

DAY 153
No Matter What

Always be joyful. Never stop praying. Give thanks no matter what happens. God wants you to thank him because you believe in Christ Jesus.

—1 Thessalonians 5:16–18

Are you joyful? You can't control whether you feel happy or sad, but you can choose to be joyful no matter what happens. How? By changing the way you think. Yes, being joyful is a choice! You can be joyful because God loves you.

Do you pray? The Bible says you are to never stop praying. Does that mean you can't eat, sleep, or do anything else? Of course not! Praying continually means having a close relationship with God by talking with him throughout your day. You can tell him anything you want. He will listen. When you tell him what's going on in your life, it builds a deeper relationship with him.

Are you grateful? The more you understand how much God loves you, the more grateful you're going to be. There are many things you can be thankful for even when life stinks. Yes, you can be grateful in all circumstances.

So choose joy. Pray always. And give thanks no matter what!

Choose joy by using this acronym: J=Jesus, O=others, Y=you! When you put Jesus first, others second, and yourself third, you will have more joy in your life!

DAY 154
Rain Makes Everything Grow

"'Then I will send you rain at the right time. The ground will produce its crops. The trees will bear their fruit.'"

—Leviticus 26:4

Rain makes plants grow and grass green. Have you ever wondered how it all works? One step in the water cycle is precipitation, which is rain, snow, or hail. Clouds form in the sky when a lot of water droplets clump together. When the water droplets in the clouds become heavy, gravity causes them to fall from the sky. Without rain, the earth would dry up, there wouldn't be crops for food, and the trees wouldn't bear fruit.

Did you know God planted you on this earth to bear fruit? Just like rain helps plants grow, God helps you grow into the person he wants you to be. When you trust and obey him, you will be able to bear the type of fruit God wants in your life, such as love, joy, peace, patience, kindness, gentleness, and self-control. Without God in your life, your spirit will dry up like earth without rain. Thank God for rain and your relationship with him today.

Draw on the sidewalk with sidewalk chalk a couple of hours after it rains. The colors will be brighter because of the rain.

DAY 155
Rainbows and Promises

"When the rainbow appears in the clouds, I will see it. I will remember that my covenant will last forever. It is a covenant between me and every kind of living creature on earth."

—Genesis 9:16

Have you ever seen a rainbow after it rains? What about a double rainbow? Did you know a rainbow is a full circle of light? You only see a semicircle or arc because you are looking at the rainbow from the ground. Rainbows form when light bends and reflects in the water droplets in the air. The colors of a rainbow are always in the same order. Can you name them?

A rainbow appeared after God made a promise to Noah that he will never again destroy the whole earth with a flood. Every time there is a rainbow, God is showing you that he remembers the promise he made to Noah. Wouldn't you like it if God gave you a special promise too? He did! God gave you many cool promises in the Bible to show you how much he is looking out for you like he looked out for Noah. So go on! Open your Bible and discover the wonderful promises he has for you.

Open your Bible and check out the promise from Joshua 1:9. How does that promise make you feel?

DAY 156
Say What?

"But love your enemies. Do good to them. Lend to them without expecting to get anything back. Then you will receive a lot in return. And you will be children of the Most High God."

—Luke 6:35

Do you have an enemy? You might be thinking of someone right now who has been mean to you in the past or bugs you on a daily basis. Does this person call you names? Pull mean pranks? Spread rumors about you that are not true? Maybe they embarrassed you in front of a crowd or lied to get you in trouble. What do you do about a person like that?

The Bible says you are to love your enemies and do good to them. You might be wrinkling your nose, shaking your head, and saying, "No way! That's impossible!" Do you believe God loves you? Do you believe he loves you even when you are mean to others or make bad choices? Yes, God loves you no matter what! No, it isn't easy to love your enemies, but when you do, you are showing them the kind of love God has for you. And you never know, you might turn that enemy into a friend!

Practice loving your enemies by doing something nice for them. Say a kind word. Help them with their schoolwork. Invite them to play at recess. Remember, God loves you.

DAY 157
No Fear

So do not be afraid. I am with you. Do not be terrified. I am your God. I will make you strong and help you. I will hold you safe in my hands. I always do what is right.

—Isaiah 41:10

What are you afraid of? The dark? Bad dreams? Thunder? Being lost? Getting sick? Perhaps you think something bad is going to happen to you or someone you love. Or maybe you are afraid people won't like you. Did you know many kids your age are scared of the same things you are? It's true. So now what? How do you stop being afraid?

Talk to your mom or dad. They can give you information that might make you feel differently about it. Reading books on the subject from the library can also help you face your fear. But more importantly, God can take your fear away if you ask him. He is with you and watching over you. He will help you and make you strong. You can trust God to keep you safe. He always does what is right.

Dear God, thank you for helping me and making me strong. Help me put my trust in you. Amen.

DAY 158
Jars of Clay

Treasure is kept in clay jars. In the same way, we have the treasure of the good news in these earthly bodies of ours. That shows that the mighty power of the good news comes from God. It doesn't come from us.

—2 Corinthians 4:7

Do you get sick often? Maybe you get ear infections or catch colds easily. Or maybe you're allergic to peanuts or milk. Sometimes kids need to wear glasses or hearing aids. Sometimes kids use wheelchairs or crutches.

God created us as "earthen vessels" or "jars of clay." Bodies can be weak and sometimes get sick. But God put his treasure of eternal life inside you when you accepted Jesus. So even if your body isn't working the way you'd like, you still can praise God that you have this special treasure. Even though you may be weak, God is strong. Trust God that he will take care of you. Your body is special and exactly the way God intended it to be.

Find a special box to keep treasures, such as the shell or rock you picked up from your last vacation or your favorite stuffed animal. Remember the special treasure God gave you when you accepted Jesus into your heart.

Stand Strong

Daniel decided not to make himself "unclean" by eating the king's food and drinking his wine. . . . He wanted permission not to make himself "unclean" with the king's food and wine.

—Daniel 1:8

In the Old Testament, King Nebuchadnezzar told his chief official to find young healthy men to train to become his servants. Daniel was one of the men chosen from Judah.

Daniel did not want to eat the food and wine given to him by the king because it was "unclean" according to God's laws. Instead, he only ate vegetables and drank water. After a time, Daniel was more fit and healthier than the other men. By choosing to rely on God, Daniel stood strong against the pressure of the king.

What "unclean" situation are you facing? Maybe kids are pressuring you to say bad words or watch a movie you shouldn't. The only way you will be able to take a stand like Daniel is by deciding you won't join in. When you stand strong, God will honor you for your faith.

Make an exit plan for "unclean" situations you might face. Be like Daniel!

DAY 160
The B-I-B-L-E

God has breathed life into all Scripture. It is useful for teaching us what is true. It is useful for correcting our mistakes. It is useful for making our lives whole again. It is useful for training us to do what is right.

—2 Timothy 3:16

When you read a book, do you ever skip to the end? It wouldn't be much of a story if you only read the first and last pages. Sure, you might know how the story ends, but you'd miss the entire journey of what the characters learned and how they got there.

Some people do that with the Bible too. They skip over the parts they don't want to read and ignore the parts they don't want to obey. The purpose of the Bible is to teach you what is true and right and correct your mistakes. God gave you the Bible to help you live out your faith. So don't skip pages when you read books—or God's Word. Otherwise, you'll miss all the exciting things you could learn!

Read an entire chapter or story in the Bible. Don't skip the parts you don't want to read. God always has good things to say.

DAY 161
On Top

"You live in the safety of the rocks. You make your home high up in the mountains. But your proud heart has tricked you. So you say to yourself, 'No one can bring me down to the ground.'"

—Obadiah v. 3

Have you ever been the best at something? Maybe you're the smartest person in your class. Maybe you beat your whole family at a board game. Maybe you always get picked to be team captain. It's nice to feel as if you're on top or the best at what you do. You might even start to think nobody could ever beat you or be better than you. But that kind of thinking will get you in trouble.

The people of Edom in the Bible had a prideful attitude. They built their city on top of rocky cliffs high in the mountains. They thought no one could beat them in battle because of how high they were.

Being humble when you are on top is hard, but it's super important if you want to have the same attitude as Jesus. He IS the best, but he humbled himself and served others. When you are humble, you think of others before yourself. It won't matter to you if you're the smartest, coolest, or the best. When you are humble, it won't matter how "high" or "low" you are. When you are humble, God is number one.

Dear God, help me to always have a humble attitude. Amen.

DAY 162
Too Tired

"Come to me, all you who are tired and are carrying heavy loads. I will give you rest. Become my servants and learn from me. I am gentle and free of pride. You will find rest for your souls."

—Matthew 11:28-29

Is something making you tired? You could be tired because you're not getting enough sleep or you're hungry and need something to eat. But there might be another reason too. Are you sick? Do you have too much homework? Is somebody bothering you? Maybe you wish a certain situation would change or go away. Or maybe you are tired of the tough stuff going on in your family. Whatever your burden, you feel weighed down and need rest.

There is someone who can give you rest. He will carry your load. Yes, it's Jesus! Pray to him. Tell him what is making you tired. Give your worries to him. It is good to know that when life feels heavy, God is there to give you rest.

Fill a glass with water and hold it with one hand. It might seem light at first, but the longer you hold it, the heavier it seems. After a while you'll need to put it down. That's the same with your burdens. If you try to carry them yourself, they get heavier and heavier. But when you give your burden to Jesus, your load will be light.

DAY 163
Something Super Cool

It is time to seek the Lord. When you do, he will come and shower his blessings on you.
—Hosea 10:12

When was the last time your mom or dad asked you to do something that you didn't want to do? Maybe it was to take an older neighbor's dog for a walk. Perhaps they wanted you to help your little sister or brother. Or maybe they asked you to go with them to bring a meal to a sick friend. At first you may have wrinkled your nose and let out a big sigh, but then you obeyed and discovered something super cool. Helping others makes you feel good inside. You not only blessed someone else, but you received the blessing too.

When you seek God, the same thing happens. He will shower you with his blessings when you obey him. Many times it's the small things you do, like feeding your dog or taking out the trash without being asked, that bring about the biggest rewards. The reason is that when you obey God, it also blesses others. (Think about how happy it makes your dog and parents!) God showers you with blessings in other ways too. He loves you, forgives you, and cares about you. Now there's good reason to pass the blessing to others.

Ask God how you can bless someone today, then do it! You will discover something really cool—you will be blessed too.

DAY 164
Secrets

"What is hidden will be seen. And what is out of sight will be brought into the open and made known."

—Luke 8:17

Has anyone ever told you a secret? There are good secrets, like when your friend's mom invites you to a surprise birthday party for your friend. And there are secrets that you shouldn't keep to yourself, like if your friend is making bad choices and you're the only one who knows. Those types of secrets, where someone is doing something hurtful or wrong, should be told to an adult who can help. Your friend may get mad at you at first, but soon they will know it was the right thing to do.

Do you keep your faith a secret? God wants you to let your light shine and share the good things he has done. Have you ever tried to hide a light? It's impossible! You can even see a flashlight glow under the covers. When you listen to what the Bible says, you will shine for him and let the secret out!

With parent permission, light a candle and turn out the lights. Just like the glow of the candle, your love for God will show when you listen to him. Now that's a secret that shouldn't stay hidden!

Do the Right Thing

The ways of the Lord are right. People who are right with God live the way he wants them to. But those who refuse to obey him trip and fall.
—Hosea 14:9

Do you like to be told what to do? How about when your mom asks you to put the dishes in the dishwasher or when your teacher tells you to focus on your work? Do you do the right thing and obey, or do you do your own thing instead? What about when a friend wants to do something you know is wrong? Do you do the right thing and obey God, or do you follow your friend and mess up?

There is a word for doing the opposite of what God wants you to do—it's called being rebellious. People who have a hard time obeying end up in trouble. They trip up and stumble and make life difficult for themselves. God wants you to obey and do what the Bible says. When you live the way God wants you to live, you are obedient and wise. Everyone trips up sometimes, but dust yourself off and learn from your mistakes.

Practice doing the right thing by obeying what the Bible says and choosing friends who follow God. You've got this!

DAY 166
Shine Your Light

> "In the same way, let your light shine so others can see it. Then they will see the good things you do. And they will bring glory to your Father who is in heaven."
>
> —Matthew 5:16

The sun is a star in the center of solar system. It's over 109 times larger than Earth, and it is closer to Earth than any other star. Light from the sun reaches Earth in eight minutes. Now that is one bright light!

In the Bible, it says Jesus is the Light of the World. Without Jesus, the world is in darkness. When you believe in Jesus, the Bible says you are also light. People will see the good things you do because of your light, and they will praise God's name. What type of good things? You don't have to try very hard to shine your light. Be a friend to someone who needs one. Treat people with kindness and respect. Be humble. When you love others like Jesus did, you will be one bright light for him.

Cut a few small holes in a paper lunch bag. Shine a flashlight inside the bag and turn off the lights. Just like the light shines through the holes, you can shine your light too.

DAY 167
What Is a Bribe?

"Have respect for the Lord. Judge carefully. He is always right. He treats everyone the same. Our God doesn't want his judges to take money from people who want special favors."

—2 Chronicles 19:7

Has a friend or a sibling ever offered you a bribe? A bribe is when someone gives you something to get their own way. Maybe a friend gave you money so that you wouldn't tell the teacher they cheated on a test. Maybe a sibling told you they'd do your chores for a week as long as you didn't tell your parents they were hanging out with the wrong crowd.

You might think you are being rewarded for keeping their secret, but you are really stopping yourself and others from doing the right thing. You are encouraging their bad behavior. Did you know God sees everything? He knows when you make good and bad choices. The next time someone offers you a bribe, tell them no. Encourage them to be honest. The Bible says God doesn't want anyone to take a bribe. He rewards those who tell the truth.

If you've offered someone a bribe to keep quiet about a bad choice you've made, go to them and apologize. God will help you do the right thing.

DAY 168
Put On These Things

You are God's chosen people. You are holy and dearly loved. So put on tender mercy and kindness as if they were your clothes. Don't be proud. Be gentle and patient.

—Colossians 3:12

Do you have a favorite piece of clothing? Maybe it's a T-shirt or a pair of jeans. Maybe it's a fun pair of socks. Whatever it is, you love wearing it and would put it on every day if you could.

The Bible says you are to put on mercy and kindness as if they were your clothes. That means you should show compassion to your friends and family even when you feel like they don't deserve it, and you should be kind and caring to everyone you meet. When you put on mercy and kindness, you are making your relationships stronger, doing what God says, and showing how much you love God. Are you wearing mercy and kindness today?

As you put on your favorite piece of clothing, consider how you can show mercy and kindness to the people in your life.

DAY 169
You Are Priceless

God, your thoughts about me are priceless. No one can possibly add them all up.

—Psalm 139:17

Have you ever seen a diamond ring? A diamond is very valuable and is the hardest gemstone. There are many other unique and cool gemstones. Perhaps the most colorful gemstone is the opal, which has an iridescent rainbow effect. Garnet, a dark red gemstone, was named after the seeds of a pomegranate. And it takes between one and three years to grow a cultured pearl.

Did you know God thinks of you as his precious gemstone? You are unique, wonderfully made, and priceless in his eyes. God not only created you, but he loves you and wants a close relationship with you. On the days when you think nobody cares, remember God not only thinks you are valuable, but he paid the highest price for you by sending Jesus to die on the cross so that you can spend eternity with him. Yes, like a precious gemstone, you are valuable and priceless to God!

Dear God, thank you for creating me and for sending Jesus to earth to die for my sins. Help me remember that I am priceless in your eyes. Amen.

DAY 170
On Your Own?

But the kindness and love of God our Savior appeared. He saved us. It wasn't because of the good things we had done. It was because of his mercy. He saved us by washing away our sins. We were born again. The Holy Spirit gave us new life.

—Titus 3:4-5

What can you do all by yourself? You might be able to hit a baseball or kick a soccer ball because you are getting stronger and more coordinated every year. You might be able to solve difficult math problems because you are logical in the way you think. You might be able to make friends easily because you are self-confident in who God made you to be. But that's not all! You can help your parents do chores around the house, help your teacher at school, and help a friend when they need you.

However, there is one thing you can't do by yourself. There is nothing you can do to save yourself from your sins. You need God's kindness, love, and mercy. You need Jesus as your Savior. You need God's power. God made you, and he gives you new life when you trust in him. When you get frustrated that you can't change or do things on your own, remember to trust in Jesus your Savior.

Name one thing you can do all by yourself. Thank God for the good things you can do and for the gift of Jesus, the one who saves you from your sins.

DAY 171
My Heavenly Dad

There is one God and Father of all. He is over everything. He is through everything. He is in everything.

—Ephesians 4:6

How would you describe your dad? Is he tall? Short? Muscular? Thin? Does your dad live with you? Do you see him every day or only on the weekends? Can you talk easily with your dad, or do you have a difficult time sharing how you feel? Maybe you have a super cool dad. Maybe you haven't seen your dad in a long time. Maybe you've never met him.

You have a heavenly dad who loves and adores you. The Bible describes him as kind, loyal, and strong. There is no doubt that he will keep his promises because of his unfailing love and might. God led the people in the Old Testament to the promised land, and he will lead you too. He is faithful and will guide you where he wants you to go. Aren't you glad you have a heavenly dad to take care of you?

Write a letter to your heavenly dad. Tell him five things about yourself. Thank him for his great love and strength.

DAY 172
Are You Bored?

Be filled with joy in the sight of the Lord your God. Be joyful in everything you do.
—Deuteronomy 12:18

Are you bored even though you have a closet full of toys and a bookcase full of books? That's not even counting all your video games or the bike in your garage. Do you walk around with a frown on your face and a bad attitude, hoping someone will notice and go out of their way to make you happy?

If you are sad or bored all the time and don't know why, talk with your parents. There might be something going on. But if you act bored because you hope it'll get you attention, then stop right now! When you act bored, it makes your parents tired and zaps everyone's energy—yours included. God wants you to enjoy life. Look around! There are plenty of things to get excited about. God created an amazing world!

Take a nature walk. Bake a batch of chocolate chip cookies. Pet your dog. Play a game with a friend. Watch a movie with your parents. Have fun!

DAY 173
It's Not Fair!

Let us not become proud. Let us not make each other angry. Let us not want what belongs to others.
—Galatians 5:26

Have you ever wondered why some kids seem to have it all? Maybe you know someone who's super talented, has lots of friends, and lives in the best neighborhood. Their life seems perfect. You might start complaining to God that it's not fair! You might be full of envy and anger. You might do or say something you will later regret.

Instead of thinking about someone else's life, focus on your own. God has a plan just for you. In fact, he planned your life before you were born. His plan is better than anything you could ever dream of for yourself. Once you start going after God's plan for your life instead of someone else's, you won't be envious anymore. The next time you are tempted to want what others have, remember that God didn't make you like anybody else. He made you to be YOU! So enjoy the life he's given you.

Dear God, thank you for the life you've given me. Help me not to be envious of others. Amen.

DAY 174
Work It Out!

Then the LORD said to Cain, "Where is your brother Abel?" "I don't know," Cain replied. "Am I supposed to take care of my brother?"

—Genesis 4:9

Do you have a brother or a sister? What about a cousin or a close friend? Do you ever get jealous of them? Maybe they are better at something or get more attention than you. Have you ever gotten so angry that you wanted to hurt them?

That's what happened to two brothers in the book of Genesis. Cain was jealous of his brother Abel. Abel was a shepherd while Cain worked in the fields. When it came time to give God a gift, Cain gave some of his crops and Abel gave the best portions of the firstborn lambs from his flock. God was happy with Abel's gift, but he did not accept Cain and his gift. Cain was so angry, he killed his brother Abel! When God asked Cain where Abel was, Cain lied. One sin led to another. Cain never told God he was sorry. He never asked for forgiveness.

Is there someone you need to say sorry to and ask for forgiveness? Don't let jealousy come between you. Even though Cain sinned, God protected him and kept him safe. God loves you too, and he will help you work it out!

Do you need to apologize to someone? Do it now! Remember, God loves you and will help you make things right!

DAY 175
Spittin' Mad

The LORD is gracious, kind and tender. He is slow to get angry and full of love.
—Psalm 145:8

Do you ever have temper tantrums? You know, when you slam doors, kick and scream, and throw things on the floor? This type of anger is so out-of-control that you can't see past the hurt and frustration. It's like you become a monster ready to destroy anything in your path. But when it passes, you might be surprised and embarrassed about letting it go that far. You might even wish you could take it all back. How can you keep your cool and let go of your anger? Is it possible? What about God? Does he get angry?

Sure, God gets angry. He doesn't like sin. But the Bible says he is slow to get angry and is full of love. That means he doesn't explode when he's upset. Can you slow down and keep your cool too? There are many ways to get your energy out when you are angry. Run around the block, punch a pillow, write in a journal, talk with a friend. When you follow God's example by being gracious, kind, and tender, you will be slow to become angry and full of love too.

Are you angry? Talk to God. Be totally honest about how you feel. By getting out your energy in a positive way, you will be able to handle whatever has you spittin' mad.

DAY 176
Every Good Gift

Every good and perfect gift is from God. This kind of gift comes down from the Father who created the heavenly lights. These lights create shadows that move. But the Father does not change like these shadows.

—James 1:17

Do you have a comfortable bed to sleep in? Clothes to wear? Food to eat? What about a book to read or a ball to play with? Do you know who gave you all those gifts? God did! He gave you your life, family, and everything else you have. Did you know pretty flowers, rainbows, and sunsets are also gifts for you to enjoy? Every breath you take is a gift from God. You didn't do anything to earn them. God gives you good gifts because he loves you.

Has anyone ever given you a gift and then wanted it back? Ouch, that hurts! Other times people give gifts because they want something in return. But God gives you gifts with no strings attached, and he doesn't change his mind. His love never changes. God gives you good gifts, and he is the same yesterday, today, and forever!

When you give like God does, you don't expect anything in return. Give a gift to someone just because you love them. It could be a flower, a note, or anything else you can think of— even a smile.

DAY 177
No Dirty Jokes Allowed

There must not be any bad language or foolish talk or dirty jokes. They are out of place. Instead, you should give thanks.
—Ephesians 5:4

Do you like to play practical jokes on your friends? Like the time you tapped someone on the shoulder and hid so they couldn't see you. Or when you took part of your friend's lunch when they weren't looking. Or the time you pulled something away before your friend had a chance to grab it. Silly pranks are meant to be fun. Hopefully your friend laughed and took it well. But sometimes pranks don't go the way you plan. Sometimes the person you play the joke on doesn't think it's funny. There is a difference between being funny and being mean.

So what type of joke does God think is okay? God is holy and pure and wants you to tell jokes that don't use bad words, make fun of other people, or fill anyone's mind with wrong thoughts. God created you to laugh and have fun, but not if it is sinful or hurts others. Joking around with your friends and acting silly is fun. Tell them jokes that would make God smile too!

Go to the library and find a good clean joke book to share with your family and friends. That is one sure way to make them laugh!

DAY 178
Counting Stars

The LORD took Abram outside and said, "Look up at the sky. Count the stars, if you can." Then he said to him, "That's how many children will be born into your family."
—Genesis 15:5

Have you ever tried to count the stars? How many did you count? Twenty-five? Fifty? One hundred? Maybe you lost track because there were too many. As you look up into the night sky, do you imagine God sitting on his throne? Do you wonder if he keeps his promises?

Abram wondered the same thing. God appeared to him in a vision and said, "Abram, do not be afraid. I am like a shield to you. I am your very great reward." Then God took Abram out beneath the starry sky and told him to count the stars because that is how many children would be born into his family. How could this be? Abram was an old man. He did not have any children. But God made a promise that from Abram would come a great nation and because of Abram all people on earth would be blessed. Abram believed God's promise, and it came true. Do you have faith like Abram?

Go outside and look up at the stars. Count as many as you can and consider how you can have faith like Abram.

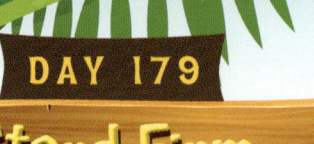

Stand Firm

So obey God. Stand up to the devil. He will run away from you.

—James 4:7

When was the last time you made a choice to do the right thing? Maybe it was when you chose to listen to your mom instead of sneaking a cookie from the cookie jar. Maybe it was when you chose to be safe instead of taking a dare from a friend. Maybe it was the time you said no when someone wanted you to do something you knew you shouldn't. Did you know Jesus was also tempted by the devil?

In Matthew 4:1–11, the Holy Spirit led Jesus into the wilderness. After forty days and forty nights of not eating, Jesus was hungry. Three times the devil tried to tempt Jesus. The first time he wanted Jesus to turn stones into bread. The second time he wanted Jesus to throw himself down from the highest point of the temple so God could rescue him. The third time he offered Jesus all the kingdoms of the world if only Jesus would worship him. But Jesus didn't fall for the devil's evil plan! Each time Jesus used words from the Bible to show the devil he knew what was right. Just as Satan left Jesus, he will run away from you too when you obey God and stand up to the devil.

Read your Bible every day so that you will know right from wrong and can stand firm when the devil tempts you.

DAY 180
Dream BIG

God is able to do far more than we could ever ask for or imagine. He does everything by his power that is working in us.

—Ephesians 3:20

Do you have a dream? Maybe you want to be a good dancer, learn how to play the drums, or get a role in the school play. Maybe you want to make a new friend or join a sports team. Sometimes reaching your dream seems easy. Other times it feels impossible. Maybe you are afraid. What do you do then?

God wants you to have faith and go after your dreams. He doesn't want you to be afraid, but to take small steps to make your dreams happen. That means taking dance classes if you want to be a good dancer, drum lessons if you want to play the drums, or practicing lines if you want to get a role in the school play. It means putting your nerves aside to make a new friend or trying out for the sports team. Don't let anyone tell you that you can't reach your dreams. God has the power to do more than you could ever ask or imagine. So dream BIG and never give up!

Dear God, thank you for giving me a big dream. Help me to not be afraid and take small steps to make it happen. Amen.

DAY 181
Wise Worker

You people who don't want to work, think about the ant! Consider its ways and be wise! It has no commander. It has no leader or ruler. But it stores up its food in summer. It gathers its food at harvest time.

—Proverbs 6:6–8

Have you ever seen an ant colony? Ants may be very small critters, but they are very powerful! An ant can carry fifty times its body weight, and when ants work together, they can move big objects. Did you know there are over twelve thousand different types of ants? In 2000, the largest known ant's nest was found in Argentina, and it had thirty-three ant populations. This giant ant colony held millions of nests and billions of workers!

God wants you to work like an ant. Ants work every day, know where to find food, and line up to get it. Ants also work together. Can you work every day? Can you look for ways you can be a team player? If you do those things, you will be a wise worker, like the ant!

Make ants on a log by putting peanut butter or cream cheese on a celery stick and placing raisins (ants) on top. As you eat your snack, think about how you can work like an ant.

Day 182
Like Honey

Kind words are like honey. They are sweet to the spirit and bring healing to the body.

—Proverbs 16:24

Do you like to eat honey? Do you know where honey comes from? Honeybees, of course! During the spring and summer months, bees collect the sweet nectar from flowers and mix it in their mouths before taking the nectar to their hive. Then the bees drop the nectar into the honeycomb. Once the nectar becomes thicker, the bees cover it with wax. Then the beekeeper knows it's time to collect the honey.

The Bible says kind words are like honey. That means when you say kind words, your words will be sweet to those who listen. So encourage a friend who is sad, speak to your parents in a kind way, and be nice to your siblings. Kind words not only build others up, but they can lead people to Jesus.

What types of words are coming out of your mouth? Kind words that build up, or hurtful words that tear down? Ask Jesus to help you say kind words today!

DAY 183
New Creation

> When anyone lives in Christ, the new creation has come. The old is gone! The new is here! All this is from God. He brought us back to himself through Christ's death on the cross.
> —2 Corinthians 5:17-18

When was the last time you saw a butterfly? What color was it? Butterflies have many different colors and patterns, but all butterflies have one thing in common. They all were caterpillars. After a caterpillar sheds its skin multiple times, it hangs from a branch and a hard shell forms on the outside. Inside the cocoon, the caterpillar is transforming into a butterfly. When the hard shell splits open, the butterfly comes out, but it's not ready to fly yet. The wings are soft, wet, and wrinkled. Once the wings are dry, the butterfly is ready to take flight.

Just like a butterfly, you are a new creation when you believe in Jesus. No, you don't look different on the outside, but there is a change that happens inside. When you become a new creation, your heart will change. You will want to be more like Jesus. Just like a caterpillar can't go back into a cocoon after it becomes a butterfly, you have a brand-new life in Christ when you accept Jesus into your heart.

Draw a picture of a butterfly and color it. Just like a butterfly, you are a new creation when you believe in Jesus.

DAY 184
Forever and Ever

"'The grass dries up. The flowers fall to the ground. But what our God says will stand forever.'"

—Isaiah 40:8

Have you ever noticed what happens to grass and flowers during winter? Grass dries up and turns brown. Flowers fall to the ground. The truth is, nothing lasts forever. Your new video game won't be new anymore. Your favorite television show will end. And your latest tech gadget will be a thing of the past. People can change too. Your friends might move away, go to a different school, or want to hang out with someone else. With everything changing around you, it's easy to feel sad and lost.

But there is one thing that will never change, and that is God's Word. The Bible was written a long time ago, but it never goes out of style. God loved people during Bible times, and he loves you now! Even though the world around you changes all the time, the Word of God lasts forever and ever.

Put a flower in a vase with water. It will last only for a few days, but you can be glad God's Word never changes.

What to Wear

"And why do you worry about clothes? See how the wild flowers grow. They don't work or make clothing. But here is what I tell you. Not even Solomon in all his royal robes was dressed like one of these flowers."

—Matthew 6:28-29

Do you take a long time getting dressed for school? Maybe you have too many choices and can't decide what to wear. Maybe you take a long time because you want to look just right. Or maybe you don't have many clothes and are embarrassed to wear the same thing over and over again.

Have you ever seen a field of brightly colored wildflowers? Beautiful, huh? Wildflowers don't worry about what they look like. God wants you to be like the wildflower. He doesn't want you to worry about clothes and what you wear. Just as God helps the wildflowers grow and multiply through animals, bees, and the wind, he will take care of you.

Dear God, thank you for taking care of me. Help me not to worry about clothes and what I wear. Amen.

DAY 186
Mom Hugs

"As a mother comforts her child, I will comfort you. You will find comfort in Jerusalem."
—Isaiah 66:13

How would you describe your mom? Is she tall? Short? Is she kind? Funny? What do you like to do with your mom? Maybe you are super close with your mom. Or maybe you only see her on weekends. Maybe you live with a foster mom, an aunt, or your grandma.

The Bible says God comforts you like a mom comforts her child. That means you can turn to God when you are sick or hurting and he will give you peace. He will wipe away your tears when you are sad and give you rest when you are tired. You can tell your problems to God, and he will listen to you. When you go through good times and bad times, remember God is there for you even if your mom is not.

Give your mom a big hug or write her or the mother figure in your life a card or letter. Tell her how much you love her!

DAY 187
Good Manners

Finally, I want all of you to agree with one another. Be understanding. Love one another. Be kind and tender. Be humble.

—1 Peter 3:8

Do you have good manners? Do you say *please*, *thank you*, and *you're welcome*? What about *I'm sorry* and *excuse me*? Your parents probably taught you to say all these things when you were younger. Having good manners shows good behavior and that you can be kind to others. Having good manners shows what is in your heart.

But what if you don't get along with your sibling or your best friend snaps at you? Do you need to have good manners then, or can you let them have it? Don't they deserve what's coming to them? Snapping back might feel good in the moment, but if you listened back to your words later, you would probably feel embarrassed. So instead of lashing out, remember that you are made in God's image, and he wants you to be understanding, kind, and tender. When you remember to have good manners even when it's tough, you show God's love.

Practice good manners by thinking of others first, listening before you speak, and being helpful whenever you can.

DAY 188
What Is Your Choice?

A person who has a pure and loving heart and speaks kindly will be a friend of the king.

—Proverbs 22:11

What is your favorite color? Is it red? Blue? Purple? Green? When you open a box of crayons, what color do you choose first? Coloring the pages of a coloring book is fun. It's as if the picture comes to life! You can color with bright, happy colors, or you can color with dark, gloomy colors. It's up to you.

Just as you choose the colors for your coloring book, you can also choose your attitude. You can choose to be happy or grumpy. You can choose to be loving or angry. You can choose to be polite or rude. It's up to YOU! But guess what? With God's help, you can be happy, loving, and polite no matter the circumstances. The Bible says a person who has a pure and loving heart and speaks with kind words will be a friend. What color is your attitude today?

Take out paper and crayons and color! Just as you choose crayons, remember to choose a positive attitude as well.

DAY 189
Strong Faith

Even if we are not faithful, he remains faithful. He must be true to himself.

—2 Timothy 2:13

Have you ever had an arm-wrestling match? You know, when you grip the hand of an opponent and try to push the back of their hand to the table? Whichever one of you is stronger will win.

Have you ever wrestled with your faith? The truth is, everyone has doubts from time to time. There are many people in the Bible who doubted Jesus. Peter denied Jesus three times, and Thomas didn't believe Jesus was raised from the dead until he saw him and touched the wounds in his hands. Both Peter and Thomas became strong in their faith, and God used them in big ways! So don't be afraid to wrestle with your faith. God will use you too. When you search the Bible for the answers to your questions, God will make your faith strong.

Talk to your parent, a Sunday school teacher, or your pastor if you are wrestling with your faith. They can help you find the answers to your questions. Remember, even during Bible times people wrestled with their faith.

DAY 190
Live It OUT!

I have no greater joy than to hear that my children are living by the truth.

—3 John v. 4

Have you ever played a game called Truth or Dare? To play the game, you need to decide if you want to answer a question truthfully or act out a dare. You might be asked to share your most embarrassing moment or to dance like a chicken. But don't worry! You are not the only one. Each person takes turns answering a truth or acting out a dare. And if you can laugh at yourself, the game will be a lot of fun!

Did you know the Bible is full of truth *and* dare? You can find what God says is true from Genesis to Revelation. He wants you to know the truth of his Word and be able to answer questions about your faith. He also dares you to act out your faith by showing God's love to others and doing BIG things for him, such as sharing your lunch with someone in need, helping your neighbor rake the leaves, or encouraging a friend. It makes God happy when his children live out their faith. Are you living by the truth?

Read your Bible every day to find out what God says is true and what exciting things he wants you to do!

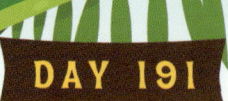

DAY 191
Forever Kind of Love

The LORD appeared to us in the past. He said, "I have loved you with a love that lasts forever. I have kept on loving you with a kindness that never fails."

—Jeremiah 31:3

Have you ever done something you know is wrong? You may be slouching in your seat right now just thinking about it. Maybe you lied to your parents. Maybe you cheated in a game or on a test. Maybe you broke something and chose not to fess up. Or maybe you hurt someone's feelings. All of these can make you feel down on yourself. You may be wondering if God still loves you.

The truth is, nothing can separate you from God's love! No, he doesn't want you to lie, cheat, or hurt others, but even when you do these things, God still loves you. God's love lasts forever, and his kindness never fails. He loves you on your best day and on your worst. The best thing to do is confess your sins to him and thank him for loving you no matter what!

Dear God, thank you for loving me even when I do bad stuff. Help me to be more like you. Amen.

DAY 192
Who Is Your Neighbor?

The whole law is fulfilled by obeying this one command. "Love your neighbor as you love yourself."

—Galatians 5:14

How do you love yourself? Do you get a drink of water when you are thirsty? Eat when you are hungry? Sleep when you are tired? Good! It's important to take care of the body God gave you. But does your whole day focus on you and what you want? Here are some hints. Maybe you interrupt your mom when she's on the phone. Maybe you argue with your siblings and demand your own way. Or maybe you sulk and complain when your friend can't hang out. The real question is, do you always put yourself first?

If you answered yes, it's time to learn how to love your neighbor as you love yourself. That means you think about their needs like you do your own. So when your mom is on the phone, wait until she hangs up before you talk with her. Think about someone else instead of demanding your own way. When you love God above everything else, you will be able to love your neighbor as you love yourself.

Maybe the hardest neighbors to love are the people who live next door. Do something nice for them today. Bake them cookies, offer to wash their car, or walk their dog.

DAY 193
Noise Maker

Lord, you will give perfect peace to those who commit themselves to be faithful to you. That's because they trust in you.

—Isaiah 26:3

Have you ever been distracted by noise? A loud truck driving down the street. People talking. Music blaring. Noise is everywhere. But did you know you create your own noise inside your head? It's when you think super hard about stuff, like whether your teacher likes you or whether or not someone wants to be your friend. Or when you worry about your family or your sick pet. That kind of noise will keep you from having peace.

But you can quiet the noise in your head when you think about God and trust in him. When you think about how much God loves you, you won't worry about whether your teacher likes you or if someone wants to be your friend. And when you put your faith in God, you will trust him to care for your family and pets. When you trust God, you will have peace.

How many different noises can you make? Can you cluck like a chicken? Squeal like a pig? Can you whistle? Make popping sounds? Making noise that you can hear is fun!

DAY 194
Help Wanted

Carry one another's heavy loads. If you do, you will fulfill the law of Christ.

—Galatians 6:2

God made people to help each other. Sure, you can tie your own shoes, get a bowl of cereal, and turn on the television, but you need a parent to drive you to school, pay the bills, and keep a roof over your head. People need each other. And when you carry someone else's load, you are doing what the Bible says you should.

Every day God puts people in your life for you to help and encourage. You could help your baby brother or sister get dressed. You could reach for something on the top shelf for someone in a wheelchair. You could help an older person load groceries in their car. You could listen to a friend. Look around you! When you see a way to help someone, do it—even if it seems small. If everyone helped each other, our world would be a better place.

Do a chore for your sibling. Pass out papers for your teacher. Encourage a friend. Ask God how you can help someone today.

DAY 195

Strong and Brave

Here is what I am commanding you to do. Be strong and brave. Do not be afraid. Do not lose hope. I am the Lord your God. I will be with you everywhere you go.

—Joshua 1:9

Do you need to be strong and brave right now? You might be scared because your mom is going to have another baby and you feel invisible. You might be scared because your audition is tomorrow and you really want the part. Or you might be scared because there is a big hairy spider dangling above your bed. EEEK! It's easy to lose hope when you are afraid. But whatever has you worried doesn't have to take over your life. So how do you become strong and brave when you are afraid?

God commanded people throughout the Bible not to be afraid, and he says it to YOU too! He wants you to face your fear and not lose hope. That means talk with your parents when you feel invisible, practice your lines for the audition, and tackle your fear of spiders by learning more about them—after you call someone to remove the one on your ceiling, of course! You don't need to be afraid of *anything* because God is with you wherever you go.

Take one small step to face your fear. You don't need to be afraid; God is with you wherever you go.

DAY 196
Don't Take That

Anyone who has been stealing must never steal again. Instead, they must work. They must do something useful with their own hands.

—Ephesians 4:28

Have you ever stolen something? Maybe you put a pack of gum in your pocket at the store and forgot about it until you got home. Maybe you didn't return the books you borrowed from the library. Or maybe you took money from your sibling's piggy bank so that you could buy ice cream with your friends. Yes, those things are stealing! Even if it was a long time ago, you may still feel a bit guilty about it. So what should you do now?

The best thing to do is make it right with the person or store you stole from. That means you pay for whatever you took, go to the library and return the books, and put money in your sibling's piggy bank. As you grow older, you'll face many situations when you'll need to make a choice between stealing and being honest. The Bible says anyone who has been stealing should never steal again. Instead, you should work hard and earn the money to pay for it. You'll feel good inside, and God will be happy too!

Think about a time you chose to be honest. Tell God all about it and thank him for helping you make the right choice.

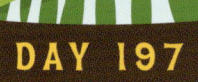

Second Chances

Then he prayed to the Lord. Samson said, "Lord and King, show me that you still have concern for me. Please, God, make me strong just one more time."

—Judges 16:28

Have you ever made a huge mistake? You know, the kind that makes you wonder if things can ever be made right. Maybe you hurt a friend's feelings. Maybe you got in trouble at school. Or maybe your parent caught you doing something wrong. Will you be given a second chance?

There was a man in the Bible named Samson who was super strong. He was so strong that he could kill a lion with his bare hands, defeat an army, and pull apart the doors of the town gate. But Samson had a weakness. He told Delilah the secret of his strength. After Delilah cut his hair, the Philistine enemy captured him. But because Samson prayed, God allowed him to be strong one more time. With one big push the temple where he was chained came crashing down and he was able to get rid of the bad guys. Like Samson, you can call on God to help you make things right. Everyone deserves a second chance!

Talk with the person you have wronged, admit your mistake, and ask for forgiveness. You can do it!

DAY 198
Gossip Hurts

A person who talks about others tells secrets. So avoid anyone who talks too much.

—Proverbs 20:19

Has anyone ever told you a secret? Did you keep that secret to yourself? Truth is, it feels good when someone shares something with you that nobody else knows. You might even feel super cool if you tell someone because it shows how much you know. But guess what? When you share your friend's secret, you are tearing him down instead of building him up. When you share your friend's secret, you are gossiping. And God has plenty to say about that.

There are many verses in the Bible that speak against gossip. In fact, God despises it! So don't be the one who talks too much and tells other people's secrets. But what if somebody else is the one gossiping? What do you do then? The best thing to do is change the subject or walk away. You could also tell your friend to treat others with respect. After all, what people say isn't always true. Remember, don't gossip, and stay away from those who do. That's what Jesus would do.

Play the glitter game outside with a group of friends. The leader takes a handful of glitter and passes it to the next person in line. That person passes it to the next person and so on. When the game is over, talk about how gossip is like glitter.

DAY 199
Love in Action

When Jesus came ashore, he saw a large crowd. He felt deep concern for them. They were like sheep without a shepherd. So he began teaching them many things.
—Mark 6:34

Have you ever given some of your old toys away? What about clothes you've outgrown? Have you ever shared your lunch? Having compassion means you see when someone is hurting or needs something, and you do something to help. Compassion is taking action.

Did you know Jesus fed five thousand people with one boy's lunch of five loaves and two fish? He sure did! It was a miracle. Do you know why Jesus did that? He saw the large crowd and felt deep concern for them, and he did something about it. He asked the crowd to sit in groups, gave thanks, and broke the five loaves into pieces. He did the same thing with the two fish. The disciples passed the food around. Everyone ate and was satisfied. And guess what? There were twelve baskets left! Do you have compassion like Jesus? Can you spot a problem and do something about it? You sure can!

Read or have a parent read Mark 6:30–44. Decide how you can take action and show compassion to someone in need.

DAY 200
Are You Wise?

Don't be wise in your own eyes. Have respect for the Lord and avoid evil. That will bring health to your body. It will make your bones strong.

—Proverbs 3:7–8

Do you need to be right all the time? Are you losing friends because you are acting like a smarty-pants? There is a word for this type of behavior. It's called being a know-it-all. If you find yourself constantly saying, "Do it like this," or "You are wrong!" you may have a know-it-all attitude.

Yes, you are learning new things every day about the world around you, but it's important to let others give their thoughts and ideas too. When you give others a chance to share what they know, they will also listen to what you have to say. Besides, the Bible says you are not to be wise in your own eyes. True wisdom happens when you respect God, avoid evil, and learn from your mistakes. So remember, your family and friends won't think you're a know-it-all when you can admit you don't know it all.

Write a list of ten things you know. Now write a list of ten things you'd like to know more about. You become wise by asking God questions and searching for the truth.

DAY 201
You Can Do It!

I can do all this by the power of Christ. He gives me strength.
—Philippians 4:13

Do you need courage? Maybe you have a piano recital and you're afraid you'll mess up. Maybe your family is moving and you're afraid you won't make new friends. Or maybe it's your turn to give a speech in class and you're afraid you'll say something silly. Where do you find strength when you want to give up?

Did you know there was a man in the Bible named Gideon who felt the same way? He knew his army was too weak to defeat their enemy. Gideon felt like giving up. But God told Gideon not to worry. God would be with him, and Gideon would win the battle. And that is exactly what happened! When your strength comes from God, you can do things you never thought possible. You can face whatever you are going through because God loves you and will give you strength.

How strong are you? Go to your neighborhood playground and swing on the monkey bars. Just like a parent catches you when you lose your grip, God is strong for you in tough times too.

Boys and Girls

While our sons are young, they will be like healthy plants. Our daughters will be like pillars that have been made to decorate a palace.

—Psalm 144:12

The Bible talks about boys being like healthy plants. Sounds a bit funny, doesn't it? But what does a healthy plant need? Good soil and pruning shears. Your roots will grow deep when you read your Bible. And by cutting out the bad stuff, like anger and complaining, you will be healthy and a boy after God's heart.

How can a girl be like a pillar that decorates a palace? A pillar is important because it is strong and holds up the structure. It also adds character. When you love Jesus with all your heart, you will be strong and draw others to him.

If you're a girl, you may think God loves girls better. And if you're a boy, you may think God loves boys better. But the truth is he loves boys and girls the same. God wants you to be proud of the person he made YOU to be!

Dear God, thank you for making me the way that I am. I want to make you proud today. Amen.

DAY 203
Getting Along

If possible, live in peace with everyone. Do that as much as you can.
—Romans 12:18

Do you get along with others? What if someone takes something that is yours? Cuts in front of you in line? Calls you names? Maybe your little brother or sister plays with your toys without asking you. Maybe there is someone in your class who always wants to be first. Or maybe there is a bully in your neighborhood who is mean no matter what. How do you live in peace with someone who bothers you all the time?

The Bible says, "If possible, live in peace with everyone." That means you don't take matters into your own hands and fight back. Instead, do as much as you can to keep the peace. Talk to your sibling. Allow your classmate to go in front of you. Walk away from the neighborhood bully. No, it's not possible to get along with everyone all the time. But choosing peace should always come first.

Is there someone in your life you have a hard time getting along with? Pray for that person right now.

DAY 204
The Amazing Brain

Great is our Lord. His power is mighty. There is no limit to his understanding.
—Psalm 147:5

Your brain is one very clever organ. It is soft and squishy and weighs about three pounds. It controls everything you do. Did you know you actually see things upside down, but your brain flips it so that you see things right side up? And that the right side of your brain talks to the left side of your body, and the left side of your brain talks to the right side of your body? Cool, huh? And believe it or not, your brain is always working, even when you are asleep.

As amazing as the human brain is, you will never know everything there is to know. But God does! He knows everything that happened during Bible times, what is happening right now, and everything that will happen in the future. He knows how many stars are in the sky and how many grains of sand are on the beach. He knows your thoughts, what is in your heart, and what you are going to say next. God is mighty and powerful—there is nothing that God doesn't know!

Want to make your brain stronger and smarter? Try juggling! Start by tossing one ball up in the air, then try two and three. Thank God for being all-knowing, and for creating your brain.

DAY 205
Hide and Seek

"His eyes see how people live. He watches every step they take."

—Job 34:21

Do you like to play the game hide-and-seek? Where do you like to hide? In a closet? Under your bed? Behind a tree? It's fun to be still and quiet, waiting to be found. Maybe you like to be the one searching for family members and friends. The game of hide-and-seek is fun to play, but have you ever tried to hide from God?

No matter where you are or what you are doing, you can't hide from God. He is everywhere and always present. God created heaven, earth, and everyone in it. And because God is all-seeing, he watches every step you take. No matter where you go, he is there. So when you feel like hiding, seek God instead. You are never alone because God is by your side.

Ask a few friends to play hide-and-seek. Think about how you can't hide from God. Yes, he is everywhere and watches every step you take.

Greatest Superhero!

"'Lord and King, you have reached out your great and powerful arm. You have made the heavens and the earth. Nothing is too hard for you.'"

—Jeremiah 32:17

Who is your favorite superhero? Why do you like him or her? Do they fight crime? Do they have special powers? It's fun to pretend you are a superhero and can fly, be invisible, or have superhuman strength. You could even save someone from ultimate doom! Wouldn't it be cool if a *real* superhero existed? Guess what? There is one!

God is the greatest superhero! He is big and strong, and there is no one who is more powerful. God created the sun, moon, and stars. He controls the whole world and everything in it. There is no limit to his power. Because God is all-powerful, you can trust him to be there for you. He will always do what he promised. Now that's one superhero you should know!

Dear God, thank you for being my superhero! Help me trust in your power. Amen.

DAY 207
Great Mystery

There is no doubt that true godliness comes from this great mystery. Jesus came as a human being. The Holy Spirit proved that he was the Son of God. He was seen by angels. He was preached among the nations. People in the world believed in him. He was taken up to heaven in glory.

—1 Timothy 3:16

Do you like to solve puzzles? Each piece you find and put into place helps you see the entire picture. Have you ever misplaced something? Going back and retracing your steps can help you search. And once you find what you are looking for, you most likely will take better care of it and treasure it more. The mystery will be solved.

Did you know Jesus is the great mystery? Starting with the Old Testament, God gives clues about Jesus's coming. Then in the New Testament, it happens! Jesus was born as a baby, was seen by angels, he preached to the people, they believed in him, and Jesus was taken up to heaven. When you discover this great mystery, you will no longer be lost. You will treasure your relationship with Jesus more and want to be like him.

Unscramble these letters to solve this puzzle: Jesus is the TAERG YRETSYM!

DAY 208
Servant's Heart

"Even the Son of Man did not come to be served. Instead, he came to serve others. He came to give his life as the price for setting many people free."

—Mark 10:45

How do others serve you? Does your mom or dad cook your meals? Maybe a sibling helps you with your schoolwork. Or your grandparents stay with you when your parents are away. It feels good to be taken care of. But do you know what feels better? Serving others.

Did you know Jesus once washed the disciples' feet? That must have been a dirty job! Now you may be wondering, *What can I do?* It doesn't take much. Hold open a door for someone. Tie a little child's shoe. Help your parent in the kitchen or take out the trash. Maybe you can pass out papers for your teacher or help in your Sunday school class. When you serve others like Jesus, you will have a servant's heart.

Look for ways to serve others today. And if you don't know what to do, pray. Saying a prayer for someone is one of the best ways to serve others.

DAY 209
Be Creative

"The LORD has filled him with the Spirit of God. He has filled him with wisdom, with understanding, with knowledge and with all kinds of skill."

—Exodus 35:31

How do you like to be creative? Do you draw pictures? Write stories or poems? Maybe you like to bake cookies or act in plays. Perhaps you like to sew, build model airplanes, or plant in the garden. You might like to create math problems to solve, build things with tools, or sell lemonade to your neighbors. Do you play an instrument, dance, or sing? Or do you like to ride bikes or do tricks on your skateboard? There are all kinds of ways to be creative!

Did you know God is super creative? After all, he made the entire world! Yes, God made everyone different and designed YOU to be one-of-a-kind, with your own unique skills and talents. Maybe you don't know what you like to do yet, and that's okay. Jump in and try new things. Soon you'll discover that God made you to be creative too!

Dear God, thank you for creating me. Help me use my talents to please you. Amen.

DAY 210
My Safe Zone

You are my hiding place. You will keep me safe from trouble. You will surround me with songs sung by those who praise you because you save your people.

—Psalm 32:7

Where is your favorite spot to hide when you want to be alone? In your bedroom? Up in a tree house? Under a blanket fort? Maybe you've been going from one activity to the next and need to slow down. Maybe you're frustrated and need to take some time before you explode. Or maybe you want to get away from someone who isn't being kind. Where can you go when you need to be still? Where is your safe zone?

The Bible says God is your hiding place. Like you, David was trying to hide. He was going from cave to cave, running from Saul who was hunting him down. David knew God would keep him safe. David also knew God would forgive his sins when he confessed them to him. Just like God helped David, he will be your hiding place. He will watch over you, guide you, and keep you safe from trouble. Don't forget to read your Bible when you want to run and hide. You are safe with God.

Grab a flashlight and your Bible and read under the blankets on your bed. Remember, God is your hiding place and you'll always be safe with him.

DAY 211
Light Bulb Moment

But the Father will send the Friend in my name to help you. The Friend is the Holy Spirit. He will teach you all things. He will remind you of everything I have said to you.

—John 14:26

When the light is low, it is harder to see. The opposite is also true. The brighter the light, the easier it is to see. Have you ever tried to read in the dark? It's practically impossible! When you don't understand something, you can also feel like you are in the dark. Are there times when reading the Bible feels like you're reading in the dark? Do the words sometimes seem too difficult to understand?

God sent the Holy Spirit to be your helper. He is like a light bulb that helps you see. The Holy Spirit not only helps you understand the Bible, but he shows you how to connect the words to your life. Have you ever read something from the Bible and thought God was speaking directly to you? That's the Holy Spirit. He teaches you the truth and reminds you of everything God has said. If you're having trouble understanding the Bible, ask the Holy Spirit to be a light for you. He will help you when you need him.

Need help understanding God's Word? Turn on the light and ask the Holy Spirit to be your helper.

DAY 212
Get UP!

The Lord takes good care of all those who fall. He lifts up all those who feel helpless.

—Psalm 145:14

When was the last time you fell? Maybe you crashed your bike. Maybe you tripped playing soccer. Or maybe you fell down the stairs. No matter how it happened, it hurts to fall. Did you know it also hurts when you sin? Remember when you disobeyed your parents, gossiped about your friend, or hit your sibling? When you sin, you fall away from God.

Satan wants you to think you can't get up when you've messed up, but God loves you and wants you to be right with him. So tell God what you have done. Ask him to forgive your sins. Look to God and then get back up. God will take care of you. He will lift you up when you fall down.

Dear God, thank you for taking care of me when I fall. Help me to confess my sin, look to you, and get back up! Amen.

DAY 213
On Guard

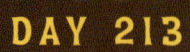

Be on your guard. Remain strong in the faith. Be brave.
—1 Corinthians 16:13

Do you like to use the computer? It's cool to go online and learn new things. It's also fun to play games and connect with other kids. It's important to talk with your parents, as well as your teacher, about the best sites to visit so that you are safe online. Another tip is to keep track of how many hours you spend on the computer. Without limits, screen time can quickly become a hard habit to break and can take over your day.

Does God care about how you use the computer? Yes, he does! In fact, he commands you to be alert and on guard. That means you need to pay close attention to what your eyes see. But what if your friends show you something you know God wouldn't approve of? It's hard to say no, but standing firm means you hold on to what you believe, speak up for what is right, and walk away when you are tempted. Don't be afraid to go against what your friends are doing. When you remain strong and take a stand, your faith grows.

Make a pact with your parents so that you will stay safe while using the computer. Remember to be on your guard, remain strong, and be brave!

DAY 214
Lighten Your Load

Let us throw off any sin that holds on to us so tightly. And let us keep on running the race marked out for us.

—Hebrews 12:1

On your mark. Get set. Go! When was the last time you raced someone? Maybe you raced your sibling to the car. Maybe you raced your friend to the playground at school. Or maybe you raced your whole class during PE. Do you think it is easier or harder to run with a backpack on? Harder, of course! The added weight slows you down.

Every day is like a race, and when you pack your day with too many activities, you're bound to get tired and fall down. Other things can slow you down too, like comparing yourself with others, holding a grudge, or trying to please your friends. The best thing to do is to lighten your load. Stop comparing yourself to others. Don't hold a grudge. And please God instead of always trying to please your friends. God wants you to run your own race. Stay in your own lane and keep running toward him.

Go outside and challenge a friend to a race. No matter whether you win or lose, run your own race by doing your best.

DAY 215
Keep Your Eyes on Jesus

Let us keep looking to Jesus. He is the one who started this journey of faith. And he is the one who completes the journey of faith.
—Hebrews 12:2

Do you like to play catch? Maybe you throw a ball in the backyard with your parent after school. Maybe you're on a baseball team and have a game every week. Or maybe you play the game four square at recess. What happens when you take your eyes off the ball? You miss, and the ball whizzes past.

The same thing happens to your faith when you take your eyes off Jesus. A man in the Bible named Peter learned this the hard way. When Jesus walked on water, he called to Peter to come to him. Peter climbed over the side of a boat and walked toward Jesus. When Peter kept his eyes on Jesus, he did the impossible and walked on water! But when Peter focused on the wind and waves, he looked away from Jesus and sank. When you play catch, you need to keep your eyes on the ball. When you follow Jesus, you need to keep your focus on him.

Play catch with a parent, sibling, or friend. As you keep your eyes on the ball, remember to keep your eyes on Jesus.

DAY 216
God's Fingertips

I think about the heavens. I think about what your fingers have created. I think about the moon and stars that you have set in place.

—Psalm 8:3

When was the last time you looked up at the moon? Did you know the side of the moon that faces the sun is very hot, and the side that faces away is very cold? Here are some other interesting facts. The moon orbits, or goes around the Earth, approximately every twenty-eight days. The surface of the moon has a large number of craters made when comets and asteroids collided with the moon over time. And a lunar eclipse occurs when the Earth is between the sun and the moon.

Like David who wrote Psalm 8, have you considered the hugeness of the universe? It's pretty amazing to think that God created the moon and the stars and set each one in place. God is so much bigger than the universe. And the God who made the universe is also the God who made YOU! When was the last time you created something with your fingers?

Create something using clay. Thank God for creating the moon and stars—and for creating you!

DAY 217
Three Things

And do everything you can to live a quiet life. You should mind your own business. And work with your hands, just as we told you to.

—1 Thessalonians 4:11

Your day might look something like this: You get up. Get dressed. Eat breakfast. Go to school. Go to soccer or piano practice. Do homework. Eat dinner. Watch television. Take a shower. Go to bed. Phew! Are you always busy, or do you have time in your day to be still and quiet? You can write your thoughts in a journal. Spend time with God. By doing these things, you will live a quiet life.

Do you like to give your opinion all the time and tell people what to do? If so, it's time to stop being a busybody and mind your own business. Do you help around the house, or do you expect your parents to do everything for you? Instead of watching everyone else, jump in and do some work!

When you live a quiet life, mind your own business, and work with your hands, you are living the kind of life God wants you to live.

Dear God, thank you for showing me how you want me to live. Help me do these things. Amen.

Giant Rock!

Be my rock of safety that I can always go to. Give the command to save me. You are my rock and my fort.
—Psalm 71:3

Have you ever seen a giant rock? Did you stop and stare at it? Did you try to lift it or move it? A large rock is solid and super heavy. When camping, you might have used a few smaller rocks as weights to hold down the corners of a tarp, or to form the circle of a bonfire. The reason why is because rocks act like anchors and will not burn. Even though rocks might turn black from the fire, their shape doesn't change.

In the Bible, Jesus is compared to a rock. He is your anchor because you can find safety and security in him. Like rocks around a campfire, Jesus will protect you so you won't get burned, and he will rescue you and do what is right. Like a giant rock, Jesus never changes. So lean on Jesus and put your trust in him.

Create a rock structure by collecting rocks of various sizes and stacking them on top of each other, using the biggest on the bottom to the smallest on top. When you finish, thank Jesus for being your rock.

DAY 219
Got the Gimmies?

"Father, I want those you have given me to be with me where I am. I want them to see my glory, the glory you have given me. You gave it to me because you loved me before the world was created."

—John 17:24

When was the last time you got the "gimmies"? You know, when you went grocery shopping with your parents and wanted them to buy you something in *every* aisle? Maybe you wanted your favorite cereal, cookies, or ice cream. Maybe you begged your dad for a bag of chips or tugged on your mom's arm for a pack of gum or a candy bar. The truth is, your parents don't love you any less because they didn't buy you the gallon of chocolate ice cream or a giant bag of potato chips.

When you talk to God, do you get the gimmies? Do you only pray for what you want, or do you pray for others? Yes, you can ask God for anything, but it doesn't mean he loves you any less when you don't get what you want. He knows what's best for you. The thing God wants most is to be with you. He created you to have a relationship with him. In fact, he sent Jesus to die for your sins to make that happen. The next time you get the gimmies, remember God knows best—and that's to spend eternity with you!

Count how many times during the day you ask for something. Consider how God wants you to have a relationship with him so that you will be with him forever in heaven.

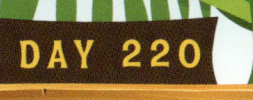

DAY 220
God's Tender Care

"May the LORD bless you and take good care of you."

—Numbers 6:24

Do people ever say, "God bless you!" when you sneeze? It's another way to say, "I hope you are well." There are other types of blessings too. You pray a blessing to thank God for your food before you eat. God can bless you by giving you gifts, like the home you live in or the clothes you wear. Another blessing is how God takes care of you by providing help, sometimes in the nick of time. When you pray, do you ever say a blessing for others?

In the book of Numbers, God commanded the priests to bless the people when they were wandering in the wilderness. He wanted the blessing to be said again and again. Why? Because he wanted them to remember that God would take care of them. The next time your pastor says, "May the Lord bless you and take good care of you," remember it's a special blessing for YOU too.

Dear God, thank you for taking special care of me. Help me remember to bless others. Amen.

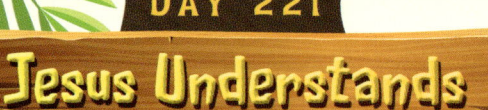

Jesus Understands

Jesus wept.
—John 11:35

Have you ever cried yourself to sleep? Maybe someone you loved died. Maybe your best friend moved away. Other situations may also bring you to tears. During those times, you may feel as if no one understands.

Did you know Jesus experienced sadness and grief? The Bible says that Jesus cried when his close friend Lazarus died. He grieved the loss of his friend, and he comforted Mary and Martha even though he knew he was going to raise Lazarus back to life. Jesus feels your pain too. You can be comforted knowing Jesus understands exactly what you are going through. He loves you and sees your tears.

Put some drops of water into a clear jar with a lid to remind yourself that Jesus weeps with you when you cry.

DAY 222
He's Got Your Back

The LORD is a place of safety for those who have been treated badly. He keeps them safe in times of trouble. LORD, those who know you will trust in you. You have never deserted those who look to you.
—Psalm 9:9-10

Have you ever been treated badly? Maybe you were the only one from your class not invited to a party. Maybe your best friend doesn't want to be friends anymore. Or maybe you missed the goal, and your team blames you for the loss. If you feel zapped of your strength and want to hide in your room and never come out, you are not alone. It hurts when others treat you badly. You might even blame yourself.

God wants you to go to him when you are hurting. Tell him what happened and how you feel. God will listen. You are safe with him. Then when you are ready, find your parents or an adult and tell them how you were mistreated. It will take courage, but you will become stronger if you do. Above all, trust God. He's got your back no matter what.

Dear God, thank you for always being there when others hurt me. Give me courage so I can talk to my parents about it. Amen.

DAY 223
Yesterday and Today and Forever

Jesus Christ is the same yesterday and today and forever.

—Hebrews 13:8

The world is always changing. The Earth spins. The seasons come and go. Popular television shows and fashion trends fade over time. Friends move away. People change their minds. Every day you are growing and changing too. With everything changing all around you, can you count on anything to stay the same?

Yes, you can count on Jesus! He never changes. The Bible says Jesus is the same yesterday and today and forever. He is always there for you when you need him. He always loves you and keeps his promises, and you can always depend on him. Even though the world is always changing, you can hold on to the truth that Jesus is the same.

Draw a picture of something that changes. Write "Jesus never changes" on your picture and hang it in your room.

DAY 224
Near Jesus

Jesus had healed many people. So those who were sick were pushing forward to touch him.

—Mark 3:10

Who is someone you like to be around? Maybe it's a friend from school because she makes you laugh. Maybe it's your older brother because he looks out for you, or your sister because she lets you hang out with her and her friends. Maybe it's your mom because she takes care of you when you are sick, or your dad because he plays with you. One of the best parts about being around someone you like is being able to give a hug or a high five.

Many people during Bible times wanted to be near Jesus. He was compassionate, kind, and healed people who were sick. People even pushed their way to get close so they could touch him. God is just as powerful today. Do you want to get close to Jesus? Even though you can't physically touch Jesus with your hands, you can spend time with him each day. The good news is that God can touch your heart when you believe in him.

Dear God, thank you for the special people in my life. Help me to believe in you and grow close to Jesus. Amen.

DAY 225
Sunrise to Sunset

From the sunrise in the east to the sunset in the west, may the name of the LORD be praised.

—Psalm 113:3

Where do you live? Near the ocean? Maybe by a desert? Perhaps you live smack-dab in the middle of your country. No matter where you live, the sun always rises in the east and sets in the west. Did you know it takes twenty-four hours for the Earth to spin all the way around? As the Earth rotates, the portion of Earth that is lit up by the sun experiences day while the portion that faces away from the sun experiences night.

From sunrise in the morning to sunset in the evening, God wants you to praise him. That means throughout your day you need to look for reasons to thank God for who he is and the blessings he has given you. Thank him for the stack of pancakes you ate for breakfast. The new friend you made at recess. The dog waiting for you at home. There are many reasons to praise God. After all, he created the sun and the moon, and each new day is a gift from him.

Get up early and watch the sunrise. Remember to look for reasons to praise God all day long.

DAY 226
Grab Your Life Vest!

If any of you needs wisdom, you should ask God for it. He will give it to you. God gives freely to everyone and doesn't find fault. But when you ask, you must believe. You must not doubt. That's because a person who doubts is like a wave of the sea. The wind blows and tosses them around.

—James 1:5-6

Do you talk to yourself? Most people do. What do you say? "God loves me. I'm special!" or "Nobody likes me. I'm a loser!" What about when you look in the mirror? Do you say, "God created me. I like the way I look!" or "Yuck. I'm ugly." What do you say when you make a mistake? "I'm sorry. Please forgive me." or "I'm so stupid!" We all have those little voices in our heads that tell us wise words or foolish things. Which voice do you listen to?

If you are listening to the foolish voice telling you hurtful things, ask God for wisdom. God freely gives wisdom, but you must first believe. But if you are having trouble, talk to an adult. Because if you doubt, you will be like someone on a boat in the middle of a storm being tossed around by the wind and waves. You won't know what to think. So instead of getting seasick, grab onto your life vest—God! When you believe in him, the wise voice will get louder and louder.

Draw a picture of yourself. What do you see? Ask God to give you wisdom.

DAY 227
Remember

"Remember what happened in the past. Think about what took place long ago. I am God. There is no other God. I am God. There is no one like me."

—Isaiah 46:9

Do you like to write letters to God? If you don't know how or what to pray, a journal is a good way to see what God is doing in your life. That way, you can look back and remember how God took care of you when you were afraid, when you didn't know what to do, and when your faith was tested.

Do you remember when you were a baby? How about when you were two? Four? It's hard to recall what happened when you were very young. However, if you look at pictures, it might nudge a memory. Keeping a journal does the same thing. When you go back and remember what God has done for you in the past, you will have confidence that God will take care of you in the future. Remember, he is God. And there is no one like him.

Create a prayer journal by placing notebook paper between two pieces of construction paper. Put three staples down the left side to hold it all together. Design and color the front cover any way you like. Write a letter to God in your new journal today.

Washing Feet

I, your Lord and Teacher, have washed your feet. So you also should wash one another's feet.

—John 13:14

What type of shoes are you wearing today? Maybe it's a snowy day and you're wearing boots. Maybe it's hot outside and you're wearing flip-flops. Maybe you're going for a run and need your athletic shoes, or you're headed to dance practice with your ballet slippers.

During Bible times people wore sandals, and their feet would get very dirty and grimy. It was typical for a servant to wash the feet of guests. One day, Jesus demonstrated his love for his disciples by washing his disciples' feet. It surprised the disciples, but Jesus wanted to show them how to be humble like a servant. Did you know God wants you to humble yourself and serve others as well? No job is too small when you are willing to do it for him. In God's eyes, the greatest person is the one who serves others. Jesus, your Lord and Teacher, is the greatest servant of all. He put others first and gave his life so you can spend eternity with him.

Get a bucket of water and a bar of soap and offer to wash someone's feet. Tell him about how Jesus washed the disciples' feet and how we are to serve one another.

Different Colors

There is no difference between those who are Jews and those who are not. The same Lord is Lord of all. He richly blesses everyone who calls on him.

—Romans 10:12

Did you know the different colors in fruity cereal taste the same? It's true! Red, orange, yellow, green, purple, and blue have the same fruit flavor. They may look different on the outside, but they are the same on the inside. It would be boring if they were all the same color, don't you think?

God made people to look different on the outside too. Some people have dark skin, and some people have light skin. Some people have blond hair, and some people have red hair. Some people have brown eyes, and some people have blue. Treating people differently because they don't look like you is wrong. God made people with different color skin, hair, and eyes, and he loves us all the same.

Dear God, thank you for making each person special. Please help me to love everyone the same, just like you do. Amen.

DAY 230
I Do!

And may you commit your lives completely to the Lord our God. May you live by his rules. May you obey his commands. May you always do as you are doing now.

—1 Kings 8:61

Have you ever been to a wedding? During the ceremony, the people getting married promise to love each other in good times and in bad, for richer or poorer, in sickness and in health, for as long as they both shall live. Wow, that's a big commitment!

But you don't have to wait until you are older to commit your life to someone. God wants you to have a relationship with him right now. You can promise to love him when times are good, and when times are tough. You can promise to love him when you have money or if your piggy bank is empty. You can promise to love him when you are healthy or if you are sick. Loving God means you want to follow what the Bible says because you believe it is true. Committing your life to Jesus is the best commitment of all.

Dear God, thank you for wanting a relationship with me. Help me follow what the Bible says and always remember to say "I do" to YOU!

DAY 231
Who's In Charge?

God, see what is in my heart. Know what is there. Test me. Know what I'm thinking. See if there's anything in my life you don't like. Help me live in the way that is always right.

—Psalm 139:23-24

Have you ever asked God to help you see the bad things you are doing? You may already know what those sins are. Maybe you are mean to your sibling. Maybe you are jealous of a friend. Or maybe you disobey your parents. If you can't think of anything, ask God to show you what is in your heart, so that you can live in a way that honors him.

Now that you're thinking about something God wants you to change, what's next? Of course, you can be nice to your sibling, stop being jealous of your friend, and obey your parents. But is that it? Is changing your behavior enough? No, because you can change your behavior without changing what is in your heart. When you ask God to change your heart, you are admitting you are not the boss and putting him back on the throne. Truth is, God's in charge and it's important to live for him!

Point heavenward and say, "God." Now point to yourself and say, "Not." When you think or do something you know you shouldn't, stop and remember God is in charge.

DAY 232
Encouraging Words

Don't let any evil talk come out of your mouths. Say only what will help to build others up and meet their needs. Then what you say will help those who listen.

—Ephesians 4:29

Have you ever said something that hurt someone's feelings? Maybe you said something without thinking first. Maybe you were joking around, but it didn't come out that way. Or maybe you tore someone down and were careless with your words. Words are powerful, and if you're not careful, you can destroy someone with your mouth. Just ask your parents! They probably still remember when someone said something hurtful when they were young.

God wants you to use your words to make others feel good about who they are. So instead of jumping in to say something, listen. Instead of having to apologize for saying something careless, think of words you can say to build the other person up. Saying encouraging words will make a positive difference in your friend's life. Encouraging words help those who listen.

Say positive, encouraging words to those you meet today.

DAY 233
Judging Others

"'Do not make something wrong appear to be right. Treat poor people and rich people in the same way. Do not favor one person over another. Instead, judge everyone fairly.'"

—Leviticus 19:15

Have you ever eaten something that looked or smelled terrible, but tasted great? Maybe the vegetables your parents wanted you to try smelled disgusting, but after one bite you were pleasantly surprised. Maybe the hamburgers your dad barbequed looked burnt but tasted amazing. Maybe your mom made a lopsided cake for your birthday, but it was melt-in-your-mouth delicious. Have you ever judged someone by how they look? Most everyone has at some point in their lives.

Judging is basing an opinion on an assumption rather than a fact. Just like you might have been wrong about the vegetables, hamburger, or cake, your judgment of people can be wrong too. Jesus loves everyone. It doesn't matter if they're rich or poor; every person has value to God. The next time you catch yourself judging others, remember everyone is important.

Dear God, thank you for loving me! Help me to judge people fairly. Amen.

DAY 234
Keep Going!

Brothers and sisters, don't ever get tired of doing what is good.

—2 Thessalonians 3:13

Do you ever wonder if the good things you do matter to God? You know, like the time you held a door open when someone was going into the store, or when you let someone else have the last slice of pepperoni pizza even though you were still hungry. Maybe you sat quietly in class or did your chores before being asked. Maybe you helped a friend. Doing good for others is something you can control.

Did you know there are a lot of things you don't control? You didn't choose your parents. You didn't choose what you look like or how many brothers or sisters you have. You didn't choose when or where you were born. You also didn't choose what gifts and talents you have. But you do have control over how much you believe in God. When we give our hearts to God, he will help faith grow in us. When you have faith, you please God. So don't get tired of doing what is good! It matters to him.

Do something good for someone today!

DAY 235
God's Reward

"May the Lord reward you for what you have done. May the Lord, the God of Israel, bless you richly. You have come to him to find safety under his care."

—Ruth 2:12

Have you ever been rewarded for doing a great job? Maybe your class won a pizza party for selling the most in the school fundraiser or maybe you read the most books in the library's reading program. Whatever it is, being rewarded for a job well done feels great. Did you know God sees everything you do? That means he sees when you do something good, when you say no to temptation, when you choose what is right, and when you stand firm because of your faith.

The Bible says every good thing you do will be rewarded, no matter how small. God sees when you encourage your friends, get along with your siblings, and show love to your parents. And guess what? It doesn't matter if nobody else sees the good that you do. God sees it all! Just like God rewarded Ruth because of her faithfulness to her mother-in-law, Naomi, he will reward YOU too.

Dear God, thank you for seeing every good thing I do. Help me continue doing what you want me to do. Amen.

DAY 236
Growing Up

Grow in the grace and knowledge of our Lord and Savior Jesus Christ. Glory belongs to him both now and forever. Amen.

—2 Peter 3:18

Do you know how much you weighed when you were born? You might have been six pounds, seven pounds, or possibly eight. Some babies arrive early and are very small, while others are big. By drinking breast milk or formula, you grew very quickly. And when you started eating solid food, you grew even more!

The Bible says you are also to grow in your faith. In order to know God better, you need to read your Bible and do what it says. There are other ways to grow your faith. You can grow by going to church, praying every day, and singing worship songs. When you are a baby, you need milk and food to grow. By knowing God and what the Bible says, you are growing as well.

Do you own a Bible? If not, ask for one for Christmas or your birthday. You will grow your faith when you spend time with God.

DAY 237
Time to Get Clean

God, create a pure heart in me. Give me a new spirit that is faithful to you.

—Psalm 51:10

How often do you take a bath? It's important to bathe a few times a week, and maybe every day if you went swimming in a pool, lake, or ocean. Of course, you'd definitely want a bath if you played in the mud, got sweaty, or have body odor. In addition to your hair and skin, your heart also needs cleansing.

In Psalm 51, David asks God to create a pure heart inside him. David is not only asking God to cleanse him of his sins, but to take out his old heart and make him a brand-new one. David wants God to change him on the inside. Like David, you can ask God to clean your heart by asking for forgiveness. You can't change on your own, even if you try really hard. Remember, God can and will forgive you of your sins, and he will change your heart too.

The next time you take a bath to wash your hair and skin, ask God to create a pure heart inside you.

DAY 238
Bit of Honey

It isn't good for you to eat too much honey. And you shouldn't try to search out matters too deep for you.

—Proverbs 25:27

Do you eat honey on toast or with the crust of your pizza? Maybe you like to eat honey on cornbread or pancakes. Some adults put honey in their tea. Bears eat honey, but they also eat the bees and larvae inside the beehive because they're a good source of protein. Did you know the Bible says too much honey can make you sick? It's true! A little honey goes a long way. Just like eating too much honey isn't good for you, it also isn't good to seek attention for yourself. Talk about a sticky situation!

Constantly wanting compliments from others or hoping to be popular will only push people away. Seeking praise is as foolish as eating too much honey. But what if someone gives you a compliment? Is that okay? Of course! You will know when someone is genuine when you don't ask for praise or search it out. So let others pat you on the back instead of doing it yourself. Just as food only needs a bit of honey to taste sweet, you will be sweet when you praise God instead of praising yourself.

Cut up an apple into slices and arrange on a plate. Drizzle a little honey and melted peanut butter on top. Delicious! As you eat your snack, think about how too much honey, and seeking attention for yourself, can make you sick.

DAY 239
You've Got a Friend in Me

Be willing to be a friend of people who aren't considered important. Don't think that you are better than others.

—Romans 12:16

Has someone ever ignored you? How did it make you feel? Hurt? Rejected? There are people who would like to be your friend, but they might feel ignored by you. Don't think so? Look around. Is there a girl at school who eats lunch by herself? Is there a boy who doesn't join in at recess? Does your little sister or brother ask you to play?

When you are considerate of others, you will have a humble attitude and treat others the same way you'd like to be treated. God wants you to be willing to be a friend to the people who need one. But how? Go up to the girl who eats alone and invite her to sit with you. Ask the boy to play at recess. Tell your little sister or brother that you'd like to spend time with them. When you remember what it feels like to be ignored, you'll be more understanding of others.

Ask God to show you someone who needs a friend. Invite that person to hang out with you. Remember, in order to have a friend, you need to be a friend.

DAY 240
Why Me?

But Moses spoke to God. "Who am I that I should go to Pharaoh?" he said. "Who am I that I should bring the Israelites out of Egypt?"

—Exodus 3:11

When your parents ask you to do something, do you ever ask, "Why me?" Maybe you don't feel like doing whatever they are asking of you, or maybe, like Moses, you don't feel qualified for the job. What do you do then? Do you beg your parents to pick someone else, or do you step up and do it?

God called to Moses from the middle of a burning bush and told Moses that he was sending him to Pharaoh to lead the Israelites out of Egypt. One problem: Moses didn't want to go. He gave God all kinds of excuses: He didn't know what to say. The people might not believe him or listen to him. He might get tongue-tied or trip over his words. Finally, Moses begged, "Lord, please send someone else to do it!" God became angry with Moses, but he agreed to send his brother Aaron with him, to help Moses speak.

What is God calling you to do that feels scary right now? Just like God was with Moses, ready to help with a solution, God will be with you. He will give you strength, courage, and the right words to say. So be brave and go for it!

The next time God asks you to do something, try saying, "Why *not* me?" and do it.

No Complaining, Please!

Don't be proud at all. Be completely gentle. Be patient. Put up with one another in love.

—Ephesians 4:2

Are you patient? What do you do when someone interrupts you? Do you tell that person to leave you alone, or do you stop what you are doing and listen? What about when someone is chewing loudly or tapping their foot? Do you yell at that person to be quiet, or do you put up with the noise? It's hard to put up with others when they do things that bother you, but God wants you to be completely gentle and patient.

Patience is waiting without complaining. Did you know having patience is one of the fruits of the Spirit? When you follow Jesus and spend time with God, you will have more patience in your life. By trusting God, you will be able to listen when someone interrupts you and to put up with the things that bother you. When you are patient, you will be able to put others first.

Practice patience by going to the park and waiting for your turn on the swings, by being gentle to a friend who insists on having their way, or by waiting without complaining when your parent is making dinner.

DAY 242
The "P" Word

Don't brag about tomorrow. You don't know what a day will bring.
—Proverbs 27:1

Do you procrastinate? That means you put something off until later even though you can do it today. Maybe you doodle in your notebook instead of doing your homework. Maybe you lie on your bed instead of cleaning your room. Or maybe you put off practicing an instrument because you're afraid you won't play it perfectly. You know you are procrastinating if you find yourself saying, "I can't do it," or "I'll do it later."

Two of the biggest reasons you might put off doing something are because it isn't important to you, or because you don't feel like you will do a good job. Does the task feel boring? Overwhelming? Instead of making excuses, talk with your mom or dad. Sometimes all you need to do is to break the task down into smaller, more easily handled actions. When you feel like procrastinating, just do it or ask for help! God wants you to be responsible with the time you've been given.

Do your schoolwork, clean your room, practice your instrument. Don't procrastinate any longer. Once you finish the task, you'll feel great!

DAY 243
God Is with Me

But I am always with you. You hold me by my right hand.
—Psalm 73:23

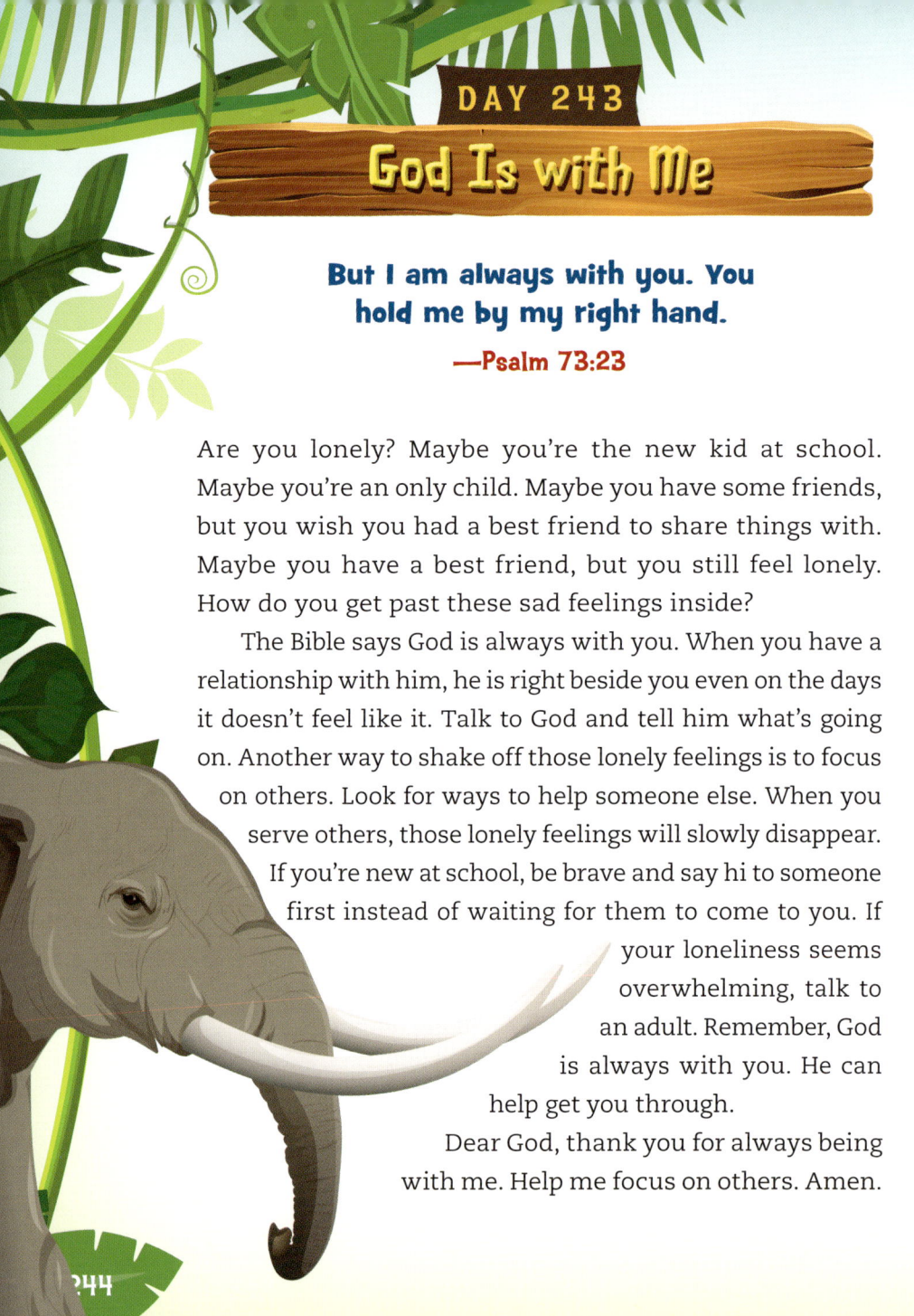

Are you lonely? Maybe you're the new kid at school. Maybe you're an only child. Maybe you have some friends, but you wish you had a best friend to share things with. Maybe you have a best friend, but you still feel lonely. How do you get past these sad feelings inside?

The Bible says God is always with you. When you have a relationship with him, he is right beside you even on the days it doesn't feel like it. Talk to God and tell him what's going on. Another way to shake off those lonely feelings is to focus on others. Look for ways to help someone else. When you serve others, those lonely feelings will slowly disappear. If you're new at school, be brave and say hi to someone first instead of waiting for them to come to you. If your loneliness seems overwhelming, talk to an adult. Remember, God is always with you. He can help get you through.

Dear God, thank you for always being with me. Help me focus on others. Amen.

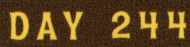

Seasons Change

There is a time for everything. There's a time for everything that is done on earth.

—Ecclesiastes 3:1

Which is your favorite season? Summer? Fall? Winter? Spring? Have you ever wondered what makes the seasons change? The Earth not only spins on its axis every day, but the Earth travels around the sun once a year. As the Earth moves, its position in relation to the sun changes. During summer, the Earth tilts toward the sun, and in winter the Earth tilts away from the sun. The amazing thing is seasons can be different depending on where you live. When it's winter in North America, it's summer in Australia!

Just as the seasons change throughout the year, life has different seasons. There are good times and bad times. You might be going through a difficult season right now. Maybe you are sick, had a fight with a friend, or have family problems. Or you might be going through a fun season. Maybe you are doing well in school, have lots of friends, and your family is great. Seasons change. Trust God. He created every season for a purpose, and he can turn a bad season into something good!

What season is it where you live? Go outside and collect something from nature to remind yourself that life has seasons too.

DAY 245
Bigger Than the Ocean

May you have power together with all the Lord's holy people to understand Christ's love. May you know how wide and long and high and deep it is.

—Ephesians 3:18

God's love for you is bigger than the ocean. How big is that? HUGE! Oceans cover around seventy percent of the Earth's surface. The largest ocean is the Pacific Ocean, which means "peaceful sea." And did you know the longest mountain range in the world is underwater? It's called the Mid-Oceanic Ridge. It runs more than 35,000 miles and has taller peaks than the Alps in Switzerland!

Just like the ocean, God's love for you is wide, long, high, and deep! No matter what you do, God's love for you never changes. He will never love you any more than he does right now, and he will never love you any less. You cannot do anything to earn God's love because he gives it freely! All you have to do is accept his love and praise him.

Dear God, thank you for loving me no matter what. Help me accept your love and worship you. Amen.

DAY 246

Hello?

Even before they call out to me, I will answer them. While they are still speaking, I will hear them.

—Isaiah 65:24

Have you ever played the telephone game? Players form a line and the first person in the line whispers a message in the ear of the next player. That player whispers the message into the next person's ear, and so on. The last player in line announces the message to the entire group. Usually, most of what the last player says is different than what the first person whispered. The message is all jumbled up, and everyone laughs.

When you pray to God, the message is never messed up. He hears what you are saying and listens to you. In fact, God knows what you are going to say even before you say it! Even before you call out to God, he answers your prayers because he knows what you need before you do. His answer may surprise you and be different than what you wanted, but God loves you and knows best.

Play the telephone game with a group of friends. Unlike in the game, God hears your message loud and clear when you pray to him.

DAY 247
Don't Fight Back

Put up with one another. Forgive one another if you are holding something against someone. Forgive, just as the Lord forgave you.

—Colossians 3:13

Has someone ever picked a fight with you? What did you do? Did you let them get the better of you? Or did you ignore them and walk away? If you walked away from the situation, you did the right thing by keeping the peace.

It's hard to walk away when someone has said or done something mean to you. It's even harder to forgive. You may be wondering how you can forgive that person if they haven't apologized. They may never say they're sorry, but that doesn't mean you shouldn't forgive them. If you stay upset, you're the one who continues to hurt. Fighting never solves anything. And forgiving, like Jesus forgives you, is a surefire way to show and accept God's love.

The next time someone tries to pick a fight with you, don't hold it against them. Forgive and walk away.

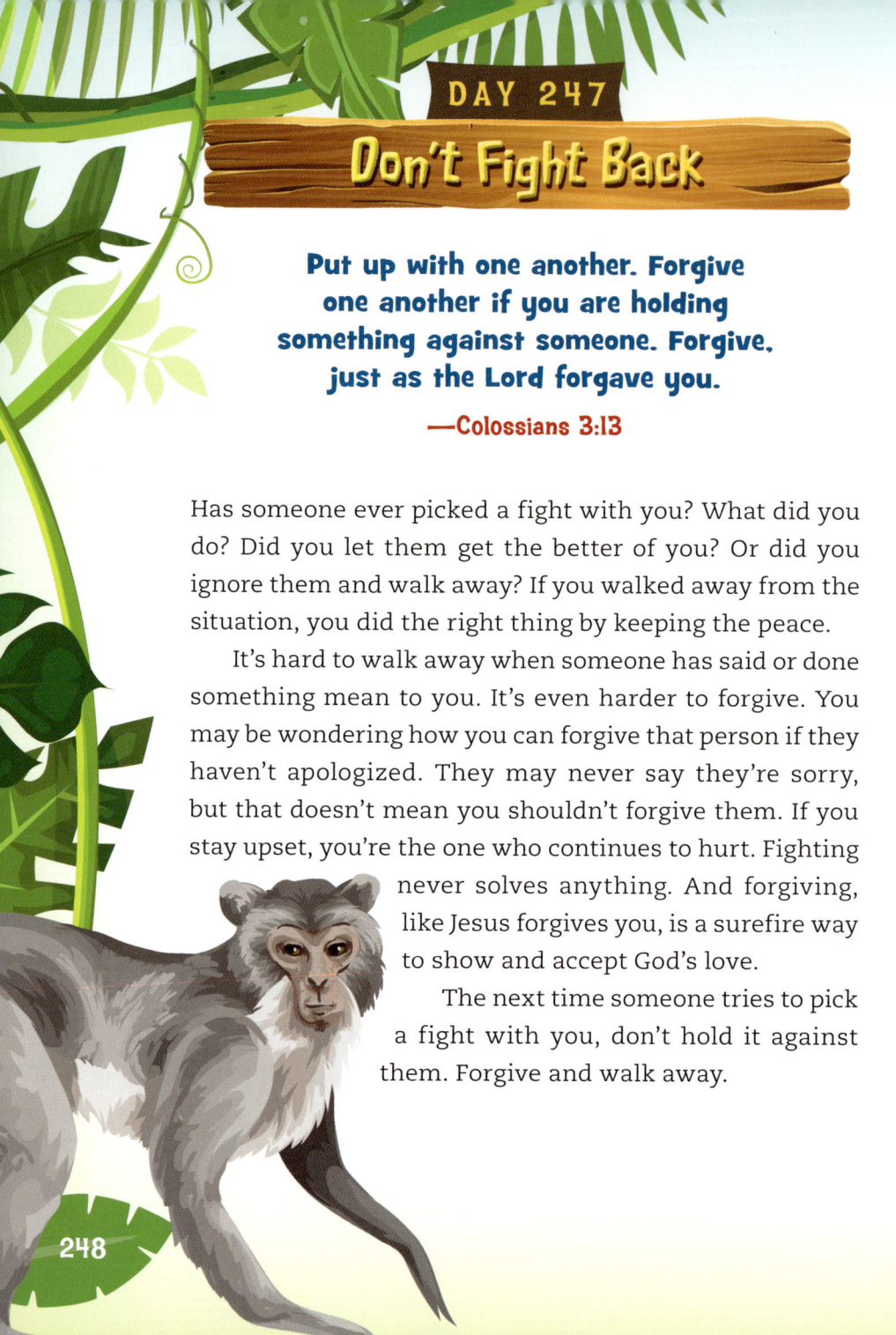

DAY 248
Safe Place

Wise people see danger and go to a safe place. But childish people keep going and suffer for it.

—Proverbs 22:3

Has a stranger ever called you over to their car, asking for directions or to help them find a puppy? Maybe someone followed you when you were walking down the street, or an adult asked you to keep a "secret." Whether or not these things have happened to you, you need to know what to do in potentially dangerous situations like these.

God wants you to use your voice when you don't feel safe. That means you need to yell super loud so someone will know you need help! By taking a deep breath and using a low, loud voice, you will get oxygen in your lungs and energy in your brain, which will give you the courage to move your feet and run if you need to.

The important thing is to go to a safe place, away from strangers or anyone that makes you feel unsafe. Remember, you have the right to say "No!" Talk with a parent or an adult you trust, keep your eyes open to danger, and be wise. You don't need to be afraid. God is with you and will protect you.

Dear God, thank you for watching over me. Keep me safe and help me to be wise. Amen.

DAY 249
Keep Out

Do what is good. Set an example for them in everything.
—Titus 2:7

Have you ever picked flowers from your neighbor's garden? Ridden your bike across someone's yard? What if you are with a group of friends and they want to go on private property? Unless you have asked permission to be there, you need to keep out. Trespassing is against the law, and it's also disrespectful because you are putting what you want above the rules and above others.

The next time you are tempted to go on private property, set an example for your friends about what it means to care for others. When you show respect for something that isn't yours, you understand that other people matter. When you respect others and their property, you are doing what is right and good. Remember that God wants you to respect other people and set a good example.

Think your neighbor's flowers are beautiful? Knock on their door and ask if you can pick one. Asking for permission is the best way to go!

DAY 250
Caught!

Anyone who lives without blame walks safely. But anyone who takes a crooked path will get caught.

—Proverbs 10:9

People cheat because they want to get a reward without having to work for it. Have you ever cheated? Maybe you moved your player a few spaces across the game board so that you had a better chance of winning. Maybe your eyes roamed to another person's paper while you were taking a test. Or maybe you cheated by pretending something was yours when it wasn't.

Cheating is dishonest and is a shortcut to getting something you don't deserve. The trouble is, once you start cheating, it's hard to stop. Eventually, you will get caught. It's never too late to start being honest. Instead of cheating, work hard to get the things you want. When you are honest, you will earn the respect of others and be the type of person God wants you to be.

Play a board game with some friends and remember to play with honesty and follow the rules. You'll earn the respect of the other players and be the type of person God wants you to be.

DAY 251
Kid of Your Word

Peter replied, "All the others may turn away because of you. But I never will."

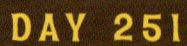
—Matthew 26:33

Have you ever said you'd do something, but then you didn't do it? You might have promised to clean your room, but you got distracted. You might have set aside some money for charity, but then you spent it on yourself instead. You might have even broken a promise to your best friend. Ouch!

In the Bible the same thing happened to a disciple named Peter. He promised Jesus that he would stick by him no matter what. But when people asked if he knew Jesus, Peter denied knowing him—not once or twice, but three times! Why? Peter was scared. Like Peter, maybe you are scared to admit you have a relationship with Jesus. Like Peter, maybe you have good intentions, but have a hard time following through. It takes courage to be a kid of your word. The next time you say you're going to do something, do it!

Be a kid of your word by following through. Clean your room. Save your money. Be the kind of friend who sticks by others. Have courage to admit you have a relationship with Jesus, the greatest friend of all.

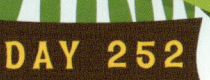

DAY 252
All the Time

"People who have an easy life look down on those who have problems. They think trouble comes only to those whose feet are slipping."

—Job 12:5

Is your life easy, or do you have problems? If your family is doing well, you have tons of friends, and you are getting good grades in school, you might think that God is good and that he really loves you. But if your family is struggling, you are having friend trouble, or you're having a hard time in school, you might think that God is punishing you for something you did wrong. Is that how it works? Does God love you when times are good, and punish you when times are bad? That's what Job's friends thought. Lots of bad stuff was happening in Job's life, so God had to have been punishing him. Right? Wrong!

God always loved Job, and he always loves you! He loves you when you get an A on your test, and he loves you when you make mistakes. He loves you when you are healthy, and he loves you when you are sick. Bad stuff happens and trouble comes to everyone, but when you remember the good things, pray about the tough times, and take time to laugh and have fun, you will make it through with God by your side.

Dear God, thank you for being good all the time and for loving me every single day.

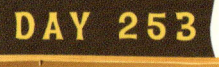

The Wise Thing

Wise people act with knowledge.
—Proverbs 13:16

Have you ever gone to the animal shelter to look at the animals? You might have wanted to take home a cute dog or cat. Did you adopt an animal right then, or did you go home to think about it? Taking care of an animal is a lot of work and a big decision. The last thing you want to do is jump into something without thinking about it first.

God wants you to be wise when making decisions. How? Get the facts and find out everything you need to know before you take the next step. Read books from the library and talk to friends to get their advice. Figure out how much time and money it's going to cost. Prepare for possible problems. Pray about it and ask God what he thinks. When you take your time, you will make a wise choice.

Spend some time with your pet or a friend's pet, or research an animal you may want to get. As you learn more about them, thank God for all the wisdom and knowledge he has given you.

DAY 254
Doubt No More

Then Jesus told him, "Because you have seen me, you have believed. Blessed are those who have not seen me but still have believed."

—John 20:29

Do you tend to doubt things? If a friend told you a story that was hard to believe, would you say, "There's no way that happened!" or "That's amazing!" What if a sibling told you he did a flip trick on his skateboard or a wheelie on his bike? Would you believe him, or would you have to see it with your own eyes?

In the Bible, Thomas didn't believe the other disciples when they told him Jesus had risen from the dead. Thomas only believed when he touched Jesus's side and saw the nail marks in his hands. Jesus let Thomas touch his hands where the nails had held him to the cross and said, "Stop doubting and believe." Thomas never doubted Jesus again. Without faith, it's impossible to believe something unless you see it first. But with faith, you can make a choice to trust and believe God.

With a pencil, trace your hands on a piece of paper. Now draw hearts in the center of each hand and color them red. Write the verse above on your paper. Remember Jesus's words to stop doubting and believe.

DAY 255
Faith Factor

"My ways are higher than your ways. My thoughts are higher than your thoughts."
—Isaiah 55:9

What do you need right now? A special friend? Better grades in school? Your parents to get along? Have you ever tried to help God make it happen? When you pray, do you give God ideas about what he should do? Guess what? That never works! You can't control God. Besides, you only see what's going on right now, but God sees the whole picture. So what can you do?

Talk to God. Tell him how you're feeling. Let him know what's going on and what you need. The answer may not be what you wanted or hoped for, but God knows what's best. Trust in God's plan even when it doesn't make sense. His ways are higher than your ways, and his thoughts are higher than your thoughts. Even when you don't understand what he's doing, have faith. God is good. Trust in him.

Dear God, thank you for knowing what's best. Help me to trust in you. Amen.

DAY 256

Roar!

"You serve the living God. You always serve him faithfully. So has he been able to save you from the lions?"

—Daniel 6:20

Have you ever seen a lion at the zoo? Lions are amazing creatures. The average male weighs 400 pounds, while the female lion weighs just under 300. Female lions do most of the hunting, while the male lions protect the pride. In the wild, they can live between 12–16 years.

In the Bible, a man named Daniel was thrown into a lions' den because he prayed to God three times a day instead of following the king's command to worship only him. The royal officials caught Daniel praying and spoke to the king about it. The king didn't want Daniel to be harmed, but there was nothing he could do. Into the lions' den Daniel went. All night the king could not eat or sleep for fear of what was happening to Daniel. The next morning, the king hurried to the lions' den. Daniel was saved because he trusted God! When you serve God with your whole heart, he will protect you too.

Create a lion's mane by cutting out the center of a paper plate and coloring the ring yellow and brown. Hold the ring up to your face and give a loud ROAR! God protected Daniel, and he can protect you too!

DAY 257
No More Pity Parties

Blessed are those who have learned to shout praise to you. Lord, they live in the light of your kindness. All day long they are full of joy because of who you are. They celebrate the fact that you do what is right.

—Psalm 89:15-16

When was the last time you felt sorry for yourself? Maybe your friends didn't include you. Maybe you had a bad day. Or maybe you are disappointed about something. It's okay to feel down, but don't let those feelings last too long, otherwise whatever you are sad about will seem worse than it really is, and the devil would like nothing better than for you to fall into his trap.

When you begin to feel down, turn the focus away from yourself and think about how much God loves you. Listen to praise songs and remember all the good things God has done. You may have had a bad day, but you can have hope that tomorrow will be better. If you are feeling sad and you can't pull yourself out of it, talk to an adult you trust about your feelings so that they can help you. God has good plans for you. Keep your eyes on Jesus. Amazing things are going to happen in your life.

Dear God, thank you for your kindness and for doing what is right. Help me not to feel sorry for myself. Amen.

DAY 258
Birthday Wishes

You planned how many days I would live. You wrote down the number of them in your book before I had lived through even one of them.

—Psalm 139:16

Happy Birthday! It may not be your birthday today, but God knows exactly when you were born. What do you like to do on your birthday? Have a party with friends? Open presents? Eat chocolate cake and vanilla ice cream? Your birthday is special and definitely should be celebrated, but is that all birthdays are about?

This verse from Psalm 139 says God planned your days. God is the one who created you, protected you, and brought your family and friends into your life. This year on your birthday, thank God for all he has done. Celebrate that you are another year older. You are special to God, and he wants you to be grateful for the life he's given you. Praise God!

Blow up a balloon and tie the end. Write something special on the balloon with a marker to thank God for your birthday.

DAY 259
All About God

"'Love the Lord your God with all your heart and with all your soul. Love him with all your mind and with all your strength.'"

—Mark 12:30

Life is all about God and putting him first. But how does that happen when you have family and friends and school and soccer? How do you make time for God when your days are filled up?

Love God with all your heart when you're at the dinner table with your family. Love God with all your soul when you are hanging out with friends. Love God with your mind as you go to school and do your best. Love God with all your strength as you use your muscles to play sports. Include God in every area of your life. Talk to him throughout the day. The most important thing in life is to love the God who created you!

Dear God, thank you for creating me. Help me love you with my heart, soul, mind, and strength. Amen.

DAY 260
Great Joy

May the God who gives hope fill you with great joy.

—Romans 15:13

Are you happy or grumpy when you first wake up? You might be the type of person who loves to get up early in the morning and looks forward to starting your day. Eating breakfast, getting dressed, and going to school might be easy for you. Or you might be someone who'd rather sleep in late. Eating breakfast makes you sick to your stomach, getting dressed is a chore, and going to school takes a lot of effort. How can you be joyful when you'd rather go back to sleep?

Being joyful doesn't have anything to do with whether or not you are happy in the moment. You can choose joy in the morning and throughout the day, even when you don't want to do something you know you have to do. You can be filled with joy because you know that God is in control and that everything is going to be all right. You can be joyful because you know Jesus. That type of joy lasts forever.

Write the verse above on a piece of paper and attach it to the bathroom mirror (with parent permission). Read it every morning and choose to be joyful.

DAY 261
It's Good to Give

Anyone who gives a lot will succeed. Anyone who renews others will be renewed.

—Proverbs 11:25

Do you share your things with others, or do you keep them all to yourself? What about if someone forgot their lunch at school? Or needed help? Would you walk by and ignore them, or stop and offer help?

There is a story in the Bible about a man who was attacked by robbers as he was traveling from Jerusalem to Jericho. He was stripped and beaten and left to die. A priest and a Levite happened to go down that road, but they passed him by. But when a Samaritan saw the injured man, he cleaned and bandaged the man's wounds. Then he brought him to an inn and paid the innkeeper to take care of him.

There are many verses in the Bible about giving. Why? Because it makes God happy when you give! You can give money, your time, or you can do something nice for someone else. Everything you have is a gift from God. He loves to give, and he wants you to give too.

Read the story of the Good Samaritan in Luke 10:25–37. Ask God how he wants you to give to others.

DAY 262
Dear God

At all times, pray by the power of the Spirit. Pray all kinds of prayers. Be watchful, so that you can pray. Always keep on praying for all the Lord's people.

—Ephesians 6:18

Do you pray before you go to sleep at night? Do you say the same thing every night without thinking about the words, or do you talk to God like a friend? He wants to hear about your day, what your plans are, and even how you might have messed up. God also wants you to pray for others. You can pray for your friends. You can pray for your classmates and teachers. You can pray for the leaders of your city, state, and country. It doesn't matter when or where you pray because you can talk to God anytime and anyplace. And when you keep your eyes open to the world around you, you will discover new things to talk to God about.

But like with all relationships, there is a time to listen. The Holy Spirit talks in a gentle whisper inside you, so you have to be quiet to hear him. What might he say? Is he nudging you to encourage a friend, give a gift to your teacher, or show your parents how much you love them? By telling God what is on your heart, he will listen and show you what to do.

Dear God, I love that I can talk to you about anything. Help me pray for others and listen to the Holy Spirit. Amen.

DAY 263
Time for Fun!

A cheerful heart makes you healthy. But a broken spirit dries you up.

—Proverbs 17:22

What do you like to do for fun? Do you like to draw cartoon characters, make up silly songs, bake cupcakes, or play in the yard? Maybe you like to build things, ride your bike, make homemade pizza, or grow flowers in your garden. Maybe your idea of having fun would be to have a picnic in the park, take a hike in the mountains, or go to the beach.

God wants you to enjoy life. He made you to laugh, relax, and play. Throughout Bible times, people who loved God had fun. They danced and celebrated at weddings and feasts. God gave you a mouth so you can enjoy food. He gave you ears to listen to music. He gave you hands and feet to dance and serve others. God wants you to enjoy his creations. Use your gifts and hobbies to have fun and glorify him.

Time for fun! Dance, sing, bake, build, ride, play! Whatever you do, praise God for creating the world for you to enjoy.

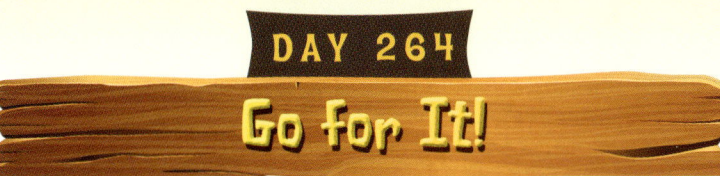

DAY 264
Go For It!

All of us get tripped up in many ways.
—James 3:2

Are you afraid to fail? Maybe you don't want to learn a new instrument because you're afraid to play all the wrong notes. Maybe you don't want to be on the baseball team because you're afraid to strike out. Or maybe you won't raise your hand in class because you're afraid to make a mistake. Truth is, you're going to trip up if you're constantly wondering what other people think of you. Did you know everyone fails from time to time?

The only way to have success is to try. That means you're going to have to put yourself out there and attempt new things. Start piano lessons, join the baseball team, volunteer in class. Yes, you might mess up, but you can step out in confidence knowing that God is with you no matter what. When you trust God and go for it, you are one step closer to achieving your dream, and you'll feel closer to him as well!

Name one thing you're afraid to try, then do it. Ask God to help you keep going even if you fail. What you learn from failure can be the best lesson of all.

DAY 265
More Like Jesus

The Spirit of God has made me. The breath of the Mighty One gives me life.

—Job 33:4

Did you know God cares about what you wear and how you look? Why? Because God made you, and he wants you to glorify him in everything you do, including what you put on. It's important to discover who you are and express yourself through your appearance, but you don't want to go about it in a negative way. Remember, you are made in God's image, and your body is a temple of the Holy Spirit.

As God's child, the most important thing you can put on is love. When you care about others, you become more like Jesus and guide others to him. Yes, you can wear T-shirts that have a Christian message, and wear jewelry with a fish or cross, but those things won't let your light shine for Jesus like giving the clothes you've outgrown to those in need or offering to help a neighbor. When you put on love, you will be respectful in what you wear and how you treat others.

As you get dressed tomorrow, think about the ways you can put on love as well. Then go out and do it!

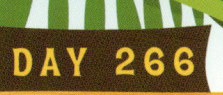

DAY 266
Abigail's Example

Then David accepted from her what she had brought him. He said, "Go home in peace. I've heard your words. I'll do what you have asked."

—1 Samuel 25:35

Have you ever helped a friend or sibling in order to keep the peace? Maybe you tried to resolve an argument between two of your friends, even though they were saying mean things. Maybe you pleaded with your parents to go easy on your sibling even though they did something wrong. Or maybe you brought a gift to your teacher after your classmates were rude.

There was a wise woman in the Bible named Abigail who also helped someone to keep the peace. She was the wife of a man named Nabal. Even though he was rich, Nabal refused to be kind to David and his men after they had protected Nabal's shepherds. David gathered his four hundred men and was prepared to fight Nabal and his household when Abigail arrived and stopped them. She gave David a generous gift and pleaded for her husband's life. David agreed to do what Abigail asked and spared Nabal. When you seek peace, God will reward you. Are you a peacekeeper like Abigail?

Read 1 Samuel 25 to find out more. Ask God to show you how you can help others by keeping the peace.

Jesus Paid the Price

He gave his life to pay for our sins. But he not only paid for our sins. He also paid for the sins of the whole world.

—1 John 2:2

What is sin? Sins are thoughts and actions that separate you from God. Like if you stole something from your sibling's closet, thought of ways to get back at an enemy, or told your parents a lie. No one is perfect, so everybody sins sometimes. And nothing you can do will take away your sin. You need a Savior.

Did you know Jesus came to earth to die? Jesus paid the price for your sins and the sins of the world when he died on the cross. But the story doesn't end there. Three days later Jesus rose from the dead and defeated sin once and for all.

Because Jesus died and rose again, you can have a personal relationship with God and live forever with him. When you believe in Jesus and confess your sins to God, he will forgive you.

Dear God, thank you for dying on the cross and forgiving my sins. Help me trust in you. Amen.

DAY 268
Seeds

Here is something to remember. The one who plants only a little will gather only a little. And the one who plants a lot will gather a lot.

—2 Corinthians 9:6

What type of seeds would you like to plant in a garden? Would you choose to plant flowers, or fruits and vegetables? Some easy foods to grow are strawberries, sugar snap peas, radishes, carrots, potatoes, tomatoes, and pumpkins. The amount of seeds you plant will determine the size of your garden. If you plant only a few seeds, your garden will be small. But if you plant many seeds, your garden will be big.

The same thing happens when you sow other types of seeds. If you sow kindness, you'll receive kindness in return. If you sow generosity, you'll reap generosity. The opposite is also true. If you sow anger, you are going to reap anger from others. You don't just reap what you sow; you actually reap more than you sow! When you give to others, you are becoming more like Jesus. What type of seeds are you going to plant today?

Ask God to help you sow seeds of kindness, generosity, and love. When you sow good seeds, your faith will grow.

DAY 269
Gray Hair and Wrinkles

"'Stand up in order to show your respect for old people. Also have respect for me. I am the Lord your God.'"

—Leviticus 19:32

When is someone old? Is forty old? What about fifty? How about sixty or seventy? As people get older, they don't move as fast as they used to, can have a harder time remembering things, and often get gray hair and wrinkles. Did you know that it doesn't matter how old someone is? God loves everyone the same.

In the Old Testament, God taught the Israelites to stand up when older people were near to show them respect and let them know they were important. You can show respect to older people too. You can open doors and let them go first. You can reach for things on the bottom shelf at the grocery store for them. And you can listen to them when they are talking. Most of all, you can show respect by being patient. Older people have lived a long time, and they deserve to be treated with kindness and respect.

Ask God to help you show respect to an older person today.

DAY 270
Outsiders

Don't forget to welcome outsiders. By doing that, some people have welcomed angels without knowing it.

—Hebrews 13:2

How has your family shown hospitality to strangers? Your parents might have asked someone over for dinner, given a warm blanket to a person in need, or invited someone to spend the night. How can you help? You can help clean the house by tidying up. You can set the table. And you can have good manners when your guest arrives. Most of all, you can have a good attitude! But why is showing hospitality important?

The Bible says you are to be hospitable or friendly with those you don't know because they might be angels in disguise. How does that work? Sometimes God sends an angel to your home because he knows what your family needs. Other times, God wants you to tend to the needs of others and share their burdens. No matter what, when you are kind to other people, you are making a difference. God gave you and your family many blessings, and he wants you to share them with others.

Think of ways you and your family can welcome someone you don't know very well. You never know, this outsider could be an angel or a new friend!

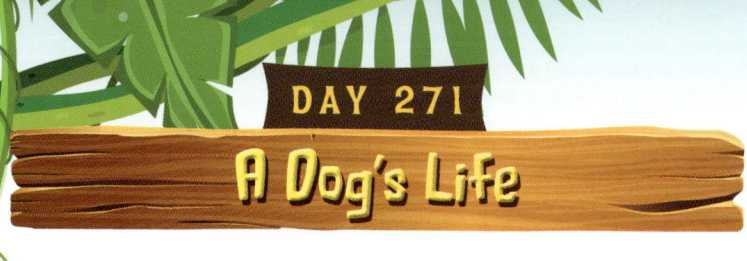

DAY 271
A Dog's Life

"He holds the life of every creature in his hand. He controls the breath of every human being."

—Job 12:10

Do you know someone who has a dog? What is the dog's name? Did you know there are more than two hundred dog breeds? There are big dogs like the Great Dane, medium-sized dogs like the Australian shepherd, and small dogs like the Chihuahua. Most big dogs live between ten and thirteen years, and some smaller dogs can live closer to fifteen. That's not a very long time compared to humans. That doesn't seem fair, does it? It's hard to lose a pet, and it's normal to be very sad when that time comes.

You might wonder if pets go to heaven and whether you will see your dog again. The truth is, no one knows the answer. The Bible doesn't make it clear. But we do know that God loves and cares about animals. While your pet is part of your family, God wants you to love it and take care of it the best you can.

If you have a pet, give it a big hug! Thank God for bringing it into your life.

DAY 272
Good Soil

"But the seed that fell on good soil is like those who hear the message and understand it. They produce a crop 100, 60 or 30 times more than the farmer planted."

—Matthew 13:23

If you were a farmer, where would you plant seeds? The answer seems obvious, doesn't it? For the best crop, farmers should plant seeds in good soil.

In the Bible, Jesus told a story about a farmer and his seeds. The seeds are God's message. The path is a person who hears God's message, but the devil takes the message away from them. The rocky ground is a person who hears God's message and accepts it with joy, but when hard times come, they fall away. The thorny ground is a person who hears God's message, but money and worldly things choke out their love for God and they don't produce the fruit of the Spirit. Good soil is a person who hears the Word of God, believes it, and produces love, joy, peace, patience, kindness, goodness, faithfulness, gentleness, and self-control. God is like a farmer who plants his Word in your heart. Will you be good soil for God?

Dear God, thank you for planting your Word in my heart. Help me to be good soil for you so that I produce the fruit of the Spirit. Amen.

DAY 273
Take a Break

Then Jesus said to his apostles, "Come with me by yourselves to a quiet place. You need to get some rest." So they went away by themselves in a boat to a quiet place.

—Mark 6:31-32

Have you been busy lately? School, sports, church, family, friends—it's important to make time for each one. But when you are rushing around from one activity to the next, you can feel overloaded in a hurry. Even if you squeeze in time for everything, you can still feel as if you're running on an empty tank of gas. Then what?

The surefire way to get filled up is to take a break and get some rest. Jesus told the apostles they needed a break too. He told them to come with him to get some rest. So they went away with him in a boat to a quiet place. You might take a break by relaxing under a tree, lying on the grass and looking up at the clouds, or dipping your feet into a pool or a creek. The important thing is to unplug from your busy life and get some much-needed rest.

Need some rest? You might feel as if you're too old to take a nap, but lying down for twenty minutes will give you the energy you need to make it through your day. Try it!

DAY 274
Dark Stuff

Don't use magic to try to explain the meaning of warnings in the sky or of any other signs. Don't take part in worshiping evil powers.

—Deuteronomy 18:10

Do you know someone who has visited a psychic? Have you ever read your horoscope and wondered if it was true? Has a friend ever invited you to play with tarot cards or a Ouija board? You might be curious about these things, but God wants you to stay far away from palm readings, astrological signs, fortune-telling, and anything to do with dark magic.

Did you know the Bible tells you that God doesn't want you to use magic to explain warnings in the sky or to worship evil powers? He doesn't want you to put a spell on anyone, or to ask for advice from the dead. God doesn't want you to practice any kind of evil magic at all. When you love God, you won't look to dark stuff for answers about your future. Pray to God. The Bible says he holds the future in his hands.

Dear God, thank you for being in control of my future. Help me stay away from evil magic. Amen.

DAY 275
Finders Keepers

The Lord rewards everyone for doing what is right and being faithful.
—1 Samuel 26:23

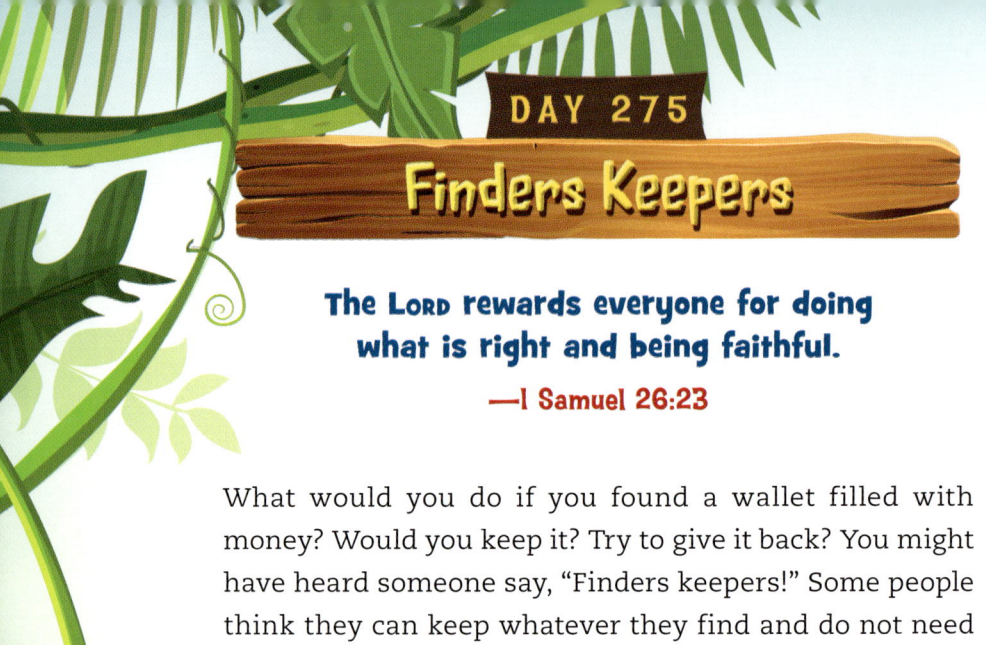

What would you do if you found a wallet filled with money? Would you keep it? Try to give it back? You might have heard someone say, "Finders keepers!" Some people think they can keep whatever they find and do not need to give the item back to the person who lost it. Is it true? Can you keep something that doesn't belong to you just because you found it?

The best thing to do is to try to find the owner and give the item back. God doesn't want you to be greedy for money or things that don't belong to you. By doing what is right, you are being faithful to God. So the next time you are tempted to say, "Finders keepers," remember that people are more important than treasure, and helping others find their lost item is the best gift of all.

If you find a sweatshirt, water bottle, or other item on the playground, take it to the lost and found. Doing what is right makes God happy.

DAY 276
Heavenly Home

But we are citizens of heaven. And we can hardly wait for a Savior from there. He is the Lord Jesus Christ.

—Philippians 3:20

What does it mean to be a citizen? A citizen is a person who has a right to be a member of a country. There are many ways to become a citizen. For example, you could be born in the country, marry someone who lives there, or take steps to become a citizen after moving to a country. As a citizen, you have certain rights. You can vote, are protected by laws, and can work for the government.

The Bible says when you love God and believe in him, you are a citizen of heaven. That means your home is in heaven with God. It doesn't matter if you were born into a Christian family or if a friend brought you to church. When you accepted Jesus into your heart, you became God's child. Now you have all the rights as God's child, and one day you will spend eternity with him!

Draw a picture of what you think heaven will be like. You are God's child and a citizen of heaven. Super cool!

DAY 277
Stand By Me

A friend loves at all times. They are there to help when trouble comes.
—Proverbs 17:17

How many friends do you have? Two? Six? More? You might have friends at school, friends at church, and friends in your neighborhood. What do you and your friends talk about? Shared interests? Your family? How much you might be struggling at home or in school?

The number of friends you have doesn't matter. The important thing is whether your friends will stick by you when trouble comes. A loyal friend is someone who loves you at all times. In order to have loyal friends, you need to be a loyal friend too. That means you stand up for a friend if they're getting picked on, listen to them if they're hurt, and help them when times are tough. God is a loyal friend to you and wants you to be a loyal friend to others.

Dear God, thank you for my friends. Help me to be a loyal friend to others. Amen.

DAY 278
The Star

When they saw the star, they were filled with joy. The Wise Men went to the house. There they saw the child with his mother Mary. They bowed down and worshiped him.

—Matthew 2:10-11

Have you ever wondered about the star the wise men followed to find baby Jesus? Scientists think it could have been a comet or a supernova, which is an explosion in the sky that slowly fades from sight over several weeks or months. The star could also have been the planets Jupiter and Venus lining up together to form a bright light in the sky. Whatever it was, God placed the star in the sky to help the wise men search for baby Jesus.

What or who has God used in your life to bring you closer to him? Maybe a friend invited you to church. Maybe someone cheered you up when you felt sad. Or maybe you have a parent or grandparent who reads the Bible with you. You might not have a star to follow like the wise men, but God places people and things in your life to guide you to him.

Draw a large star on a piece of cardboard. Cut it out and wrap it in aluminum foil. Hang it up in your room to remind you to keep seeking God.

DAY 279
Too Many Gifts

"Suppose someone offers all their wealth to buy love. That won't even come close to being enough."

—Song of Songs 8:7

Do you like it when someone gives you a gift? Your mom and dad might have brought you a souvenir from a trip. A friend might have given you a present when you were sick. Your teacher might have given you a book, or your sibling might have baked you brownies. All these gifts are special because they were given out of love.

But what if kids want to buy you stuff so that you'll be their friend? Is that okay? Buying someone's friendship is never okay. People who use gifts to earn your friendship think they need to be overly generous to be liked. But that's not true! Accepting bribes is not a good way to start a friendship and will only make you feel uncomfortable in the end. Instead, God wants you to be friends with people for the right reasons.

Dear God, help me be a good friend to others, and to be friends with someone for the right reasons.

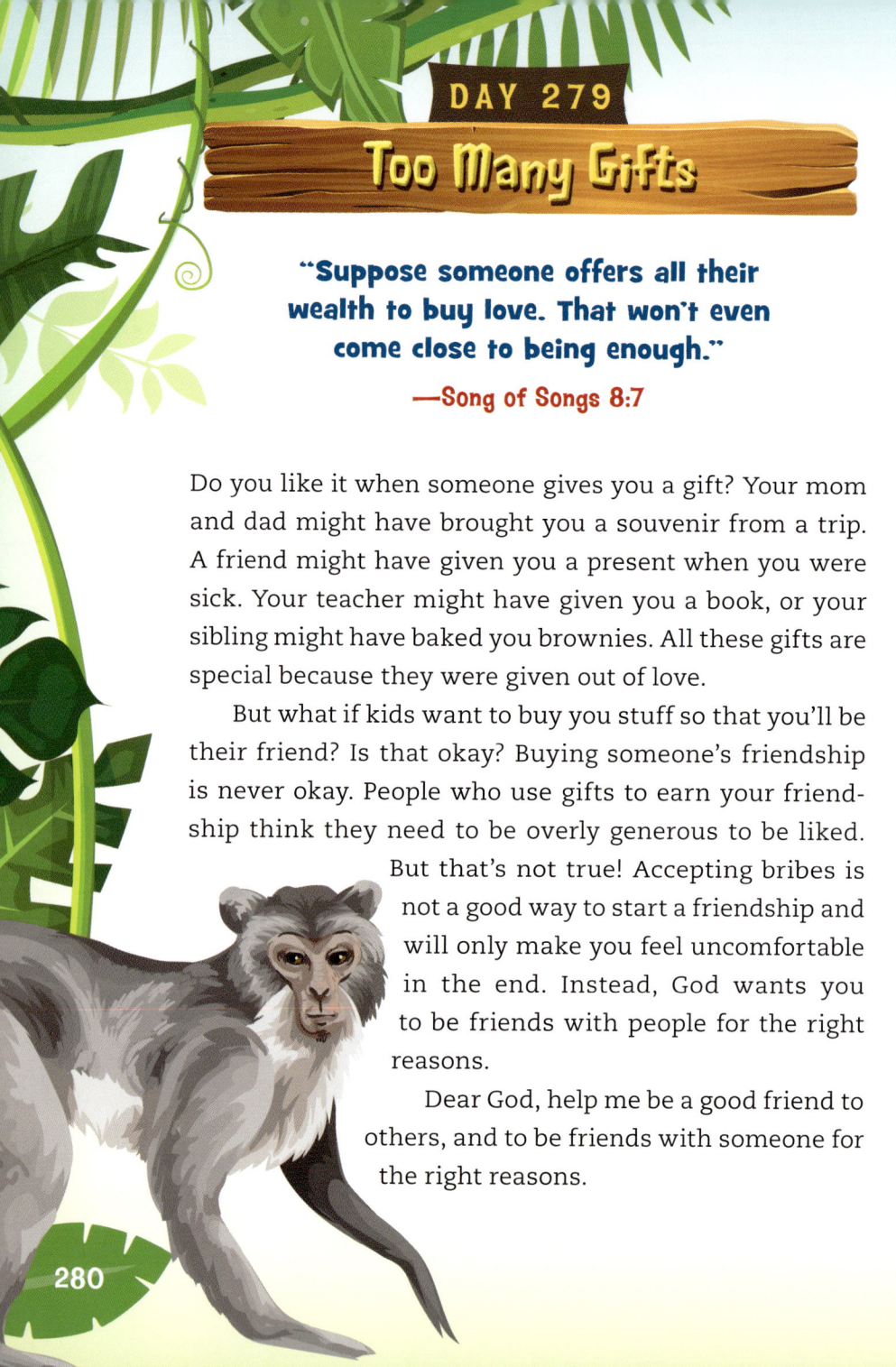

One for the Team

Show proper respect to everyone.
—I Peter 2:17

Are you a good sport? To be a team player, you need to respect other players, win without bragging, and lose without complaining. A good team player plays by the rules, encourages their teammates when they mess up, and doesn't lose their cool when the ref makes a call they don't like. A good sport also listens to the coach and follows directions. Does that describe you?

If you are on a team or part of a club, show respect by having a good attitude and treating others with kindness. When someone makes a bad play, stay focused on the game instead of arguing or yelling. Yes, winning is fun, but not as important as playing the way God wants you to. So make sure you give high fives to the other team at the end of the game, no matter if you win or lose. The best way to show proper respect to everyone is to be humble and think of others as better than yourself.

Dear God, thank you for my team. Help me to be a good team player. Amen.

DAY 281
Kind Words

Worry makes the heart heavy. But a kind word cheers it up.

—**Proverbs 12:25**

Do you have a friend who is worried about something? Maybe they are having family trouble. Maybe they're afraid of failing a test. Or maybe they're tired of sitting on the bench instead of playing in the game. What do you say when someone is down in the dumps and comes to you for advice?

There might not be anything you can do to change what's going on in your friend's life, but you can encourage them by saying something kind. You can tell them how happy you are that they are your friend. You can encourage them to study or get help so they can pass the test. And you can tell them that no matter what, they are a valuable part of the team. Kind words cheer people up, and God wants us to be a source of encouragement for others. So look for ways to lift up someone who's carrying a heavy heart.

Do you know someone who seems sad? Offer a kind word to cheer them up.

DAY 282
Lookin' Good!

Fancy hairstyles don't make you beautiful. Wearing gold jewelry or fine clothes doesn't make you beautiful. Instead, your beauty comes from inside you. It is the beauty of a gentle and quiet spirit. Beauty like this doesn't fade away. God places great value on it.

—1 Peter 3:3-4

Do you take a long time to get dressed in the morning? Are you fussy about your clothes or how you comb your hair? There is nothing wrong with wanting to look your best or expressing yourself through your appearance. In fact, looking nice shows others you care about the body God gave you. But is your outward appearance what matters most? Is that where your beauty comes from?

The Bible says God is more interested in whether you have a gentle and quiet spirit than if you have a fancy hairstyle or fine clothes. True beauty comes from inside. By having a gentle and quiet spirit, you will be able to love others when it's tough, choose kindness over anger, and trust God even when life doesn't make sense. That kind of beauty never fades, and God places great value on it.

Dear God, thank you for being gentle with me. Help me to have a gentle and quiet spirit. Amen.

DAY 283
Step in the Right Direction

Your word is like a lamp that shows me the way. It is like a light that guides me.
—Psalm 119:105

Have you ever tried reading a book as the sun goes down? The darker it gets, the harder it is to see. You need light from a lamp or flashlight to show you the words on the page. The more light you have, the easier it is to see. Have you ever tried taking a walk in the dark? Without streetlights to guide you, you could lose your way.

God gave you the Bible so that you will have light. When you read the Bible, you will discover the truth of who God is, and you will know what steps he wants you to take. One way to have more light is to memorize Bible verses. That way, when you need God's light to guide you, you will be able to make a good choice. When you have God's Word in your heart, you will step in the right direction.

Take a night hike with a parent. Use a flashlight to guide you. The Bible is like a flashlight that guides you and shows you the way.

DAY 284
God Loves Everyone, Including YOU!

God so loved the world that he gave his one and only Son. Anyone who believes in him will not die but will have eternal life.

—John 3:16

How much do you love others? You can show love to your parents by obeying their words and giving them hugs. You can show love to your siblings by getting along and being kind. You can show love to a friend by spending time together. What about the people who are harder to love? You can say something kind to the bully in your class. You can give a care package to a homeless person on the street. And you can sponsor a child from another country.

Did you know God loves everyone in the entire world? God loves all people—good and bad, rich and poor, and those who look different than you. God loves everyone, even if they make poor choices. There's nothing you need to do to earn God's love. In fact, God loves you so much that he gave up his one and only Son to die on a cross so that you can live forever with him. Amazing stuff!

Glue wooden craft sticks on a piece of paper in the shape of a cross. Pin it to your bulletin board or wall to remember how much God loves you.

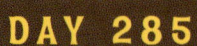

Gentle Like Jesus

Let everyone know how gentle you are. The Lord is coming soon.

—Philippians 4:5

Are you rough on your stuff, or are you gentle? A simple way to know if you are rough or gentle is judging how well you take care of your things. Do you break your toys? Ruin your clothes? Bend or tear the pages of your books? When you don't take care of things, they don't last. Being gentle takes effort. Did you know you can be rough or gentle with friends and family too?

If you ignore someone, say rude things, or put someone down, you are being rough and not how God wants you to act. But if you include others, say kind words, and treat people with respect, you are being gentle. Jesus was gentle in his words and actions by putting others first and speaking the truth in love. To be gentle like Jesus, ask God to give you strength so that you don't yell at someone or lash out the next time you're angry. Are you ready to be gentle?

Dear God, thank you for showing me how to be gentle. Help me to be like Jesus. Amen.

DAY 286
Shield of Honor

Lord, you are like a shield that keeps me safe. You bring me honor. You help me win the battle.

—Psalm 3:3

When was the last time you didn't feel safe? Maybe you heard something scary on the news or at home. Maybe you or a family member needed to go to the hospital. Or maybe you were the new kid at school, and you were afraid nobody would like you. All these events can make you feel nervous and unsafe. What do you do when you feel scared?

In the Bible, King David fled to the wilderness when his son Absalom tried to take over his kingdom. Even though David was scared, he knew God would protect him. David counted on God to keep him safe. He also asked God to help him win the battle. Like David, you can count on God. Ask God to watch over you. He will keep you safe.

Cut out the shape of a shield from a piece of cardboard. Decorate it any way you like, using crayons, markers, or aluminum foil to make it shiny. Remember, God is your shield, and he will keep you safe.

DAY 287
Stand Tall

But suppose you suffer for being a Christian. Then don't be ashamed. Instead, praise God because you are known by the name of Christ.

—1 Peter 4:16

Has anyone ever made fun of you for believing in Jesus? Maybe someone has teased you because you go to church or pray before meals. Or maybe someone made fun of you for living out your Christian values. How did it make you feel? You should never feel embarrassed for believing in God and standing for the truth. Yes, it's hard to be picked on, but you can stand tall because you're doing what is right. When you know the truth and focus on God, you can stand firm, and it won't matter to you what other people think. But sometimes it still does. Then what? The kids who tease you know it bugs you. Learn to tease-proof yourself. Let their words roll off your back, and respond in a quick and confident way. The bottom line is God loves you and his opinion is what matters most. Praise God that you know Jesus!

Tell someone about Jesus. And if that person makes fun of you, that's okay. God loves you, and his opinion matters most.

DAY 288
Turn Around

But the Lord wants to have mercy on you. So he will rise up to give you his tender love. The Lord is a God who is always fair. Blessed are all those who wait for him to act!

—Isaiah 30:18

Have you ever turned your back on a friend? Maybe you hurt their feelings. Maybe you didn't include them on purpose. Or maybe you were mean to them because of a misunderstanding. What do you do when that happens? Do you stay away from your friend, or do you ask them for forgiveness?

The same thing can happen with your relationship with God when you turn away from him. There was a prophet in the Old Testament named Isaiah who told the Israelites to stop turning away from God. But the Israelites didn't listen, and because of their disobedience, Israel was conquered and the people had to leave their land. What about you? Do you spend time with God? Do you pray? Read your Bible? Go to church? If not, now is the time to turn back to him. Ask God to forgive you.

Dear God, thank you for your love and mercy. Help me turn to you instead of away from you. Amen.

DAY 289
Scrub-a-Dub-Dub

But God is faithful and fair. If we confess our sins, he will forgive our sins. He will forgive every wrong thing we have done. He will make us pure.

—1 John 1:9

Have you ever gotten super dirty? Maybe you jumped in a mud puddle after it rained, took a nature hike along a dirt path, or climbed on rocks in the wilderness. After a day spent in the dirt, you will definitely need a shower or bath to get all the dirt and grime off your skin. It feels good to be super clean!

Did you know your heart also needs to be washed? The Bible says you can get rid of all the dirt and grime from your life to be right with God. When you tell him about all your bad thoughts or the wrong things you have done, God forgives you and wipes away your sins. It's true! God is faithful and fair, and he will not only forgive your sins, but he will also make you pure.

Grab a bucket and shovel and dig in the dirt. Consider how God washes you clean when you confess your sins to him.

DAY 290
God Makes Things Right

I will give thanks to the L‍ord because he does what is right. I will sing the praises of the name of the L‍ord Most High.

—Psalm 7:17

Is it okay to hang around people who get caught doing bad things? Maybe you have a friend who has made some bad choices lately or gotten in trouble with a teacher. What should you do?

God tells us in the Bible that you should stay away from people who do bad things. Instead, hang around friends and family who make good choices. You will be able to tell if someone is who they say they are by what they do. And if you've been hurt by someone, you can trust God to make things right. Rely on him to take care of the person or people involved, and be thankful God is who he says he is and always does what he promises.

Dear God, thank you for being who you say you are. Help me rely on you to make things right. Amen.

DAY 291
Strong Roots

You received Christ Jesus as Lord. So keep on living your lives in him. Have your roots in him. Build yourselves up in him. Grow strong in what you believe, just as you were taught. Be more thankful than ever before.

—Colossians 2:6-7

Roots hold plants in the ground and are the part of the plant usually buried under the ground. Roots keep a plant upright and take water and nutrients from the soil. They also store food to help the plant grow. Did you know there are two different types of roots? A taproot is one large root with smaller roots growing out of its sides, and a fibrous root has many branching roots growing from the stem.

Did you know when you ask Jesus into your heart, you start building roots that grow your faith? Just like trees and plants get all their food through their root systems, you can be fed by reading your Bible and building your life in Jesus. When your roots grow deep, you will grow strong in your faith and be able to share what you believe with others. If you have deep roots in Jesus, you will be able to stand upright when the tough times come.

Draw a picture of a tree to remind you to have deep roots in Jesus. Write the verse from Colossians on the top, and praise God for all he has given you.

DAY 292
What's Your Nickname?

So Jesus appointed the 12 disciples. Simon was one of them. Jesus gave him the name Peter. There were James, son of Zebedee, and his brother John. Jesus gave them the name Boanerges. Boanerges means Sons of Thunder.

—Mark 3:16-17

Do you have a nickname? Maybe your parents call you something cute, like Sweet Pea or Squirt. Or maybe you got your nickname because one of your siblings had a hard time pronouncing your name. Most of the time, nicknames are said in a loving way, but nicknames can also be used to harm. If that happens, talk with your parents and let them know it bothers you. Name-calling is never okay.

When Jesus chose his twelve disciples, he called some of them by different names. Jesus changed Simon's name to Peter, and he gave James and John, two brothers, the name Sons of Thunder. Jesus has many names too. He is called Christ, Immanuel, Lamb of God, Messiah, Savior, and Lord of All. He is also called Wonderful Counselor, Mighty God, and Prince of Peace. Having many names can be a good thing when it describes who you are and gives you a special role. How do you think of Jesus?

Write down all your nicknames. Do you like all of them? If you don't, let your mom or dad know so that you can scratch that one off your list.

DAY 293
Not All About Me

None of you should look out just for your own good. Each of you should also look out for the good of others.
—Philippians 2:4

Have you ever thought about all the things others do for you? Your parents take care of you. Your siblings watch out for you. Your teachers help you learn. Your coach encourages your team. Your piano teacher boosts your confidence. And that's not counting your grandparents, aunts and uncles, and anyone else in your life. If you only think of yourself, it's easy to take people for granted and expect them to give without giving back in return.

But when you think about others, you look for ways to care for them too. Offer to help your mom or dad with chores. Listen to your brother when he's had a bad day. Hand out papers for your teacher. Call your grandparents and ask how they are doing. When you look out for the good of others, you take the focus off yourself and please God in the process.

Make a list of all the people in your life who do something for you. Go back through the list and write down some nice things you can do for them.

DAY 294
Make a Difference

Here is what the Lord who rules over all said to his people. "Treat everyone with justice. Show mercy and tender concern to one another."

—Zechariah 7:9

Have you ever wondered how you can make a difference in the world? You might not be able to help people in another country or even another state, but you can make an impact in your neighborhood, church, and school. How? Pick up trash in your neighborhood to keep it clean. Give money to your church. Donate books to your school. Get a group of kids together and do yard work or have a bake sale to earn money for a new playground. There are many ways to change the world for the better!

By using the gifts and talents God gave you, you will make a big difference in the lives of the people around you. When you look for ways to help others and act, you will make the world a better place.

Dear God, thank you for all that you have given me. Help me to make a difference in my neighborhood, church, and school. Amen.

DAY 295
Change of Attitude

"Who can ever know what is in the Lord's mind? Can anyone ever teach him?" But we have the mind of Christ.

—1 Corinthians 2:16

When your mom or dad asks you to do something, do you do it? Or do you just say you're going to do it and forget? Maybe you don't forget, but you choose to do something else. Or maybe you're having so much fun that you don't want to stop what you're doing. Sound familiar?

Jesus told a story about a man with two sons. The man told the older boy to go out into the vineyard and work. The older son answered, "No, I won't go," but later changed his mind and went. Then the father told the younger son to go. The son answered, "Yes, I will." But he chose not to work. Which one of the brothers obeyed his dad? The older son, of course! He had a change of attitude and did what his father asked. When you obey, you have the same attitude as Jesus.

What chores do you have around the house? Remember to have the mindset of Jesus and obey your parents.

DAY 296
Sticky Situations

Sin is not ended by using many words. But those who are wise control their tongues.

—Proverbs 10:19

Have you ever tried to get out of a sticky situation by using a bunch of words? Maybe you lied to your parents and the more you talked, the bigger and more outrageous the story became. Or maybe you gossiped about your friend and the more you shared, the worse it made you feel. How can you use your words and be wise at the same time?

The Bible says those who are wise control their tongues. That means you can apologize and ask your parents to forgive you for lying to them. You can apologize and ask your friend to forgive you for spreading gossip. And you can ask God to forgive you and help you make better choices. It doesn't take many words to make things right. Are you wise?

Dear God, help me to choose my words wisely today and avoid sticky situations. Thank you for your guidance. Amen.

DAY 297
God Notices You

But God continues to give us more grace. That's why Scripture says, "God opposes those who are proud. But he gives grace to those who are humble."

—James 4:6

When was the last time you worked hard at something and wanted people to notice? Maybe you raised the most money for your school's fundraiser. Maybe you created a super cool science project and were chosen to go to the state fair. Or maybe you sang at your school's talent show. Are you trying to make a name for yourself to impress others, or are you doing these things to share the gifts God gave you?

When you are humble, your goal isn't to get a lot of attention. God knows whether you are showing off or trying your best. Did you know you can make a bigger impact by being gracious and humble? How, you ask? By raising the most money for your school because you want to help. By making a super cool science project because you want to make a difference in the world. And by singing in the talent show because you are thankful God gave you a nice voice. When you do your best with a humble attitude, God notices.

Dear God, thank you for noticing me. Help me to do my best and be humble. Amen.

DAY 298
Too Young?

Don't let anyone look down on you because you are young. Set an example for the believers in what you say and in how you live.

—1 Timothy 4:12

How old are you? Do you think you are too young to tell others about Jesus? Many kids think they have to wait until they are older before they are taken seriously. The truth is, you are never too young to do big things for God.

In the Bible, there was a man named Paul. He traveled around preaching the good news of Jesus to thousands of people. He met a young man named Timothy and asked if he'd join him on his journey. Together they started many churches. Even though Paul was thrown into prison for sharing about Jesus, Timothy continued to set a good example for other Christians to follow. Timothy understood that he wasn't too young to show others how to follow God. You can join the adventure *right now* and show others what it means to follow Jesus. Will you do it?

Braid a piece of yarn and tie it around your wrist to remind you to be a Christian example to others. Speak kind words and love people the way Jesus would.

DAY 299
Can I Be Older, Please?

Remember your Creator. Remember him while you are still young.

—Ecclesiastes 12:1

Do you or any of your friends have an older sibling? It's fun to imagine what it would be like to be older. You can shave, wear makeup, drive a car, and go out on dates. Sometimes it's tempting to want those things right now. Some kids try to act older instead of being the age they are. You might think it sounds cool to be more independent, but the older you get, the more responsibility you will have.

There was a boy in the Bible named Josiah who was eight years old when he became king. He ruled in Jerusalem for years and years! Talk about having to grow up quickly. But Josiah did what was right in the eyes of the Lord. He lived the way King David had lived by keeping his eyes on God and not turning away from him. Are you ready to be king or queen? Don't worry! You don't have to be ready now, but you can live like Josiah and David by remembering God, your Creator, while you are still young.

Run, play, and thank God for the age you are right now.

DAY 300
Growing and Changing

When I was a child, I talked like a child. I thought like a child. I had the understanding of a child. When I became a man, I put the ways of childhood behind me.

—1 Corinthians 13:11

Remember when your mom or dad took the training wheels off your bike? Or when you didn't need your car seat anymore? What about when you outgrew some of your clothes or when you gave away some of your childhood toys? You are growing and changing all the time. But maybe you don't want to grow up. Maybe you like things just the way they are. Maybe, if you had a choice, you'd be a kid forever.

As fun as it is to be a kid, God created you to grow and change. He made you to start as a baby and grow up to be an adult. There are many things you can do now that you couldn't when you were younger. You can learn more in school, have better coordination playing sports, and go to slumber parties with your friends. As you grow and change, talk to God about what you're feeling and how you're changing. That's the way God designed it to be.

Trace your hands on a piece of paper with a crayon. Write the date on it. Thank God for creating you to grow and change.

Ready for Battle

The weapons I fight with are not the weapons the world uses. In fact, it is just the opposite. My weapons have the power of God to destroy the camps of the enemy.

—2 Corinthians 10:4

Who is your biggest enemy? The bully on the playground? The mean neighbor down the street? A sibling? Actually, your worst enemy is Satan. He can get into your mind and cause you to think bad thoughts and do bad things. But God has given you weapons to fight against Satan. No, not guns and knives, but armor to fight against Satan and his lies.

First, you need the *belt of truth*. When you read the Bible every day, you will be able to know the truth and fight evil. The *breastplate of righteousness* protects your heart. By confessing your sins to God, your heart will be right with him. *Sandals of peace* protect your feet from going where you shouldn't go, and help you stand firm when difficult times come. The *shield of faith* stops the bad thoughts Satan sends your way when you believe in God and his promises. The *helmet of salvation* protects your mind. Remember, you are God's child. The *sword of the Spirit* is memorizing God's Word in order to tell the difference between good and evil. By putting on God's armor, you will be ready for battle!

Dear God, thank you for giving me your armor to fight against Satan. Help me to have strong faith and to know the truth. Amen.

DAY 302
Grandma and Grandpa

Grandchildren are like a crown to older people. And children are proud of their parents.

—Proverbs 17:6

Do you live near your grandparents? Maybe your grandparents live in another state. Maybe your grandparents live with you. Or maybe you don't have grandparents but have someone who is like a grandparent in your life. Did you know you are like a crown to them? That means you are more valuable to them than jewels. Think of ways you can let your grandparents know how special they are. You can make them a card, draw them a picture, or give them a hug. The important thing is to let them know how much you love them.

What do you like to do with your grandparents? Read books? Take nature walks? Get ice cream? It doesn't matter what you do. Your grandparents are happy to spend time with you, even if you just hang out together and visit. Do your grandparents talk to you about Jesus? If not, you might think about reading the Bible with them. Remember, you are never too young to share the good news of Jesus.

Show your grandparents or that special adult in your life how much you love them. Do it today!

Sibling Rivalry

Why do you fight and argue among yourselves? Isn't it because of your sinful desires? They fight within you.

—James 4:1

Do you love your siblings one minute and hate them the next? Maybe hate is a strong word and not allowed in your house, but it seems like the right word to describe what you are feeling. Living with siblings or stepsiblings can drive you bonkers. They play with your stuff, follow you around, and get in your way. And sometimes Mom and Dad seem to treat them better than they treat you. It's hard not to be jealous when they are getting attention and you are not.

That is what happened to two brothers in one of Jesus's parables. One brother left the family, made bad choices, and spent all his money, while the older brother stayed at home and helped his father. One day, the younger brother came to his senses and returned home, and the father had a big party for him. When the older brother learned of his brother's return, he was angry and jealous. He had been faithful to his father all that time, and his brother was the one getting the party! It didn't seem fair. But loving your siblings means choosing to forgive them when they do wrong. Can you do it?

Hang out with your siblings and take turns choosing which game to play. Try to get along and enjoy their company. Remember to forgive them if they do something wrong.

DAY 304
Letters to God

"So write down what you have seen. Write about what is happening now and what will happen later."

—Revelation 1:19

The Sumerians were the first people to create a written language, called cuneiform, around 3500–3000 BC. Their language started as pictures used to mean certain words or ideas. They did not use paper and ink, but tools made of wood or stiff reeds that pressed the symbols into clay tablets. Eventually other written languages took the place of cuneiform.

Do you write things down in a journal? You might like to share your thoughts, draw pictures, or collect souvenirs of where you've gone or what you've done. Maybe you also like to write letters to God. You can tell him all about your day, what you are feeling, and how thankful you are for what he's done in your life. And when the book is full, you can look through it and see all the blessings God has given you and how he's answered your prayers.

Dear God, thank you that I can write about all that I've seen and done. Help me trust you with the future. Amen.

DAY 305
My Body

We don't give up. Our bodies are becoming weaker and weaker. But our spirits are being renewed day by day.

—2 Corinthians 4:16

How do you feel about the body God gave you? You might be tempted to compare yourself with someone you see on television or in a magazine. You might think of yourself in a certain way because of what a family member has said. Or you might have heard someone at school say something about the way you look or how they feel about their own body.

God wants you to feel good about the body he gave you. How you feel about your body can affect how confident you are in other areas too. When you are grateful, you will eat healthy food because you know it's better for you. You will run and play outside because it is fun. And you will remember that even when your body is weak and tired, you can be strong because God loves you and is building you up each day.

Look at yourself in the mirror. Name three things you like about yourself. Thank God for the body he gave you.

Brag Much?

Joseph had a dream. When he told it to his brothers, they hated him even more.

—Genesis 37:5

Have you ever bragged about something and made others angry? Maybe you boasted to your friends about being the best reader in the whole class. Maybe you bragged to your siblings about being better at sports. Maybe you took all the credit for something even though you had help. Did you know bragging about yourself pushes people away?

Something similar happened to a boy in the Bible named Joseph. He was his father's favorite son, and it made his brothers upset, especially when their father gave Joseph a beautiful new coat. His brothers became more upset when Joseph bragged about his dreams. And these weren't ordinary dreams! Joseph told his brothers that one day they would bow down to him. This made his brothers so jealous that they sold him for eight ounces of silver and sent him away to Egypt. Even though the consequences won't be as dire for you, consider that the next time you are tempted to brag about your accomplishments.

Dear God, thank you for giving me gifts and talents. Help me to be humble and not to brag. Amen.

DAY 307
Different Kinds of Families

"Anyone who welcomes one of these little children in my name welcomes me."

—Mark 9:37

Do you know someone in foster care? Some kids don't live with their parents because they are unable to care for them. There are many kinds of families, and it is important not to judge others because their family is different than yours. Everyone deserves to feel safe and well taken care of.

There are several stories of foster care in the Bible. Moses was raised by one of Pharaoh's daughters after she found him in a basket floating down the river. Samuel went to live with a priest named Eli and his family to have religious lessons. Esther's cousin Mordecai raised Esther after the death of her parents. Joseph helped Mary raise Jesus. You may or may not know someone in foster care, but when you welcome someone and offer them friendship and love, you are opening your heart to Jesus.

Talk to God about how you feel about families that are different than yours. Ask him to show you how to open your heart to someone in need.

Something New

"Go in peace. The Lord is pleased with your journey."
—Judges 18:6

Do you want to try something new? How about learning to play the guitar or ukulele? Maybe you want to learn how to surf in the ocean or snowboard down a mountain. What about taking an art class or learning how to play chess? There are many new and exciting things to try.

Did you know fear can stop you from experiencing life? God made you to try new things. You may discover skills and talents you never knew you had. And if you try something new and it doesn't work out, remember life is an adventure and God wants you to enjoy the journey. So don't hold back. Try something new today!

Join a club, sign up for lessons, get out those art supplies. Talk to your parents about the new adventure you want to start and see how you can make it a reality.

Rules

"If you love me, obey my commands."
—John 14:15

Do you like rules? Even though some rules might seem silly to you, most are there to keep you safe and teach you right from wrong. Did you know even adults need rules?

God made rules for you to follow called the Ten Commandments. When you love God more than you love anything else, you will want to keep him number one in your life, say his name with love and respect, and honor him by resting one day a week. When you follow God's rules, you will love and respect your mom and dad, never hurt anyone, and you won't take anything that isn't yours. When you live the way God wants you to live, you will always tell the truth, be happy with what you have, and you won't wish for other people's things. By following God's rules, you will be happy and free.

List as many rules as you can from home and school. Is it easy or hard for you to follow rules? Thank God that he gave you a list of rules so that you stay safe and know right from wrong.

DAY 310
Missing Shoes and Other Stuff

"I tell you, it will be the same in heaven. There will be great joy when one sinner turns away from sin."

—Luke 15:7

Have you ever lost something important to you? Maybe it was a stuffed animal. Maybe you lost one of your favorite shoes. Or you might have lost your homework assignment or a signed permission slip to go on a field trip with your class. What would you do if you found it? Jump up and down, maybe do a cartwheel?

Jesus told a story about a shepherd who owned one hundred sheep. One day, one of the sheep wandered off and got lost. The shepherd went to look for it even though he had ninety-nine other sheep. When he found the missing sheep, the shepherd hugged it and put the sheep on his shoulders to bring it back to the fold. God feels the same way about you. He doesn't get angry when you stray from him, but instead lovingly brings you back.

Dear God, thank you for being a good shepherd. Help me not to stray from you. Amen.

DAY 311
If-Only Game

Forget the things that happened in the past. Do not keep on thinking about them.

—Isaiah 43:18

Do you play the "if only" game? You know, when you think . . .

If only I had listened to my mom.
If only I had studied for the test.
If only I could do it over again.

Did you know that no one is perfect? Everyone has made bad choices and has said some hurtful things, but it's how you deal with it that counts. Do you brush it off, blame someone else, or beat yourself up? Those things never work. There's a better way to deal with your mistakes. Admit what happened, ask God to forgive you, and then make sure you forgive yourself. God cares about every "if only" thought you have. He wants you to think about what happened so that you don't do it again, but he also wants you to keep moving forward.

Dear God, thank you for forgiving me. Help me look ahead instead of playing the "if only" game. Amen.

Best Prayer Ever!

It was very early in the morning and still dark. Jesus got up and left the house. He went to a place where he could be alone. There he prayed.
—Mark 1:35

> "Our Father in heaven,
> may your name be honored.
> May your kingdom come.
> May what you want to happen be done
> on earth as it is done in heaven.
> Give us today our daily bread.
> And forgive us our sins,
> just as we also have forgiven those who sin against us.
> Keep us from sinning when we are tempted.
> Save us from the evil one." (Matthew 6:9–13)

What does this prayer mean? By praying the Lord's Prayer, you are showing God how much you love and respect him. You believe that God is your Father in heaven and that he is in charge of everything. You are asking for God's forgiveness for your sins and promising to forgive others. God is the only one who can protect you from evil and help you when you are tempted.

Write down the Lord's Prayer on a piece of paper and memorize it. Go and pray this prayer to God the Father.

DAY 313
God's Wings

How priceless your faithful love is! People find safety in the shadow of your wings.

—**Psalm 36:7**

Do you ever wish you were a bird and could fly? It's fun to watch birds swoop and soar through the air. Birds are the only animals that have feathers, but not all birds use their wings to fly. Penguins use their wings to swim and guide them through the water. The ostrich, kiwi, and emu have feathers and wings, but they hardly use their wings at all. Have you ever seen a mama bird cover her babies with her wings? The small birds are protected until they are strong enough to fly.

God looks after you like a mama bird looks after her young. He comforts, protects, and loves you when you are going through tough times. Like a mama bird, he takes you under his wings so that you learn, grow, and get strong. Lean on God. You are safe there. Did you know that a mama bird also uses her wings to push her babies out of the nest? Like a baby bird, after a time of rest you'll be ready to fly.

Grab some binoculars, go outside, and look for birds. Watch how they fly. Consider how God is like a mama bird.

DAY 314
Don't Be Afraid to Get Wet

So Naaman went down to the Jordan River. He dipped himself in it seven times.

—2 Kings 5:14

When was the last time you went swimming? Maybe you have a pool in your backyard. Or maybe your friend is having a pool party. It's fun to get wet! But what if you didn't want to go swimming? Would you still go in the water?

Naaman was a brave soldier who had a skin disease. He went to see Elisha so he could be cured. Elisha's messenger said, "Go! Wash yourself in the Jordan River seven times. Then your skin will be healed." Naaman was angry. He was sure Elisha would cure him. Naaman's servants said, "What if Elisha the prophet had told you to do something difficult, wouldn't you have done it? So when he asks you to do something simple like go wash and be cured, you should obey." So Naaman did exactly what the man of God told him to do, and his skin was made pure again.

Even when you don't want to do something your parents or teacher want you to do, try it! You never know, it could be the best thing that ever happened to you. It worked for Naaman!

Hop in the shower and get wet. Think about how you can do something you don't want to do.

DAY 315
That's Enough!

"How long will you people make me suffer? How long will you crush me with your words?"

—Job 19:2

Do your friends tease you? Maybe your best friend says funny things and it makes you laugh. Or maybe your friend doesn't know how much their words sting. There's joking around in good-natured fun, and there's poking fun that hurts your feelings. When someone teases in an unkind way, it makes everyone around you feel uncomfortable. And when teasing becomes hurtful, it's time for it to stop.

But why would your friend tease you? Your friend may like it when people think they're funny. They may think it's fine to tease people because that's how they're treated at home. Or they may want people to think they sound smart. But you'd be doing them a huge favor by letting them know how their words make you feel. If you don't know what to say, go to an adult you trust and ask for help. After all, you don't want your friend to turn into a bully.

Do you have a friend or family member who teases you? If you don't like it, let them know.

DAY 316
Ready to Trade?

"So he went and sold everything he had. And he bought that field."

—Matthew 13:44

Do you like to trade? Maybe you swapped your chocolate chip cookies for a friend's bag of chips at lunch. Or maybe you traded chores with a sibling. You can trade in other ways too. You can give the grocery clerk money for a pack of gum. You can trade time to watch a movie. And you can give energy to help someone in need. To make a good trade, you need to get something that is worth more to you than what you gave up.

Jesus tells two stories about trades in the Bible. The first trade was when a man found treasure in a field. He sold everything he had to buy that field. The second trade is when a man found a valuable pearl. He sold everything he had to buy that pearl. God is like that treasure and pearl. You must be willing to give up money, time, and some energy to have a relationship with him. Are you willing to make a trade?

Ready to trade? Give up something today in order to spend time with God.

DAY 317
Mine! Or Is It?

But Esau ran to meet Jacob. He hugged him and threw his arms around his neck. He kissed him, and they cried for joy.

—Genesis 33:4

Have you ever wanted something so badly that you took it away from someone else? Maybe you borrowed a friend's sweatshirt and decided you didn't want to give it back. Maybe you wanted attention and blew out the candles of your sibling's birthday cake. What do you do now? Do you pretend it never happened, or try to make things right?

In the Bible there is a story of twin brothers named Jacob and Esau. Esau was born first, but Jacob tricked Esau into giving him the honor given to the firstborn. On top of that, Jacob and his mother fooled his dad into giving Jacob the blessing he'd intended to give Esau. Esau was angry, and Jacob ran away in fear. Years went by before Jacob decided to make things right. When he apologized, Esau hugged him and cried for joy. Do you need to apologize to someone? Don't wait! Do it right now.

Dear God, thank you for forgiving me. Help me apologize to the person I hurt. Amen.

DAY 318
Amazed

I'm amazed at how well you know me. It's more than I can understand.

—Psalm 139:6

When was the last time you were amazed? You might have been amazed when you saw a gorilla, zebra, or hippopotamus at the zoo. You might have been amazed when you hiked to the top of a mountain or walked alongside the ocean. You can also be amazed because God knows the real you.

God knows you better than you know yourself. He made you. He knows everything that happened to you in the past, what is happening to you right now, and what is going to happen in your future. He knows what you are thinking about, what you are afraid of, and what brings a smile to your face. God created you with a plan in mind. When you invite him in, he will show you that purpose. Are you amazed that God knows you so well? Guess what? By reading the Bible, you can get to know him too.

Time to be amazed! Go outside and find something that amazes you. Put it on your dresser to remember that God is amazing. He not only made creation, he made you!

DAY 319
The Outrageous

Then God said, "Take your son, your only son. He is the one you love. Take Isaac. Go to the place called Moriah. Give your son to me there as a burnt offering. Sacrifice him on the mountain I will show you."

—Genesis 22:2

Have you ever been told to do something that didn't make sense? Maybe you are super shy, but your teacher named you the leader of the group. Maybe you are afraid of heights, but your dad wanted you to ride the Ferris wheel with him. You might feel what they asked was unreasonable, or even impossible. Abraham felt the same way.

In the Bible, God told Abraham to take his only son and sacrifice him as a burnt offering. The request seemed unreasonable, but God wanted to see if Abraham trusted him. Abraham obeyed God. Because Abraham obeyed, God provided a ram to sacrifice instead. What about you? Will you obey your teacher and be the best leader you can be? Will you hold your dad's hand at the top of the Ferris wheel? Will you obey God when he calls you to do something outrageous?

Dear God, thank you for providing the ram for Abraham. Help me obey you even when it doesn't make sense to me. Amen.

DAY 320
Eraser on a Whiteboard

"So turn away from your sins. Turn to God. Then your sins will be wiped away. The time will come when the Lord will make everything new."

—Acts 3:19

Are you feeling guilty about something? Maybe you dropped your sister's cell phone in the toilet. Maybe you lied to your parents or hurt your friend's feelings. No matter what it is, after you do something you know is wrong, you usually feel bad and guilt sets in. And the more you think about what happened, the worse you feel. Is there a way to get rid of all the guilt and feel better?

Yes! Talk to God and tell him about your mistake. He will forgive you and wipe your sin away as if it never happened, like an eraser on a whiteboard. God makes everything new. Next, make things right with the person you hurt. When you apologize to your sister, tell your parents the truth, or make up with your friend, you won't need to think about your mistake or feel guilty anymore.

Dear God, please take away my guilt and shame. Help me make things right. Amen.

DAY 321
Graffiti Art

"Do not follow the crowd when they do what is wrong."

—Exodus 23:2

Graffiti is writing or a drawing that's scribbled, scratched, or spray-painted on walls or other surfaces. Most of the time, graffiti is made without the property owner's permission and is against the law. You might have seen graffiti on your desk at school, in a public bathroom, or on street signs. You might have seen graffiti on the side of a building or bridge. Maybe you think it sounds cool to spray-paint a fun design on a blank wall, but if you don't have permission, it isn't the right thing to do.

What if your friends want to do something bad? You have a choice to make. Will you follow the crowd when you know what they are doing is wrong, or will you obey God and the law? By saying no to your friends and walking away, you are standing firm in your faith and doing what is right. And if you want to paint on walls, ask your parents to help you find a legal way to do it. Your community will be better for it.

Create and color a design on a piece of paper. Ask a parent if you can paint your design on your bedroom wall. If they say yes, go for it! But if they say no, respect their wishes. Doing what is right is the right thing to do.

DAY 322
Plenty of Food

"He gives you crops in their seasons. He provides you with plenty of food."

—Acts 14:17

Are you hungry for a hamburger? What about chicken strips? A BLT? Maybe you would rather eat beans or pasta. Some people eat meat, and some don't because they are vegetarian. People have different tastes and preferences, and that's okay!

In fact, the New Testament doesn't say one way or the other what we should eat. The important thing is to respect other people's choices. To be healthy, however, it's important to make sure that you're getting enough protein (which can come from meat, beans, eggs, or dairy) along with plenty of fruits, vegetables, and grains. Did you know God is the one who gives us crops and provides us with food? So whether you eat barbecued pork ribs or a bowlful of pasta, you can thank God for the gift of food.

Be adventurous and try a new food this week! Remember to thank God at every meal.

DAY 323
Peak Performance

"The LORD gives me strength and protects me. He has saved me. He is my God. I will praise him."
—Exodus 15:2

Have you ever watched extreme sports on television? Maybe you've seen mountain bikers race down rugged hills, pro wrestlers slam each other against the mat, or snowboarders perform jaw-dropping tricks. Often these activities need a lot of speed, height, and special gear. Did you know you don't need to be extreme to keep your body healthy and strong? You can ride a bike around your neighborhood, sled down a bunny hill, and wrestle with your dad, among other sports, to keep your body fit. But you will never be at your peak performance while sitting on the couch watching other athletes. You've got to get up and do something.

The same thing is true for your relationship with God. You can watch your pastor, your Sunday school teacher, and your parents read the Bible and pray, but just like with sports, you have to be the one doing it to get strong. The best part is that you will know God for yourself instead of sitting on the sidelines. How's that for a thrilling adventure?

Dear God, thank you for giving me strength. Help me to get off the couch, move, and spend more time with you. Amen.

DAY 324
Great Faith

Then Jesus said to her, "Woman, you have great faith! You will be given what you are asking for." And her daughter was healed at that moment.

—Matthew 15:28

Do you have a goal? Maybe you want to get 100 percent on this week's math test. Maybe you want to learn how to ski, to play an instrument, or to keep your room clean. Or maybe you want to stay calm instead of being so quick to lose your temper. You will reach your goal if you take baby steps and stick with it. Do all your math homework. Join a ski class. Play in the band. Tidy up your closet. Take deep breaths before getting angry. Have faith that you can reach your goal.

What exactly is faith? Faith is complete trust or confidence in someone or something. There was a woman in the Bible whose daughter was suffering. The woman fell to her knees and cried out to Jesus to heal her. Jesus praised the woman's great faith and healed her daughter. Do you have great faith like the woman from Canaan? Do you believe God can help you achieve your goal?

What can you do today to help reach your goal? It takes a lot of hard work and great faith. You can do it!

Barnabas Wannabe

When the way you live pleases the Lord, he makes even your enemies live at peace with you.

—Proverbs 16:7

When was the last time you were nice to the kid who teases you or puts you down? You might be tempted to run and hide whenever you see your enemy, but the truth of the matter is that they might be especially in need of some kindness. When you're kind to others and love them like Jesus does, God can make even your enemy live at peace with you.

In the Bible there was a man named Barnabas who chose to stand up for Saul. Saul had many enemies in Jerusalem, and people were afraid of him. They didn't believe he was one of Jesus's followers. But Barnabas told the apostles that Saul had seen the Lord, and that the Lord had spoken to Saul. Barnabas also said that Saul had preached Jesus's name without fear. Because Barnabas chose to speak up and encourage Saul, he was able to stay with the believers. Can you be like Barnabas and encourage your enemy?

Have an enemy? Love like Jesus and show you care by being kind.

DAY 326
Do You See Him?

The Son is the exact likeness of God, who can't be seen.

—Colossians 1:15

Do you wish you could see God? Would you give him a big hug? Talk to him for hours? Ask him all sorts of questions? If you could see God, would it make a difference in your relationship? Would you spend more time with him? Pray more? Guess what? A long time ago, Jesus came to earth, and the Bible says he is the exact likeness of God! Yes, people saw God in human form. Cool, huh?

Yes, God's Son was born as a baby. He grew up to be a man to show you everything you need to know about who God is and how much he loves you. God created everything in the world so at just the right time Jesus would die for your sins and you would have a relationship with him. Now you can see God all around you—in the kindness of people, in your best friend's smile, in flowers, the pretty sunset, or when the wind blows through the trees. God is all around you!

Go outside on a windy day and watch the leaves flutter in the breeze. Just like the wind exists, you can be confident that God exists too.

DAY 327
Real Places

Then Jesus went through the towns and villages, teaching the people. He was on his way to Jerusalem.

—Luke 13:22

Do you ever wonder if the places you read about in the Bible are real? Some of the places where Jesus lived and taught, such as Bethlehem and Jerusalem, are busy towns today. You can visit the Jordan River where Jesus was baptized, the Mount of Olives where Jesus taught, and the garden of Gethsemane where Jesus prayed before he died. You can also float in the Dead Sea and walk up the same steps Jesus did to the Temple Mount. Archaeologists, or scientists who study the things of the past, are still discovering caves and uncovering temples, burial sites, and ancient cities.

But you don't need to go to Israel to know where Jesus went. You can open your Bible to the New Testament and read about it for yourself in the Gospels (Matthew, Mark, Luke, and John). You will discover all kinds of cool stuff about Jesus's life and the places he went. So buckle up. It's going to be an exciting ride!

As you read the four Gospels, keep a list of all the places Jesus visited.

DAY 328
Story Time

Then he told them many things using stories.

—Matthew 13:3

Do you like it when someone tells you a good story? Maybe your parent reads to you. Maybe your grandparents tell you stories of when they were young. Or maybe you and your friend swap stories in the dark when you have sleepovers. Did you know Jesus told stories called parables? A parable is a short story that teaches a lesson.

By telling stories, Jesus was able to talk about simple objects such as birds, flowers, seeds, and lost coins to help his followers understand God and heaven. Jesus knew a good story would get his followers' attention and help them remember the lesson.

Awesome news! You can read the parables Jesus taught in the New Testament. Afterward, talk about the stories with a pastor, parent, or Sunday school teacher. You'll discover all kinds of interesting things about God, yourself, and the kingdom of heaven.

Dear God, thank you for telling us stories in the Bible. Help me read and understand them. Amen.

Judged and Ashamed

Many of the Samaritans from the town of Sychar believed in Jesus. They believed because of what the woman had said about him. She said, "He told me everything I've ever done."

—John 4:39

Have people tried to stop you from making bad choices? Maybe you've already done something you know you shouldn't. Maybe you are making the same mistake over and over and don't know what to do about it. Maybe other people are judging you, and you feel ashamed. There is a woman from the Bible who felt the same way.

When Jesus came to a town in Samaria called Sychar, he sat down by a well because he was tired from his journey. A woman from Samaria came to get some water, and Jesus asked her to give him a drink. The Samaritan woman was surprised by his request. Then Jesus told her of her sin and revealed that he was the Messiah. Jesus knows your sin too. He loves you and wants you to spend forever with him. The next time you feel judged and ashamed for the mistakes you've made, remember the Samaritan woman. Jesus forgave her, and he will forgive you too.

Dear God, thank you for forgiving me for the mistakes I've made. Help me to come to you when I feel judged and ashamed. Amen.

DAY 330
Side-by-Side

Do two people walk together unless they've agreed to do so?

—Amos 3:3

When was the last time you had to work with someone? Maybe you had a group project for school, or a parent asked you and your sibling to do some housework together. Working as a team isn't always easy. Sometimes people disagree with each other and want their own way.

The Bible talks about many reasons two people should be on the same team. Have you ever heard the saying, "Two heads are better than one"? When you have a sibling or friend beside you, you can discover new things you never thought of before. A friend or sibling can encourage you to keep going. You are safer with someone by your side. The best part about being on a team is that you won't be lonely. You can be a part of God's team too! When you ask God to be by your side, you will have a friend for life.

Ask your sibling or friend to build or create something with you. Learn what it takes to be a team.

DAY 331
How Do You Spell L-O-V-E?

Love is patient. Love is kind. It does not want what belongs to others. It does not brag. It is not proud.

—1 Corinthians 13:4

How do you know if someone loves you? You know you are loved when someone takes care of you, says they love you, or gives you a hug. You also know you are loved when someone watches out for you or shares their stuff with you. It's nice to feel loved, and God wants you to love others too.

The Bible gives us many ways to show love, like being *patient* with your sibling when they mess up your room, being *kind* to the kid who doesn't have any friends at school, and *not being jealous* of your friend when they get something you've wanted for months. Loving others also means you *don't brag* about your accomplishments, and you are *humble* instead of acting proud. The world needs more love. Will you help make it a better place?

Spell L-O-V-E God's way by being patient, kind, and humble. Who can you show love to today?

DAY 332
The Wise Choice

So give me a heart that understands.
—1 Kings 3:9

If you could ask God for anything, what would it be? Would you ask to live a long time? Would you ask for a million dollars? Would you ask God to make a bully leave you alone? Or would you ask for a wise and understanding heart so that you could tell the difference between right and wrong?

In the Old Testament, God spoke to King Solomon in a dream. He said, "Ask for anything you want me to give you." Solomon could have asked for anything, and he chose to ask for a wise and understanding heart. God was pleased with Solomon's answer. He was so pleased that he not only gave Solomon wisdom, but he also gave him wealth and honor. No other king would be as wise as Solomon. When you pray, what do you ask for?

Dear God, thank you that I can ask you for anything. Help me to have a wise and understanding heart. Amen.

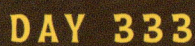

Out of This World

Do not love the world or anything in it. If anyone loves the world, love for the Father is not in them.

—1 John 2:15

Do you love God? Awesome! But do you love God more than anything in this world? Do you love him more than your house, more than all your stuff? Do you love God more than food? Do you love God more than your family and friends? It may be hard to put God above everything. But remember, God loves you! He gave his one and only Son to die on the cross for your sins. When you think of these things, you will treasure God most of all!

A man asked Jesus what he must do to receive eternal life. Jesus said, "Sell everything you have. Give the money to the poor. You will have treasure in heaven. Then come and follow me." The man went away sad because he was very rich. Jesus then told his disciples that it is harder for someone who has a lot of stuff to enter God's kingdom. When you follow God, you will receive much more than this world has to offer. When you love God, you will have eternal life. Now that's out of this world!

Dear God, thank you for loving me. Help me love you more than anything in this world. Amen.

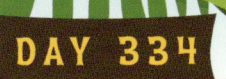

Fame and Fortune

Good things will come to those who are willing to lend freely. Good things will come to those who are fair in everything they do. Those who do what is right will always be secure. They will be remembered forever.

—Psalm 112:5-6

Do you want to be famous? Maybe you want to be a singer, an actor, or a pro basketball player. You might think it sounds fun to have people clapping, cheering, and shouting your name. Or maybe you want to have a lot of money. If you were rich, you'd be able to buy anything you want. But the truth is, fame and fortune don't last, and they definitely don't make people happy.

What is the best way for people to remember you if it's not for being rich and famous? The Bible says the best way to leave your mark on the world is by serving others. Yes, you can still sing, act, and play sports, but those things don't leave the kind of impact that lasts a lifetime. When you give generously and do what is right and fair, others will notice. Most importantly, so will God.

Want to make a difference? Ask your mom or dad how you can help them today.

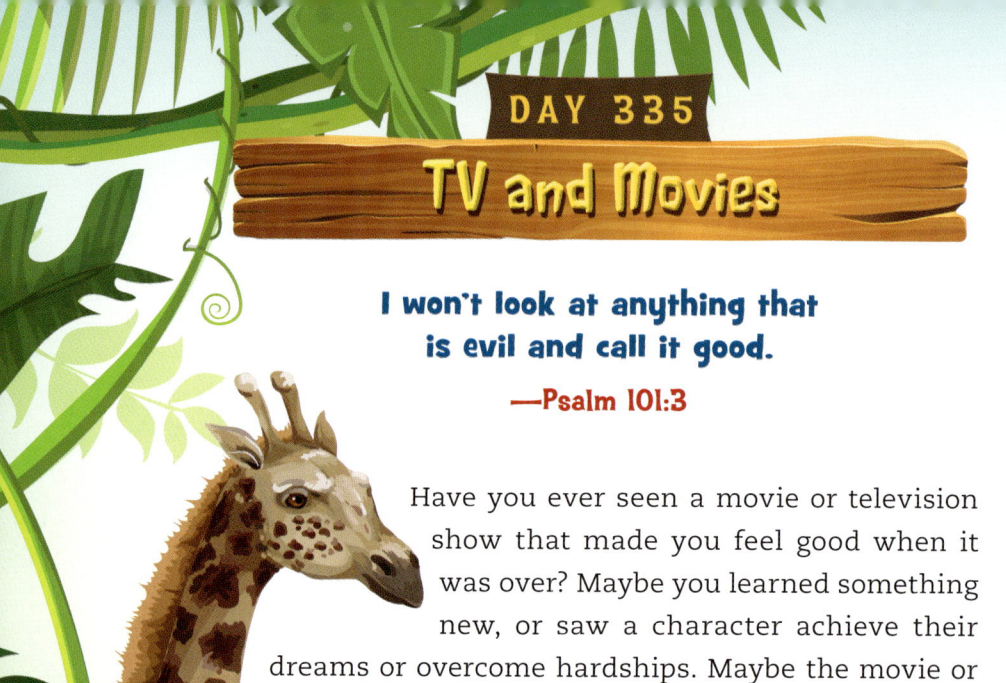

DAY 335
TV and Movies

I won't look at anything that is evil and call it good.

—Psalm 101:3

Have you ever seen a movie or television show that made you feel good when it was over? Maybe you learned something new, or saw a character achieve their dreams or overcome hardships. Maybe the movie or show made you laugh out loud or cry happy tears. Or perhaps it made you feel yucky inside. There might have been scary images, violence, or bad language.

What do you do if you are at a sleepover and your friends want to watch something you know your parents wouldn't want you to see? It can be hard to speak up, but try asking your friends to pick a different movie. God wants you to focus on things that are good and uplifting, not things that fill your head with dark or sinful thoughts. So before you watch anything, ask your parents if it's the type of show that will make you feel good inside or make you sick or scared. No show is worth having nightmares.

Dear God, thank you for giving me eyes to watch good things. Help me make good choices with the shows and movies I watch. Amen.

DAY 336
Real Friends

And let us not give up meeting together. Some are in the habit of doing this. Instead, let us encourage one another with words of hope.

—Hebrews 10:25

Who is your best friend? A kid down the street? A friend from school? Your sibling? A character from your favorite book or video game? If the only friend you're hanging out with is a fictional character, then it's time to hang out with real people. Your video game can't encourage you when you are sad, laugh at your jokes, or play outside with you.

So where can you meet real friends? You can meet kids at school, the playground, a church activity, or sports practice. If you want to get to know someone, ask questions. And when they answer you, make sure you take the time to listen. You'll be amazed at what you might have in common. A video game is fun for a while, but true friends can last a lifetime.

Time to turn off that video game and spend time with real friends. Ask God to help you find a new friend today.

DAY 337
Take Out the Trash!

So get rid of everything that is sinful. Get rid of the evil that is all around us. Don't be too proud to accept the word that is planted in you. It can save you.

—James 1:21

If you're like most people, you've probably thrown something away today. In the United States alone, people throw away 63,000 garbage trucks full each day. Talk about a lot of trash! When you throw things away, the garbage truck comes once a week to pick it up, and the trash collectors dump the garbage into landfills.

Just as we need garbage trucks to pick up the trash, you also need Jesus to take away the garbage that accumulates in your life, such as bad attitudes, bad habits, awful language, and hurtful actions. Like trash, when you forget to throw away the bad stuff in your life, it can collect and make a big, stinky smell. Taking out that kind of trash starts with telling Jesus about your sin and counting on him to get rid of it. Every day can be garbage day when you trust in Jesus.

Dear God, thank you for opening my eyes to the trash in my life. Help me to get rid of my sin and live a holy life. Amen.

DAY 338
Be a Resourceful Kid

So I went down to the potter's house. I saw him working at his wheel. His hands were shaping a pot out of clay. But he saw that something was wrong with it. So he formed it into another pot. He shaped it in the way that seemed best to him.

—Jeremiah 18:3–4

Recycling is taking something you were going to throw away and putting it through a process so it can be reused. Many things can be recycled, such as glass, metal, paper, plastic, and electrical equipment. Recycling is good for the environment, saves energy, and saves space in landfills. People have been recycling for thousands of years. In fact, even before Jesus was born, metal from swords, pots, and other household items were melted down to make new items.

In the Old Testament, God sent Jeremiah to watch the potter work at a wheel to spin a pot from a lump of clay. But the pot didn't turn out, so the potter smashed it and reused the clay to form another pot. Like the story of the potter, God can reuse the broken parts of your life to create something new. Nothing in your life is wasted. So on the days you feel like a failure, remember God can use those parts to make something good and new.

Reuse glass jars and plastic containers to store art supplies and other small toys. Another way to recycle is to buy gently used items from a secondhand shop.

God's Green Earth

The earth belongs to the Lord. And so does everything in it. The world belongs to him. And so do all those who live in it.

—Psalm 24:1

Do you have houseplants? Do you have a vegetable garden or a yard to play in? Each one needs to be taken care of. Did you know Adam was the first farmer? In the book of Genesis, God created a man and put him in the garden of Eden to farm and take care of it. So not only did Adam get to name all the animals, but he was also in charge of caring for the earth.

The Bible says everything in the earth belongs to God. That means people and animals too. So when God asked Adam to tend to the garden, he was asking him to take care of his creation. You are also called to take care of God's creation. Small changes like recycling, saving water by taking quick showers, and turning lights off when you leave the room can make a big difference for the environment. Taking care of God's green earth makes the world a better place for everyone to enjoy.

Reuse your old crayons! With parent permission, preheat the oven to 275 degrees F. Spray a muffin tin with cooking spray. Remove the paper (if still on) and place a handful of used crayons in each muffin tin. Bake for 7–8 minutes. When cool, pop them out and color on both sides of a piece of paper.

Do It Now!

You don't even know what will happen tomorrow.

—James 4:14

If you knew you were going to be sick tomorrow, how would it change what you do today? Truth is, you never know what will happen tomorrow. You might wake up with the flu or an ear infection. Or maybe a stomachache or strep throat. When that happens, it's difficult to stay indoors and rest when you wish you could go outside and play with your friends. As hard as it is to be sick, focus on how good it will feel to be healthy again.

So how can you live your best adventure? By being thankful for each day you have good health. By doing your best in school. By going to church, helping someone in need, or telling others about God. Don't miss out on the things you can do when you're at your best. After all, you don't know what will happen tomorrow. Remember, God wants you to live your best adventure no matter what.

Do you know someone who is sick right now? What can you do to help them live their best adventure?

DAY 341
What's in a Name?

A good name is better than fine perfume.
—Ecclesiastes 7:1

Does your mom or grandma wear perfume? When you smell it, does it remind you of them? Perfumes can smell tangy, fruity, flowery, fresh, or spicy. Everyone has their own opinion of what smells best. What is your favorite smell? Peach? Vanilla? Lemon? Rose?

Just like you can remember your mom or grandma because of the perfume she wears, people can remember you by what you do and the choices you make. How you act not only affects you, but your whole family as well. When you choose to do the right thing, people will think of you and your family in a positive way, and you will earn the respect of others. Honor your mom and dad and your family name by making good choices.

Dear God, thank you for my family. Help me to do what is right so that I will help others think well of my family. Amen.

DAY 342
Popular with God

What should we say then? Since God is on our side, who can be against us?
—Romans 8:31

Do you think it would be cool to fit into the popular crowd? What do you have to do to be popular? Change your clothes? Hairstyle? Do something you wouldn't normally do? It's better to choose friends who love God and enjoy doing the same things as you. The truth is, it's not always popular to believe in God. But don't give up! Finding a loyal and faithful friend is a lot less stressful than trying to gain popularity.

Instead of worrying about popularity, focus on your relationship with God. Did you know the Bible says God is always on your side? When you learn to follow the commands found in the Bible, you will be able to stand up for what you believe even if it's not popular. Besides, popularity only lasts for a short time, but your adventure with God lasts your entire life. And you will always be popular with him.

Ask God to show you friends who will value you and be on your side. Remember, God loves you!

DAY 343
Can't Decide?

Trust in the Lord with all your heart. Do not depend on your own understanding. In all your ways obey him. Then he will make your paths smooth and straight.

—Proverbs 3:5–6

Do you ever get scared you're going to make the wrong decision? Most of the time there is more than one good option, but figuring out which one is best can be tough. What should you do when the answer is difficult to figure out? Before you decide, ask God to guide you.

When you trust God, he will show you what to do. Search your Bible for answers and seek advice from godly people, such as your parents, pastor, or Sunday school teacher. Most of all, ask God to examine your heart and give you the desire to follow his will. When you seek him first, it's much easier to follow God's will and make the best choice.

Next time you have a big decision to make, talk to God about it first. Ask him to show you the best thing to do, and then don't be afraid to go for it!

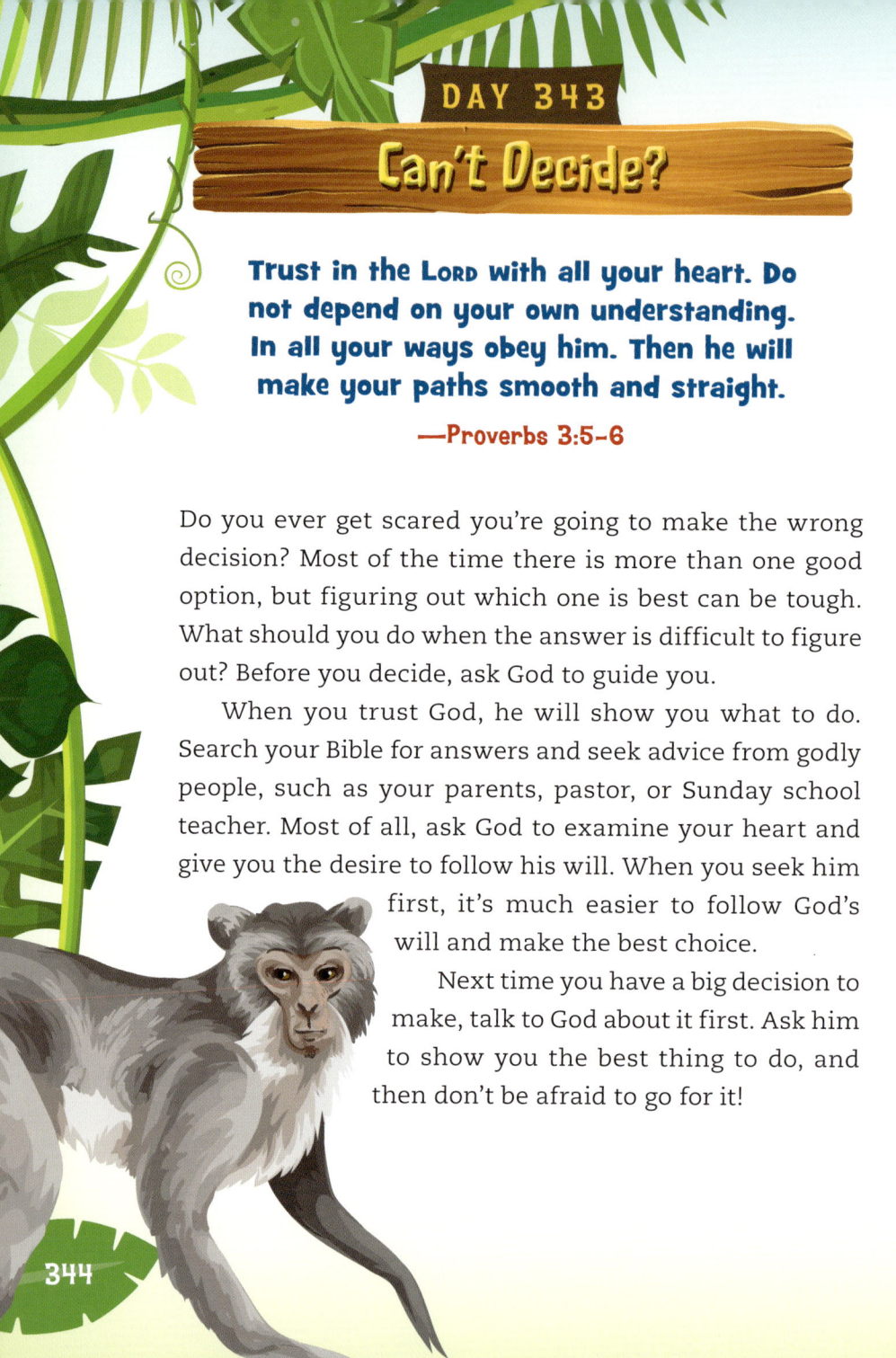

DAY 344
Got a Crush?

So God created human beings in his own likeness. He created them to be like himself. He created them as male and female.

—Genesis 1:27

Do you have a crush on someone? What makes that person special? You might get tongue-tied or your hands might sweat whenever that person is near. You might even want to change something about yourself to get them to like you back. But you don't need to figure out a way to impress your crush. God has the perfect person for you to fall in love with at just the right time. The best thing to do is to be friends and focus on your relationship with God.

Did you know God has a crush on you? He knew about you before you were born, and he knows you now. He longs to spend time with you, and he loves you beyond your wildest imagination. Nothing can separate you from God's love, and you don't need to do anything to earn it. So relax! You've already got someone in your corner who thinks you're someone special.

Dear God, thank you for bringing special people into my life. Help me focus on my relationship with you. Amen.

DAY 345
Don't Keep Count

[Love] does not keep track of other people's wrongs.

—I Corinthians 13:5

Do you like to count things? Maybe you like to count train cars as they rumble past or the seconds until the light turns green. Or maybe you like to count stickers, crayons, or coins. There are a lot of fun things to count, but the one thing you shouldn't keep track of is other people's mistakes. The Bible says love does not keep track of how many times you are wronged or how many times you've forgiven someone.

In the Gospel of Matthew, Peter asked Jesus how many times he should forgive someone who sins against him. Up to seven times? Jesus tells him not seven times, but seventy-seven times!

That means don't count how many times you've forgiven someone. And once you've forgiven them, you shouldn't bring it up again. God forgives you every single day and wants you to forgive others without keeping track.

Has someone asked you for forgiveness? True forgiveness happens when you change the way you think about the hurt. Yes, it still might sting, but when you let go of the pain and forgive, you can move on.

DAY 346
Do You Hear Me?

My dear brothers and sisters, pay attention to what I say. Everyone should be quick to listen. But they should be slow to speak. They should be slow to get angry.

—James 1:19

Do you ever feel like your parents don't listen to you? Do you try to talk to them when they are on the phone? In the middle of a task? Late for an appointment? Learning to wait until your parents are available may help you communicate better. But maybe you feel as if they don't listen no matter when you talk with them. Maybe you feel as if they don't care about your feelings or what you want. Maybe you fight with them all the time.

The Bible says everyone should be quick to listen, slow to speak, and slow to get angry. Is it possible that your parents feel as though you don't listen to them? The greatest way you can show your parents respect is by listening twice as much as you speak. God has given your parents the responsibility of providing a roof over your head, food for your stomach, and clothes for your body. Your parents have a difficult job and make choices for your family every day. If you don't know the reasons behind some of their decisions, try respectfully asking them and really listening to their answer.

Dear God, thank you for my parents. Help me listen to them and respect their decisions. Amen.

DAY 347
What Is an Angel?

Praise the Lord, you angels of his. Praise him, you mighty ones who carry out his orders and obey his word.

—Psalm 103:20

Has anyone ever said you were an angel? Maybe you are a good helper. Maybe you have a good singing voice. Or maybe you are kind or well-behaved. It's a compliment when someone calls you angelic. But what is a real angel? Angels are heavenly beings who worship God, are God's messengers, and are guardians and helpers.

Before the world began, God created angels to be his servants. Angels are often invisible, but sometimes they do appear to people. In the Bible, the prophet Isaiah saw angels with six wings flying around God's throne in a vision (Isaiah 6:1–3). God sent the angel Gabriel to tell Mary she was going to have the baby Jesus (Luke 1:31). And there are many verses about the warrior angel named Michael who helped fight in battle. Today, you have guardian angels to watch over you and protect you. God doesn't want you to worship angels, but he does want you to be grateful for them.

Draw a picture of one of the angels who appeared to Isaiah. The Bible says two wings covered their faces, two covered their feet, and with two they were flying.

DAY 348
Fallen Angel

The God who gives peace will soon crush Satan under your feet.
—Romans 16:20

Have you ever wanted to be the one in charge instead of your parents? The same thing happened to an angel God created named Satan. He was beautiful and the highest of all the angels, but he wanted to rule the universe and be God instead of one of God's servants. So God threw Satan out of heaven and down to earth as a fallen angel.

To this day Satan is trying to trick people and lead them away from God. The Bible says sometimes Satan seems pure and good like an angel of light so that he can deceive us, and other times he prowls around like a roaring lion, looking for someone to devour. Satan still wants to be in charge. The good news is that God is in control and has power over Satan. You can trust God to watch over you and protect you from the devil and his evil schemes.

Dear God, thank you for being the one in charge. Help me trust you to protect me from Satan. Amen.

DAY 349
The Blame Game

My spirit, why are you so sad? Why are you so upset deep down inside me? Put your hope in God. Once again I will have reason to praise him. He is my Savior and my God.

—Psalm 42:5

Do you ever blame yourself when someone else is having a hard time? You know, when you think . . .

It's my fault Dad is so angry.
It's my fault Mom is so stressed.
It's my fault my parents are getting divorced.

It's easy to blame yourself and think it's your fault in situations like these, but you're not in charge of other people's choices. The Bible tells you to put your hope in God. He cares about you when you are sad and upset and doesn't want you to blame yourself for what's going on with others. The truth is, kids aren't supposed to take care of adults. Grown-ups make their own decisions. And even when your parents are having a tough time, remember they still love you.

Dear God, thank you for being in control of my life. Help me trust you instead of blaming myself. Amen.

DAY 350
Do You Please God?

Without faith it is impossible to please God. Those who come to God must believe that he exists. And they must believe that he rewards those who look to him.

—Hebrews 11:6

Do you try to please others? You might say nice things to someone you want to be friends with. You might do extra chores at home to make your mom or dad happy. But as hard as you try, you won't be able to please everyone. The Bible says the one you really need to please is God.

You can please God by believing in him and having faith that Jesus died on the cross for your sins. By having faith, you will be able to do great things for God that you never imagined possible. Because of Noah's faith, he built an ark. Because of Abraham's faith, he went to a new land even though he didn't know where he was going. And because of Sarah's faith, she became a mom even though she thought she was too old to have children. There are many characters in the Bible who had great faith. God will reward you too when you have faith in him. When you do what is right in God's eyes and put your faith first, you will succeed and please him.

Read Hebrews 11:7–12. Do you have faith like Noah, Abraham, and Sarah? Ask God to help make your faith strong.

DAY 351
Sing Along!

Praise the Lord. How good it is to sing praises to our God! How pleasant and right it is to praise him!

—Psalm 147:1

Have you ever gone to a concert? Maybe you heard your favorite singer in a big arena. Or maybe you went with your parents to a music festival at a park or outdoor stadium. Maybe you went to your church for worship night. When people sing praises to God, it's called worship. You can show your love for God by singing to him yourself.

Did you know people have been singing songs about God for thousands of years? Whether you feel sad, happy, lonely, or angry, you can sing worship songs to God, and it will make a difference in your life. You can praise him at church, in a big arena, or at a park. You can sing songs to God in the shower, in your bedroom, or in your backyard. You can worship God anywhere. The Bible says it is right to praise him.

Ask your parents if they would take you to a concert. If there isn't one near you, play some Christian music and sing along. You can worship God today!

DAY 352
Bright Future Ahead

We want you to be very strong, in keeping with his glorious power. We want you to be patient. We pray that you will never give up.

—Colossians 1:11

"Lights! Camera! Action!" Those three little words the director says may seem quick and simple, but there is a lot more that goes into making a movie. The lights take hours to be set up just right. The camera angles have to be perfect. The actors need to memorize their lines and know where they need to move and stand before the director can say, "Action." A movie takes a lot of patience to create. You may need lots of patience for something in your life too, like a dream or a goal.

What do you do while you wait for your dream to happen? You may need to grow up a bit. You may need to take some classes. Or it may take your entire life before you achieve your goal. The important thing is to work hard while you wait. God has a bright future for you, and God's timing is best. So be patient and never give up hope!

Dear God, thank you for giving me a dream. Help me to do my best and work hard while I wait. Amen.

DAY 353
Prince or Princess?

But God chose you to be his people. You are royal priests. You are a holy nation. You are God's special treasure. You are all these things so that you can give him praise. God brought you out of darkness into his wonderful light.

—1 Peter 2:9

Who are you? A baseball player? A gymnast? A good student? A piano player? An artist? Somebody's friend? All those things can change. What instrument or sport you play, your friends, or your grades do not define you. Your true identity is in Jesus Christ, which is a gift from God and cannot be changed or taken away. The Bible says who you really are is a child of the King.

Yes, God says you are royalty! God adopted you as his prince or princess. God loves you and chose you to be a part of his royal family. And as his royal heir, God accepts you as you are, forgives you of your sins, and treasures you as his precious child.

Make a crown out of construction paper. Decorate it with markers or craft jewels. Thank God for choosing you as his treasured prince or princess.

Our Amazing World

The LORD has done great things. All who take delight in those things think deeply about them.

—Psalm 111:2

Do you want to be a scientist? Science is more than just being curious about the world around you. Scientists start with a question and search for answers by testing and gathering clues. There are many different types of scientists. Some study outer space, some study life and living organisms, some study the earth, and some study energy.

Many scientists believe in God, but some have a difficult time believing things they can't see. The important thing to remember is God knows all the answers scientists are trying to discover. We can find answers in the Bible, but we're still going to have a lot of questions. That's where faith comes in. Faith is trusting God for the answers. Scientists can learn as much as they can about this amazing world, but there will always be more mysteries to solve. That's because we have a big God who has done great things!

With parent permission, create an awesome chemical reaction. You will need: baking soda, vinegar, a drinking glass, and a cookie sheet. What to do: Place the drinking glass on the cookie sheet. Put some baking soda in the glass. Pour in some vinegar. Watch the reaction take place.

DAY 355

Outer Space

Look up toward the sky. Who created everything you see? The Lord causes the stars to come out at night one by one. He calls out each one of them by name. His power and strength are great. So none of the stars is missing.

—Isaiah 40:26

Have you ever looked at the night sky through a telescope? Here are some fun facts: There are many different types of objects found in our solar system, such as the sun, planets, moons, comets, asteroids, gas, and dust. The eight planets in our solar system are Mercury, Venus, Earth, Mars, Jupiter, Saturn, Uranus, and Neptune. There are between 200–400 billion stars in our galaxy, and there are billions of galaxies in the universe. Mind-blowing!

The Bible says that God created everything we see in the sky, and he calls each of the stars by name. That means he knows the names of billions and billions of stars. And the God who put each star in place is the same God who loves and cares for you. Amazing!

Create wooden craft stick stars by gluing the ends of your sticks together to make the star. Decorate with glitter, buttons, markers, etc. Add a ribbon for hanging. Consider how God created everything in the sky.

DAY 356

Be a Bible-Loving, Promise-Keeping, World-Changing Kid

Jesus saw the crowds. So he went up on a mountainside and sat down. His disciples came to him. Then he began to teach them.

—Matthew 5:1–2

Do you go to church? Do you listen when your pastor is preaching a sermon? It's easy to daydream instead of listening to your pastor. But unless you pay attention, it will be impossible to know what God thinks is important.

In the Bible, the most famous sermon ever told was called the Sermon on the Mount. One day, Jesus sat down on a mountainside and taught the people about how God wants his children to live. Just as it was important for the disciples to listen to Jesus, it's also important for you to listen in church. To help you stay focused, look up the Bible verses, take notes, and talk about the sermon with an adult. If you do these things, you'll become a Bible-loving, promise-keeping, world-changing kid.

Dear God, thank you for the Bible and for church. Help me listen during the sermon so that I learn how you want me to live. Amen.

Pass the Salt

"You are the salt of the earth."
—Matthew 5:13

Do you like salt on your food? Maybe you add a touch of salt to your french fries and popcorn, or maybe you add a dash to your veggies. Most of the time there is already enough salt in food. In fact, too much salt in your body is not good for you and makes you super thirsty. Did you know, before there were refrigerators, people salted food so that the food would last longer? Besides keeping food fresh, salt also adds flavor, which helps food taste better.

During the Sermon on the Mount, Jesus said people who love God are the salt of the earth. What does that mean? Christians are salt when they stand up for things that are right to help make our world better, like what salt did for food before refrigerators. Jesus also wants you to season your speech with kind words and show others God's love through your actions. Just like food tastes better with a dash of salt, life is better when you have a relationship with Jesus. Are you being the salt of the earth with your words and actions?

Salty foods, like pretzels or potato chips, make you thirsty for something to drink. By being the salt of the earth, you will make others thirsty for Jesus.

DAY 358
Take a Risk

A person's body without their spirit is dead. In the same way, faith without good deeds is dead.

—James 2:26

Have you ever taken a risk for your faith? Maybe you gave some of your clothes to a friend in need or helped someone who was being bullied. Maybe you told someone about Jesus or were kind to your enemy. There was a woman in the Bible named Rahab who risked her life to protect God's people. This is what happened.

Joshua, the leader of the Israelites, sent two spies to check out the land of Jericho. When the king found out, he sent messengers to Rahab's house, but Rahab hid the two spies and sent the messengers away. After the king's men left, she made the spies promise her that they would show kindness to her and her family. The spies told her to tie a bright red rope in the window as a symbol of her faith so that her whole family would be safe when the Israelites attacked. What about you? Do you have the courage to take a risk for your faith?

Dear God, thank you for my relationship with you. Help me to be bold and take risks for my faith. Amen.

DAY 359
Speak, Lord. I'm Listening!

The LORD came and stood there. He called out, just as he had done the other times. He said, "Samuel! Samuel!" Then Samuel replied, "Speak. I'm listening."

—1 Samuel 3:10

Has God given you a big idea? Maybe he wants you to sponsor a child to make sure they grow up healthy, educated, and safe. Or maybe he's asked you to help those with disabilities in your church or community. If God has given you a big idea, talk with your parents or an adult you trust. God doesn't only call grown-ups. He calls kids too!

There was a boy named Samuel who served in the temple with Eli the priest. One night while Samuel was sleeping, he heard someone call his name. He got up and ran to Eli and said, "Here I am." Eli said he hadn't called him and sent Samuel back to bed. This happened two more times. By the third time, Eli realized God was calling Samuel. God called Samuel, and God knows your name too. Will you answer by saying, "Speak. I'm listening"?

Draw a picture of Samuel sitting up in bed and saying, "Here I am. Speak. I'm listening."

DAY 360
Ups and Downs

Let the peace that Christ gives rule in your hearts. As parts of one body, you were appointed to live in peace. And be thankful.

—Colossians 3:15

Are you having a good day or a bad one? Today might be your birthday, or you might be moving away from your friends. You might have gotten a new bike, or maybe you woke up with a cold. Life is like that. One day is good and the next can be bad.

Each day teaches you lessons about life. The ups and downs won't seem so overwhelming when you keep your eyes on Jesus. To do this, you need to read your Bible every day. You will discover verses that will encourage you on the good days and help you on the bad ones. Did you know you become a stronger person when you experience both good and bad days? By learning to trust God to take care of you, you will be able to handle life no matter what happens.

Dear God, thank you for each day. Help me to trust in you and be strong, so I can be ready for both the good and bad days. Amen.

DAY 361
Do Your Best

Do your best to please God. Be a worker who doesn't need to be ashamed. Teach the message of truth correctly.

—2 Timothy 2:15

When your mom asks you to clean your room, do you go as fast as you can, or do you do a good job? When your teacher gives you an assignment, do you speed through it, or do you take your time? When your neighbor asks you to take her trash cans to the curb, do you remember, or does it slip your mind?

Whether you are doing chores, your schoolwork, or a job for someone else, do more than what is asked of you. Don't rush and just get by with doing as little as possible. You will stand out when you take pride in your work. God doesn't expect you to be perfect, but he does expect you to do your best. When you work with all your heart, the Bible says it is an act of worship, and you bring glory to God. When you do your best, it not only honors God, but it will make you feel good too.

Do you struggle with doing your best? By thinking about what Jesus did for you on the cross and how much you love him, you will be able to give him your best.

Tender Heart

So give freely to needy people. Let your heart be tender toward them. Then the Lord your God will bless you in all your work. He will bless you in everything you do.

—Deuteronomy 15:10

Do you know someone who is struggling? Maybe their house burned down in a fire. Maybe their parents are out of work. Or maybe they are homeless. Do you have a tender heart toward people in need, or do you shrug your shoulders and ignore them? If you don't want to help or have a hard time giving your things away, you might be holding too tightly to your stuff.

The Bible says we shouldn't store up treasures on earth, where things break and thieves steal. Instead, we should focus on treasures in heaven, like loving God and our family and friends and helping those in need. God has blessed you with good gifts so that you will be generous with others. The more you help others, the more God is going to bless you. You can always replace things, but you can't replace the people in your life. When you give to those in need, God will bless you in everything you do.

Go through your closet and collect some things to give to the poor. You will be amazed at how good you will feel when you help those in need.

DAY 363
Most Important

"Martha, Martha," the Lord answered. "You are worried and upset about many things. But few things are needed. Really, only one thing is needed. Mary has chosen what is better. And it will not be taken away from her."

—Luke 10:41-42

Have you ever forgotten something important? Maybe you worked hard on your homework and then forgot it at home. Maybe you got to the soccer field and realized you didn't remember to pack your cleats. Sometimes people are so busy that they forget the most important thing. The same thing happened to a woman in the Bible named Martha.

Jesus came to a village, and Martha welcomed him into her home. Martha had a sister named Mary who sat at the Lord's feet listening to what he said. But Martha was busy with everything that had to be done for her guests. She went to Jesus and complained that Mary had left her to do all the work. Jesus answered her by saying that she was worried about many things, but only one thing was needed. Mary had chosen what was better.

Have you ever made the same mistake as Martha? Did you get so busy that you forgot the most important thing, spending time with Jesus? Remember to slow down and spend time with him.

Dear God, you are the most important thing in my life. Help me spend more time with you. Amen.

DAY 364
When Things Go Wrong

> **My brothers and sisters, you will face all kinds of trouble. When you do, think of it as pure joy. Your faith will be tested. You know that when this happens it will produce in you the strength to continue.**
>
> —James 1:2-3

Have you ever been super excited about something, only to have it go terribly wrong? You might have volunteered to watch your baby brother, and then all he did was cry and scream. You might have given your friend advice, and it totally backfired. Why do things sometimes spin out of control when you try to do what is right?

Sometimes things go wrong even when you are doing what God wants you to do. But God is there for you. Whatever happens in life, he'll give you what you need to deal with it. Don't give up doing what is right and pleasing to God. Trust him to take care of even the most difficult situations. He has a plan and will work everything out.

Is something going wrong in your life? Keep doing your best and trust God to work it out.

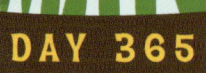

DAY 365
Love Keeps the Adventure Going

Dear children, don't just talk about love. Put your love into action. Then it will truly be love.

—1 John 3:18

Phew! You made it to the last devotion. What an adventure it's been. But it's not over! Your relationship with God lasts your entire life. By keeping him number one, you will be able to stand strong when challenges come and love others the way he commands. But how do you put your love into action?

Look around you. Do you see someone who needs your help? Maybe you could clean up the trash in your neighborhood. Or bake brownies to encourage a friend. Or paint a picture to give to your grandparents. Or help your sibling learn to read. Remember, love is not a feeling, it's something you do. This means that when you truly love someone, you will show it by your actions. Keep the adventure going by showing your love today!

Think about the people in your life. Name three things you can do to put your love into action. Then go out and do them!